LORD JAMES HARRINGTON AND THE EASTER MYSTERY

Easter Day — and the vicar's dog digs up a human bone on the Harrington estate. Retracing the dog's walk, Lord James Harrington uncovers a skeleton buried in the woods and identifies a number of expensive items. With the likelihood that the victim could be someone well-to-do, James is concerned that they may be known to him, and puts his sleuthing hat on. His questions take him from Cavendish to Boston, where more surprises await. Will he bring the killer to justice, or is he on a wild goose chase?

LYNN FLORKIEWICZ

LORD JAMES HARRINGTON AND THE EASTER MYSTERY

Complete and Unabridged

LINFORD
Leicester

First published in Great Britain

First Linford Edition
published 2019

A catalogue record for this book is available
from the British Library.

ISBN 978–1–4448–4079–7

Published by
F. A. Thorpe (Publishing)
Anstey, Leicestershire

Set by Words & Graphics Ltd.
Anstey, Leicestershire
Printed and bound in Great Britain by
T. J. International Ltd., Padstow, Cornwall

This book is printed on acid-free paper

Welcome to the world of Lord James Harrington and the small village of Cavendish.

I hope you'll feel at home during your visit and that you'll enjoy getting involved in the Easter traditions and, of course, the mystery that James stumbles upon.

Many thanks to those who have been with me from the first book and welcome to those who are new to the series. I hope that you enjoy these mysteries as much as I enjoy writing them.

1

'Who's good at making up clues?'

'Mr Bateson, he's good at clues, makes 'em rhyme too.'

'He's away at the moment, stopping with his niece.'

'Well it can't be difficult, can it? I mean it's only for the kids, it's not *The Times* crossword.'

Lord James Harrington listened to the chatter between the villagers, lit a cigarette and exchanged a wry smile with his wife, Beth. It was the week before Easter and the lead up to the festival was always like this: a host of activities to organise and far too many people wanting to pitch in with ideas and suggestions.

He was all for villagers being involved but he wondered whether they should limit the numbers at this late stage. Around a dozen individuals had been firing questions at one another but, after an hour, he didn't feel they were any further forward. And, he'd decided early on in this meeting, the Half Moon was not conducive to organising events.

It was lunch-time and Donovan and Kate Delaney, who ran the ancient pub, had placed tables and chairs to the side of the bar for those residents able to attend. The tables had been positioned as an extension to one of the booths that had a view of the village green. Everyone had a drink and this had prompted people to treat it more like a social gathering than a meeting. Even pensioners, who'd popped in for a swift half, drifted toward the group to add their opinions on how things should be run.

Kate, who wasn't the most patient individual in the world, had finished dusting the dented oak counter and was now cleaning the Toby jugs and horse brasses that helped give the bar its character. Not that it needed help. The uneven floors, ingrained smell of hops and tobacco, along with sepia photographs from the turn of the century did that. Bits of the building dated back to the sixteenth century and, together with the church, it had been the centre of Cavendish activities since that time.

In the booth and attempting to direct proceedings were James, Beth, the vicar Stephen Merryweather and Dorothy Forbes, self-appointed director of the Cavendish Players.

Before them were gathered numerous villagers, including members of the WI, making up what was loosely termed the events committee. Unfortunately, it appeared to grow year by year and had become a committee for whoever could attend at a given time. Generally, this worked out for the best in the end, ensuring everyone had a say in the matter but today James feared nothing would be finalised. With the volume of chatter coming from all sides, a stranger would have thought these people hadn't seen one another for years.

Charlie Hawkins, the librarian, had perched a blackboard on a wooden chair at the far end of the bar. On it was sketched a map of the locality. In his early thirties, Charlie wore wool trousers and a loose jumper. His dark hair was dishevelled and he had a look of resignation about him. He met James' sympathetic gaze to show they were both thinking the same thing. He picked up the wooden board-cleaner and rapped it heavily on the board: chalk dust floated up. The room hushed and all eyes turned to him.

He forced a smile and pointed to the board with a long stick. 'Let's have a bit of hush now or we'll not get anything done. Back to the Easter egg hunt. Now, Lord Harrington suggested this should take place in the forest on the Harrington estate. It'll be exciting for the kids 'cos there're loads of places to put the eggs, with plenty of trees and hidey-holes.' He traced the route with his pointer. 'It'll start off at the back of the house here, enter the little copse area here and then through this bit of forest, along the riverbank and back out into the fields. We'll end up where we started from. Along the way we'll have about twenty clues to follow.'

A murmur of approval went around the bar with people commenting that the use of woodland belonging to Harrington's would certainly be an adventurous one for the children. James' family had turned the ancestral home into Harrington's, a country hotel, and it had, over the last few years, become a thriving retreat for the well-to-do.

Stephen tapped the old oak table in front of him. 'Anne is w-walking the route as we speak,' he said with his endearing stammer. 'With R-Radley.' Radley was their Springer spaniel, a stray they'd found wandering in the fields the previous year.

James proposed that along with Anne and Charlie he should sit down and work the clues out. 'Anne's out at the moment to see where the eggs can be hidden and we're making good use of the forest environment to help with our riddles. Charlie, how about you and I walk the route as well to get some inspiration?'

Charlie gave him a thumbs-up and proposed they do that after the meeting. Dorothy, with her ever-present clipboard, checked the list of events.

She sat up straight and ordered everyone to remain quiet. She cut an imposing figure in her two-piece suit, her glasses balanced on the end of her nose. 'I think, Lord Harrington, it would be best to see where we are at the moment.'

'I think that's a good idea,' he replied, pleased to see her taking charge. There was a definite matter-of-fact attitude with Dorothy and she had the knack of giving anyone who interrupted a severe glare. 'You fire away and we'll chip in where we need to.' He was pleased to see that Beth also had a notebook and pencil at hand, ready to scribble down any instructions. Easter was such a busy time for the Cavendish community, he felt sure he'd forget something if it wasn't written down.

Dorothy gave him an enquiring look. 'Well, the Easter egg hunt is coming together nicely, so can we leave this in your hands?'

James exhaled smoke toward the ceiling and reassured her that he and Beth, along with Anne and Charlie, would mark the route out, write and place the clues and ensure there was supervision along the way.

'Jolly good,' said Dorothy as she

checked her list again. 'Maundy Thursday.'

All eyes turned to Stephen who cleared his throat. Over his dog-collar, he wore a soft mauve sweater that complemented his fair complexion. 'Ah yes, a-all in hand. It's not as if I've n-never done Maundy Thursday before.'

Maundy Thursday occurred the day before Good Friday and was celebrated in Cavendish and the neighbouring village of Charnley; it commemorated the Last Supper and heralded the start of the Easter festival.

Stephen continued: 'I'll organise the feet washing; Anne's already accumulated enough half-crowns.'

Along with many vicars, he followed the tradition of washing parishioners' feet to mirror Jesus doing the same for his disciples at the Last Supper. James remembered Stephen once saying to him that it was a stark reminder that he was here to serve. There were a number of pensioners in the village and, as had been the custom since the days of Edward I, James insisted they also offered a token gesture of charity to the elderly. In Cavendish, this meant a half-crown coin for all men and women aged 80 or over, along with two lamb chops each, supplied by local butcher, Graham Porter.

The bulky butcher, seated just along from Beth, held a large hand up. 'I've ordered the chops and I'll give them out when you're doing your thing with the half-crowns.'

The doctor's wife, Helen Jackson, volunteered to help Stephen and Anne with anything they needed doing. Dorothy and Beth jotted everything down in their respective notebooks.

While they were on the subject of food, Stephen quickly added that he would be organising a lunch after the service in the church hall.

'That'll be lovely,' said Dorothy. 'Now, Easter Sunday.'

Again, all eyes turned to Stephen. 'Easter S-Service is as usual and E-Elsie is kindly making a batch of hot cross buns.' He turned to James. 'Your grandmother's recipe, I understand.'

Another, more vocal, murmur of

approval went around the room. James salivated. Elsie Taylor, who ran the café on the road between Cavendish and Charnley was an expert baker. Just thinking about a spiced toasted bun drizzled with butter set his taste buds off.

'I-I believe Mrs Keates is also helping out with the b-baking.'

Even better, thought James. Mrs Keates, a Charnley resident, had reintroduced him and Beth to Soul Cake during Hallowe'en a couple of years ago. He turned to Beth. 'We could do Granny's simnel cake.' She gave him an encouraging smile and noted it down.

'I'm also a-adding a reflective hour b-by the river on Good Friday. It'll be mid-afternoon, around three o'clock.'

James asked exactly what that was as this was new to him: the previous vicar had only ever stuck to the traditional service on Good Friday.

Stephen's face brightened. 'I-I hope the weather will be f-fine for this. I'm leading villagers down toward the river for quiet c-contemplation. This day is all about J-Jesus dying on the cross so it will be a time for reflection. There won't be any prayers or hymns. I'm simply asking people to come and g-go in silence.'

A number of villagers expressed their delight at this new notion and promised to spread the word. James said that he and Beth would do their best to attend and added this would be a popular event, especially if the weather held.

'That leaves the races,' announced Dorothy.

A spate of chatter began and Charlie clapped his hands hard to silence them. 'Leave that with me and Mr Chrichton.'

'Where is Mr Chrichton?' asked James. The schoolmaster was normally at all of these meetings.

'Still at the school. They're a teacher down so he's doubly busy.'

Beth leaned forward. 'Are we doing the normal races?'

Charlie turned the blackboard around to show that he'd written a list. 'We are. We have the Easter cake race for the women. We need twenty cakes. That's the maximum entry this year and we've five more spaces to fill.'

'Count me in,' Kate shouted from the other side of the bar.

James tapped Beth's notebook and gestured for her to write that down. 'You'll need to remind the WI to get their recipes out.'

'It's just a sponge recipe so it's nothing complicated,' she replied. 'They normally make them the evening before.'

Charlie continued. 'The women go once around the village green while keeping their cake balanced on an upturned plate. The men have a sack of Russet apples each. Again, once around the green with that on their backs. Pete Mitchell at the orchard's bringing those so that's all organised. Then, of course, there's the traditional wooden egg rolling for the kids.'

Donovan called out from behind the bar in his syrupy Dublin accent. 'I've the eggs in the loft. I'll get up there later.'

Egg rolling had been a tradition in many villages across England and always proved popular with the children. The wooden eggs in the village had once been brightly painted but were now faded and

11

worn after decades of play. The idea was simple. The children chose an egg and rolled it the length of the village green; the first one to the finish line was the winner. James had always loved this tradition and remembered taking part when he was a boy. As the eggs were not circular, the race was not as straightforward as it appeared. If you rolled the egg too hard, it simply veered off in another direction causing great hilarity in children and parents alike.

Dorothy turned to James and enquired about prizes.

'All in hand,' he replied.

Beth flipped the pages on her notebook to remind herself of the arrangements. 'We've arranged tea for two at Elsie's for the winner of the cake race. The men are competing for a stoneware jug of Donovan's Easter beer and, for the children, we have a number of prizes. We've noticed they all seem to be playing cowboys and Indians so we have a couple of cowgirl and cowboy outfits for the winning girls and boys. We also have some skipping ropes, books and footballs.'

'And,' Charlie put in, 'Mr Chrichton's sorting out some more games on the green to keep the kids amused.'

It didn't take long for everyone to put more reminders in the mix, including asking Bob Tanner and his folk group to provide entertainment and inviting the eccentric solicitor Mr Bateson to set up a marbles competition.

Beth sat up with a start and turned to James. 'Of course, it's the world championships in Crawley! We should make time to go.'

James assured her they would. Every Good Friday at The Greyhound pub in Crawley, groups from across the world gathered at the old marble circle to compete for the world marbles championship. It seemed an out of the way place to have such a global event but it attracted many local teams and, James recalled, a fine old character by the name of 'Pop' Maynard; a man now in his late eighties who had competed in the event with the Copthorne Spitfires team several years previously. He was also a singer of traditional folk songs and a keen folklorist. He wondered if Pop would be there this year. He hoped so.

Graham checked his watch and decided it was probably time to go. He swigged down the last of his beer and set the glass on the table. 'That's my lunch over with. Sarah wants me to put up some shelves in the kitchen. She won't want me smelling of beer at this time of the day.'

This prompted the majority of villagers to leave but not without a quick announcement from Dorothy instructing everyone that they needed one last meeting for final arrangements. James suggested that only those who were involved in organising need bother. He hoped this wouldn't upset anyone but the thought of having another enormous meeting filled him with dread. Fortunately, the idea went down well. Stephen said that a couple of telephone calls to Dorothy and Beth should suffice. Thank goodness for that, James thought, as the bar emptied.

Donovan and Kate cleared the glasses away and Charlie began to tidy up the items he'd brought with him.

The bar was almost empty when Anne, smiling brightly, popped her head round the door. She wore a navy-blue shower proof jacket and an old pair of trousers. Her wellingtons shone with the wet and her hair was flat from the damp. 'Have I missed everything?'

' 'fraid so, old thing,' said James, 'we're about finished with the organising. We'll tie up any loose ends with Dorothy and Beth.'

'Oh jolly good.'

Radley raced in with muddy feet, promptly dropped a bone and barked as if to attract attention to his find. Beth reached down to make a fuss of him. 'Goodness, he's soaking. I guess it must be pretty wet in the forest.'

Anne said it was. 'It's a beautiful day but you need wellingtons. Glad I put mine on. It'll be a while before it dries out. I found some good spots for the clues though.'

Stephen frowned at Anne. 'Did you buy him a bone?'

Anne shook her head and pulled Radley back. 'No I did not. He dug that thing up when we were walking round the forest. This is the first time he's let it go.'

Charlie greeted Radley by fondling his soft ears and hinted that it was probably from a deer. Radley picked the muddy bone up again and wagged his tail.

Philip Jackson, Cavendish's handsome doctor, followed Anne in and waved to his wife. 'Ah, Helen, I thought you'd be finished by now; I'm taking a break for lunch. My next surgery isn't for an hour.'

Helen reached for her handbag and reminded James and Beth that she was ready to help with anything relating to the Easter festivities. Philip squatted down and eased the bone out of Radley's mouth. He stood up and examined it.

James, helping Beth slip her jacket on, noted Philip's concerned expression. 'Everything all right?'

The doctor studied the item and tilted his head at Anne. 'Where'd he find this?'

'In the forest,' said Anne enlarging on the success of her trip. 'I've found lots of good places to hide eggs, especially along the river. And I have to say it's invigorating! The air in the forest feels so fresh and alive. Spring is definitely around the corner.' She turned to Philip.

'Is it from a deer or perhaps a fox or something?'

'No.' He turned to James. 'This is human. It's a fibula.'

2

James knew he must have looked astounded. Stephen appeared equally horrified and Anne and Charlie grimaced at the bone and took a step back to distance themselves from it. James scanned the bar. Donovan and Kate were at the far end, moving tables and chairs back to their original positions and a number of pensioners were propping up the bar chatting. He was keen to keep this from being overheard and steered the group out of the pub with a hasty farewell to the Delaneys.

They stood on the cobbles immediately outside where the distinctive smell of a bonfire greeted them from one of the nearby gardens.

James turned to Philip. 'Are you absolutely certain?'

Philip studied the bone again and, stony-faced, said he was one hundred per cent sure. 'It's been in the ground a good few years. I'd like to tell you that this was an ancient bone but it would be in a more fragile condition if that was the case.'

Beth leant in to get a closer view. 'Is it bone? It couldn't be part of a joke skeleton; you know, like a stage prop or something?'

'I wish I could say yes but I can't.'

James groaned and asked Anne if Radley had definitely found it in the forest.

Anne explained they'd been halfway around their planned route so it had been quite a way in. 'The trouble is, James, I can't tell you where Radley went. He was off the lead. You know what he's like; he goes running off all over the place chasing rabbits and squirrels, so he could have dug this up anywhere.'

Philip suggested taking another walk round. 'I can't come, I have surgery this afternoon and a couple of house calls to make.'

'I-I must get on with my work. Easter is a busy time for the c-clergy.'

Beth gave James a look of despair. 'I said I'd visit the old people's home and I can't really put that off.'

James said he really only needed Anne. 'After all, you know the route you took. Would Radley be up for another walk?'

The spaniel's ears pricked at hearing the word 'walk'. He barked and wagged his tail in anticipation.

'I've never known him refuse,' said Anne. 'We'll have to hope we can keep up with him.'

'I'll come up with you,' said Charlie. 'We can mark the route out at the same time. I'll leave this board with Donovan and pick it up later.'

Philip suggested putting a long extension of rope on the end of Radley's lead. 'At least that'll keep him within sight.'

'Good idea,' James said, adding that he had plenty in the garage at home. He gave Anne his full attention. 'I'm not dragging you away from anything, am I?'

Anne rubbed her hands together gleefully and rushed her words. 'If I did have something on, I'd cancel it. There may be a body in the woods and I, for one, would like to find it.'

Stephen admonished his wife for being ghoulish. She shrugged her shoulders and proposed another way for him to look at it — that they could dig the body up and give it a Christian burial. He answered that he knew full well this was not the predominant reason for her wanting to return to the forest.

He turned to James. 'These mysteries you've solved in the p-past have turned my wife from being an armchair detective into w-wanting to be the real thing.'

James held his hands up in apology. 'It shouldn't take too long. The car's just at the end of the green there.' He turned to Beth. 'Darling, are you all right walking to the home?'

'Of course, it's only a five minute walk. And I want to get home and see if we've news from Meg.'

Meg Craven, who had been a flower girl at their wedding, had hinted in her last letter from Boston that romance had blossomed and that Beth would receive significant news soon.

'Right you are,' said James. 'I'll take Anne and Charlie, we'll pick up the rope and go hunting for bones.'

'Take the little wooden stakes we made

too — to mark out the route.'

Helen tapped his arm. 'Shouldn't you call your friend, Mr Lane?'

DCI George Lane was not only the area's Detective Chief Inspector, he was also one of James' oldest friends. James remembered their first meeting as if it were yesterday: George had been a young, eager-to-please constable making notes about a break-in. They had discovered a mutual love of cricket and got to know each other better through playing for the Cavendish cricket team. Over the last few years, James had exasperated his friend by getting involved in helping to solve mysteries in the area. No doubt, he would be interested in this little discovery.

James decided that he would prefer to wait until after they'd found more bones, if there were any. 'We'll have to contact him, I'm sure, but that bone could have been dropped by a fox. The rest of the skeleton could be miles away. Let's see what we come up with before bothering George. Come along, Anne, Charlie, let's make a move.'

Within twenty minutes, James had parked his gleaming red Jaguar at the back of Harrington's. Adam, the young head waiter, was standing outside with a glass of lemonade. James smiled when he straightened up on seeing him.

'Hello, your Lordship; Mrs Merryweather, Mr Hawkins. Nice day today. A bit different from yesterday.'

It certainly was a nice day. The weeks leading up to Easter were always hit and miss where the British weather was concerned. James never knew what to expect from one day to the next. A Ted Robinson poem he'd recently read describing this month so well popped into his head. He could only remember the first part and felt inclined to quote it now as he opened the boot of the car:

'So here we are in April, in showy, blowy April,
In frowsy, blowsy April, the rowdy dowdy time
In soppy, sloppy April, in wheezy

23

breezy April,
      In ringing, stinging April with a singing swinging rhyme.'

He received a gentle round of applause for his trouble. Today, the showers had cleared and left them with a bright, chilly day and a promise of dry weather to come. But, seeing Anne's bedraggled features, he knew the forest remained sopping from the previous few days' rain so he and Charlie changed their shoes for wellingtons. James reached into the boot and retrieved his Barbour jacket which he shrugged on and popped a tweed flat cap on his head.

'Everything running smoothly, Adam?'

'Yes, your Lordship. This is the calm before the storm as they say.'

'It is indeed.'

Easter at Harrington's was always busy, as were the weeks on either side of the festival. Rooms had been booked several months in advance and James and Beth had spent some considerable time sorting out activities, menus and events for residents. Didier, their temperamental yet magical chef, had spent the previous afternoon with James, going through his proposed menu. Lamb would play a predominant part in proceedings; his chef had succulent leg of lamb and lamb chops on offer. To satisfy those with other tastes, he'd included trout and beef as options.

GJ, the young man they'd helped a couple of years ago, was proving to be a success with his painting workshops. He'd transformed the old stable into a gallery and studio where artists could display their work and aspiring painters could create their own masterpieces. As part of the pursuits at the hotel, he'd arranged morning workshops over the entire Easter period and asked permission for his wife, Catherine, to set up a pottery class as well.

When James had agreed to allow GJ use of the stables, he'd thought it might prove to be an expensive disaster. How wrong he was. Many of their guests, especially the women, had been thrilled to find such a creative activity on offer. Husbands didn't feel so guilty about spending an afternoon fishing and shooting as their wives were more than happy to try their hand at drawing, especially with the handsome, blue-eyed GJ running the classes.

'Do we have many families booked in this year?' James asked, mindful of the games and celebrations the village had at this time.

'A few more than last year,' Adam replied. 'We have seven children stopping here with their parents.'

Anne confirmed the number as she tied the length of rope to Radley's lead. 'Beth let me know because we've invited them to take part in the egg hunt and I must ensure we have enough to go around.'

Two unexpected visitors clip-clopped toward them. Sebastian and Delphine, the two donkeys gifted to them by GJ, arrived for their lunchtime treat. Adam took his break at the same time every day and had got into the habit of giving them a few mints. Like Pavlov's dogs, the donkeys took their cue when they saw Adam emerge from the kitchen and meandered across for their treat. James fondled their long, furry ears and patted their necks. The donkeys nuzzled in, enjoying the attention.

He squatted down to examine their hooves. 'When's the vet due?'

'This week, your Lordship. Lady Harrington asked us to get hold of them for their routine check-up. The children will probably want rides over Easter so we need to make sure they're healthy.'

'Jolly good.' He beamed at Anne and Charlie. 'Well, this isn't getting us anywhere. Let's follow the hound and see what we can dig up.' He gave Adam a mock salute. 'Jot us down for dinner on Good Friday evening, would you Adam? Normal time.'

'Certainly your Lordship, I'll do that right away.'

The three of them strolled across the fields toward the forest. Anne steered them to an opening at the edge of the tree line. Radley, on a fifteen-yard stretch of rope, ran back and forth, sniffing and pawing the ground. 'This is my hiding place for the first of the eggs.'

Charlie took a bright yellow wooden stake, numbered one, and pushed it into the ground. 'This is a good start. There're some rabbit holes there so we could perhaps link a reference to *Alice in Wonderland*.' He jotted down a remark to that effect in his notebook.

As they entered the forest, they were thankful they'd worn their coats. Water dripped from the canopy of branches above them. Ahead was a carpet of dead ferns, moss and rotten twigs, making their path spongy and soft. There was a dampness that hung in the air but it was fresh, as if one could feel the trees waking up to greet the spring. Blackbirds and thrushes flew above them and a woodpecker drilled in the distance. Radley dragged them off in all directions but, where the bones were concerned, on a wild goose chase, it seemed.

'I say, Anne, do you think he remembers where he found this bone?'

'Oh yes. Spaniels are incredibly clever dogs. If they've found something they like and it was in a certain place, they tend to make a beeline for that same spot.'

'I read somewhere,' said Charlie stomping down hard on the undergrowth, 'that a dog's sense of smell is a few thousand times better than a human's.'

'You never fail to impress me with your knowledge,' James said, adding that working in a library must have widened his range of interests.

Over the next half hour they planted stakes and made notes about clues along the route while making detours as Radley tugged them back and forth among the trees. Before too long, the three of them felt like drowned rats as they plunged through sodden grass and drooping branches. Anne pulled for Radley to come back to the path and, for a second, he was happy to do so; but then, he yanked her back.

James stopped. 'He seems pretty insistent, doesn't he?'

Anne took a tentative step forward.

He put his hand out for the rope. 'Do you want to stay here?'

She swallowed as she passed the lead across. 'No, but I'll follow you.' She linked arms with Charlie.

James allowed Radley to pull him through the forest. Twigs and old branches snapped beneath his feet and water dripped down the back of his neck. He pulled his collar tight and began planning a nice hot bath when he returned home, and a brandy to warm him through. The damp seeped into his bones and he could feel his toes getting cold. He silently bemoaned the fact that wellingtons were all well and good but that they never kept your feet warm. Radley barked at the edge of a clearing and James let out an exasperated sigh.

'Didier!'

His chef was ahead of him, holding a small wicker trug, foraging in the undergrowth. The stout Frenchman got up from his knees and winced as he felt his back. 'Ah Lord 'arrington, it is no day for rambling in the damp forest, *non*?'

'No indeed, Didier.' He peered into the basket to see wild garlic and a number of morel mushrooms. Radley stood on his hind legs to sniff the contents. Didier held the basket above his head and gave the dog a look of disgust.

Anne caught up with them and smiled a welcome at Didier. 'Hello there, I didn't realise you foraged.'

'*Oui, oui*, fresh from the forest floor,' he beamed and brushed himself down. 'Never the same place; *non, non*. Must allow everything to grow again. Now, I 'ead to the outskirts for mint. Mint sauce to 'ave with the lamb. *Au revoir*.'

Charlie smiled. 'Looks like Radley was after Didier's selection of leaves instead of old bones.'

They turned towards the path but another yank on the lead suggested the dog had other ideas. James tilted his head for his companions to follow. Two minutes later, and much deeper into the forest, they came to a natural clearing where Radley was busy digging with fervour. His front paws scooped and his back paws flicked wet mud and leaves behind him. James handed the rope to Anne and asked that she pull the dog away. She did so and stood back.

James pulled his gloves off and squatted down. Charlie joined him. Radley had already taken a layer of soft mud from the surface and something grey-white caught his eye. With his thumb and forefinger, he gently manoeuvred the item out. He brushed the cloying soil from it and stood up to show them another length of bone.

Anne put her hands to her mouth. 'Oh dear.'

Charlie made a face, with a silent 'Ooh'.

James reached across and picked up a sturdy branch that lay on the forest floor. Then he gently scraped away dead leaves and earth. Charlie did the same from the other side and, slowly, fragments of bone surfaced. Anne edged closer, holding Radley's lead tight. James used the branch and his hands to clear the area and get a better idea of the way the body was lying. He examined an area around what appeared to be the middle of the skeleton. There were fragments of clothing, almost disintegrated. He pointed out an oval piece of leather.

'That looks like an elbow patch,' said Anne. 'You know, the sort teachers or gamekeepers sew on their jackets.'

'Mmm.'

Charlie gently cleared away strands of clothing and, over the next quarter of an hour, they identified the remnants of a jacket, tie and tie-pin. The shoes were of a good quality and appeared to be hand stitched. The wrist-watch was familiar to James; he had one similar to it.

Anne tapped him on the shoulder and jerked her head at an area toward the ribcage. He looked down and, using a handkerchief, reached across to pick up another piece of leather. This felt much sturdier. He stood up and weighed it in his hand — a wallet. The leather was soft, most likely calfskin, smooth and silky to the touch. He stared at it for some time and turned it over in his hand.

He felt bad for prying into the life of a complete stranger; it felt like an intrusion on the poor chap buried in the ground; an invasion into the person's privacy. And something else had jumped into his mind — would this be someone he knew? After all, the body was buried on the Harrington estate itself. There was only one way to find out. He flipped the wallet open. The contents were minimal: a few ten shilling notes and a flimsy piece of cardboard.

Anne tightened the lead and ordered

Radley to sit. 'What is it?'

'A driving licence.' The weather had taken its toll on the document; the words were faded and they found it difficult to make out the typed text, let alone the written. James replaced the licence and wrapped his hankie around the wallet before securing it in his inside pocket.

'Look,' said Charlie. He reached down to pick up two threepenny bits and examined the dates. 'Nothing beyond 1948, although that doesn't mean much. We don't all carry new coins around with us.'

James commented that the money and the driving licence proved one thing. The skeleton was not old.

Anne checked her watch. 'Time's getting on. The children will be out of school soon.'

'Yes,' said James brushing his hands free of dirt, 'we need to get back and I'll put in a call to George.'

Charlie stared at the ground. 'Do you think we should cover this up? The foxes or badgers may come and disturb it.'

A crow let out a raspy squawk,

reminding James of an old horror film. 'Good idea. I'm sure George will want to see everything as it is. The only thing we've touched are the coins so he shouldn't be too annoyed with me.'

Between them, they brushed loose earth over the skeleton. A few feet away, James pushed in a couple of stakes and hoped he would remember how to get back to the location.

'If you're not sure,' said Anne, 'you could borrow Radley. He'll take you straight there.'

On their way back to the car, they questioned one another about the identity of the skeleton. James assumed it was of a male bearing in mind the wallet and the shoes but how long had it been there? He had hoped it would be old; a Victorian tramp perhaps, but the items on the body had proved otherwise. He shuddered at the thought that a body had been buried on the Harrington estate. How old was this person? Did they have family? Was a wife, child or parent missing this person? The more they all thought about it, the more concerned they became.

James dropped Anne off at the vicarage and reminded her that this must be kept private. 'Tell Stephen, of course, but no one else. You know how the rumour mill starts and I'd like to make sure George is officially the first to know.'

Two minutes later, he parked alongside Charlie's cottage next door to the library. 'I wonder who that is, Charlie? Has anyone ever gone missing in Cavendish?'

Charlie pulled a face to indicate that he'd no idea. 'I don't think I've heard of anyone disappearing and going missing. But it could be someone who was due to leave but never left. It's obviously foul play.'

'Undoubtedly. A body doesn't bury itself. It doesn't look like a robbery. I know there wasn't much in the wallet but the man had a decent wristwatch on him. A Breitling. I remember that particular one coming out after the war. And his shoes are hand-made, the stitching gave that away. That gives us one clue, Charlie.'

'What's that?'

'The man in that grave had some

status. Breitling watches and bespoke shoes do not come cheap.'

Charlie got out of the car and ducked his head back in. 'Perhaps you'd better be asking that question to the people in *your* circle.'

'Ye-es,' James pondered. 'Perhaps I should.'

On the drive home, he hoped that a magnifying glass would help identify the name on the driving licence. He swung the Jaguar on to the gravelled drive and a shiver brushed over him. He liked a mystery as much as the next person but the thought that someone in Cavendish might have buried this body perturbed him. And if the person was from the same social circle as James, might he have known them?

He put the thought to one side as he trotted up the front steps. First job on his list was to telephone George.

3

The following morning, Beth placed soft boiled eggs and toast on the table and asked James about their meeting with George.

'We have to be at Harrington's in about an hour,' he said. 'I'll be interested to know if he's made anything of the licence.'

Harrington's was a short drive away from their own expansive red-brick property that James' father had built in the early 1930s.

The previous evening, George had dropped by to find out more about James' discovery and questioned why it was always James who seemed to naturally trip over a mystery.

'I don't know how you do it, I really don't,' he'd said with a disbelieving shake of the head.

The only magnifying glass to hand was not particularly powerful and no one could make out the full name on the licence although the letters J, A and U were easy to spot. George made copious notes and then returned to police headquarters with the wallet for a more in-depth analysis.

Beth cracked her egg and peeled the top from it. 'It's funny how those bones have risen to the surface, don't you think? And after so many years. Why do you think that is?'

He sliced his toast into soldiers, dipped a piece in his yolk and sprinkled a little salt over it. 'It's a damp area with lots of tree roots and rainfall. I'm not an expert but I would imagine the ground shifts a little over time. Only takes one bone to come to the surface or an animal to be intrigued by it.' He bit into his soldier. The bread had been freshly delivered that morning and was so light it had toasted in under a minute. He savoured the texture and the fresh orange yolk. 'And I can't think of anyone around here who's disappeared, rich or poor. Perhaps that watch wasn't his. For all we know, he may have been a tramp who robbed someone.'

'I guess so.'

After breakfast, they donned waxed jackets and wellingtons and drove in reflective silence to Harrington's.

The gravel crunched under the wheels as James brought the Jaguar to a stop alongside Harrington's kitchen entrance, where George was already waiting. He had two young men with him holding spades, along with a middle-aged man wearing a mackintosh. As requested by James the previous evening, George ensured everyone was out of uniform and in an unmarked police car. The last thing he wanted was his guests seeing policemen marching into the forest with shovels and bringing a body back. Although they'd done as he'd asked, for some reason, they still appeared too official for James' liking.

George tipped his trilby at Beth and nodded at the man in the mackintosh. 'James, Beth, this is Maurice Kane. He's one of our medical officers and quite an expert on skeletons so may be able to help us out a little.'

'Ah, splendid, good to meet you, Mr

Kane.' James stared at their feet and frowned. 'Do you need wellingtons? We have spare pairs in the staff cupboard if you'd like to change. If you don't mind me saying, you're likely to have extremely wet feet if you go into the forest as you are.'

George examined his footwear and those of his colleagues. 'Might be a good idea.'

With everyone kitted and booted, James led the way into the forest. Although dry, the sky was grey and a damp mist continued to hang among the trees. Beth grumbled under her breath about how this weather flattened her hair. James gave her a knowing look and said that he was sure the skeleton wouldn't mind how she presented herself.

She ignored the jibe and asked George if he had been able to make out the name on the licence.

'No. We had a few attempts with different magnifying glasses. We're pretty sure the first name is Jon but that's about it. The experts are looking at it today, they'll fathom it out. They'll have a microscope so it'll be easier to make out, I'm sure.'

'I hope so, for your sake,' said James. 'I don't think you're going to find much when you see what's left in the ground.'

They trod a muddy path through the undergrowth and held soggy branches back for one another. Every so often James stopped to get his bearings and marched off again. Thrushes and goldfinches scattered and squirrels shot up trees as they approached. Finally, they came to the clearing where he was pleased to see their two stakes still standing and the earth undisturbed. They gathered round.

James highlighted specific areas. 'I'd say you need to scrape the earth away instead of shovelling it. The majority of the skeleton is pretty near the surface. The feet are this end and the skull is up there.' He nudged George. 'And before you admonish me for interfering, I can categorically state that we didn't touch anything except the threepenny bits and the wallet. Charlie picked the coins up to look at the dates.'

George had a chat with his constables and, with an order to be particularly careful, told them to start work. The young men carefully began clearing the earth away. James and Beth watched from a distance and, after a few minutes, Maurice ordered the men to stop. The man squatted down and advised them to proceed with more caution. Bones were surfacing and, he said, it was important that things were not moved unnecessarily.

'How long has Kane been with you, George?' asked James.

'About fifteen years now. He normally does the post-mortems and all the grisly stuff.'

Beth shuddered.

'My thoughts exactly,' he continued, 'but it's good that someone likes doing the dirty work.'

Maurice told the men to stop. He squatted down and examined the bones and the few items left on the body. After a couple of minutes he beckoned them across.

'This is a male, I can tell you that but until I get the skeleton laid out properly, I can't give you a definite height or probable age.' He slipped a pencil out of his top pocket and highlighted an area at the front of the skull. 'This may be an injury that happened after death but there is a clear fracture here. I can't see any signs of arthritis or anything that relates to an older person, so I'd guess this is a younger man, no older than thirty.'

George leaned over to get a closer look. 'That fracture, is that a punch or a weapon?'

'Difficult to say, but we may find out with a more thorough examination. By the way, his name is Jonathan, Jonathan Dunhelm.' Maurice stood up and stretched his back.

James' jaw dropped. 'How on earth do you know that?'

The medical officer held the watch up with his tweezers. 'There's an inscription on the back. *To Jonathan Dunhelm, Christmas 1947.*'

George asked if there would be fingerprints on it after all this time.

'No idea. I'll keep it safe and we'll see what we can find.' He turned and instructed the constables on how best to remove and transport the skeleton, then addressed James. 'We'll need to be in and out of here today to get everything packed up and back to Lewes. We'll be as discreet as we can.'

James indicated they were to do whatever was required and Maurice set to work.

Beth squeezed his hand and whispered. 'Have you heard of Jonathan Dunhelm?'

He said he hadn't though for some reason, he felt he should have. Somewhere, in the depths of his subconscious, the name 'Dunhelm' lurked. George had overheard and asked if there was a reason why they would know him.

'Nothing jumps out specifically but the watch is interesting,' James said. 'A Breitling watch doesn't come cheap. They were, and still are in some respects, *the* watch to have in the RAF; time-keeping spot on and a lot of the officers I served with had them. They now have built-in chronographs.'

'They're Swiss-made,' added Beth.

'So this bloke could have been in the RAF?'

James shrugged. 'It's dated 1947 so there's a chance this chap served.'

George heaved a satisfied sigh. 'Well, that's been a good morning's work.'

James had to agree. They'd arrived an hour ago knowing nothing. Now they knew his name, perhaps his station in life, a possible career path and how he might have died. He checked his watch. 'Darling, why don't you and I walk the rest of the egg hunt route? Charlie marked it all out yesterday and we can put the finishing touches to the clues.' He turned to George. 'Are we still meeting for a pint later or will this spoil things?'

'Let's make it early and just a quick one. I've got quite a bit of paperwork to catch up on. But, I can't do much more with this until Maurice's report comes through. We can start doing some checks on surviving family but that's about it.'

They bade the group farewell and made their way back to the trail. Beth linked arms with him. 'I could see you recognised the name, James. Did you know him in the air force?'

'I have absolutely no idea. We were a

pretty tight unit where we were and the name Dunhelm doesn't ring any bells, as far as being on our base is concerned.'

James thought back to his brief stint in the RAF as an aircraft mechanic. Three years at RAF Upwood in Cambridgeshire had, although it was during a dark period for England, been a tremendous joy to him. He'd worked alongside a team of mechanics on the huge Lancaster bombers that took their flight crew on precarious missions across Germany.

They stopped by the river where they spotted a kingfisher nestling in the shade of a willow tree. Bluebells and cowslips were beginning to show although wouldn't be in full bloom for a couple of weeks yet.

'You know the people in the village used to line the streets to watch the aircraft take off? They'd count them out and keep watch until they returned so they could count them back.'

'Oh my goodness, how poignant. And do you think Jonathan Dunhelm might have been part of a flight crew?'

He contemplated the clear water as it trickled past. 'Impossible to say. There were so many squadrons at Upwood when I was there and thousands of personnel. It may help to have a photograph of him.'

'Did the base lose a lot of people? You rarely speak about them.'

'Very few engineers perished. We had some injuries but they were part and parcel of the job. The engineers stuck together the same as the flight crew did. You learned not to get too attached to the flight crew. You had a job to do; make their bomber as safe and operational as possible. We knew, with every mission, some wouldn't come back. There's also a camaraderie that only exists when you're in the service. Once you're out, those friendships take on a different quality and people tend to drift apart.'

'You still keep in touch with Dodger though.'

James smiled. Dodger was a few years younger than him and had been nicknamed the Artful Dodger by the rest of the engineers. In some ways, he was like his friend, Bert Briggs; a wheeler-dealer who had obtained items from the black market to sell on. They'd remained in touch with Christmas cards and meeting for the odd pint if either were close by. But, with Dodger running a pub in Suffolk, quite some distance from Cavendish, those catch-ups were few and far between.

Beth suggested that Dodger might recall the name. 'Is he on the telephone? You could contact him and ask.'

They continued along the track that followed the river and discussed final ideas for the egg-hunt clues. James made a note to have some of the trees cut back along the river's edge and announced that he'd give Dodger a call. 'Hopefully, he can shed some light on things.'

* * *

After a splendid lunch of Grandma Harrington's Welsh Rarebit with fried mushrooms, James popped into the study to call Dodger. They spent a pleasant twenty minutes giving each other an update on their lives and reminiscing about old times, but it was clear he would not be moving forward where the identity of Jonathan Dunhelm was concerned. Dodger had no recollection of the name although he promised to have a chat with a few others from the base to see if they remembered anything.

'Or,' he suggested, 'you could check the service listings.'

James decided to telephone his sister, Fiona, who lived in Wiltshire. She answered in her normal booming voice. He went through the events of the previous couple of days and threw the name out for her to think about.

'You do get involved in such unsavoury matters, James. Why don't you just run the estate like you're supposed to do? I don't think Geoffrey would have got himself mixed up in things like this. I can't believe you're digging up old bodies in the forest.'

Geoffrey, their elder brother, had died shortly after their parents and the title had come to James.

'I'm sure Geoffrey would have loved it. And, anyway, I didn't dig it up, Radley did. But never mind that, does the name

Jonathan Dunhelm ring any bells with you?'

'Yes it does, but I don't know why? I don't recall ever meeting a Jonathan Dunhelm and if I did it was a fleeting introduction at a party or something.'

'Were there Dunhelms in Cavendish? I don't recall any.'

'Not that I remember. Why don't you check the parish records?'

James kicked himself for not thinking of that. He scribbled *parish records* on the blotting paper. That would be his next job. He passed the time of day with Fi and caught up on the family news her end. Before ringing off he made a promise that he and Beth would visit soon.

His next call put him through to the vicarage.

'Ah Stephen, could I possibly pop round to look at the parish records?'

Stephen chuckled. 'You're o-on the heels of another mystery, aren't you? Of c-course. Come on over. Oh, hold on.' A few seconds later he announced that Anne, whom he had now nicknamed Miss

Marple, wondered if Beth would like to come too as Anne had some dress patterns she'd like to show her.

They drove into Cavendish and parked at the vicarage where Stephen led James into his office to peruse the records and registers held by the church. It was a small room with a latticed window looking across to the Half Moon. Stephen opened the glass-fronted bookcase in the corner.

'W-what sort of date are you l-looking at?'

'Let's start at around 1930.'

The pair of them read the spines of the antiquated books and settled on one that covered the period between 1935 and 1945. James placed it on the desk and opened the cover. A musty smell that he could only associate with old books greeted him. He turned the pages carefully and commented on the precise calligraphy on its pages.

'I-it's a dying a-art and one that I would like to be a-able to do. My w-writing is dreadful.'

James examined the looped writing of previous vicars and occasionally asked his friend to clarify an entry. After checking every page, they turned to the registers either side of that one but none of the books provided information on people by the name of Dunhelm.

He closed the book and slapped it in frustration. 'This is beginning to annoy me. Fiona said the name registered with her so it must be a Cavendish link.'

'P-perhaps linked with your parents r-rather than you.'

He didn't think so but decided not to dismiss the notion. 'I'm meeting George at the Half Moon later. Let's hope he'll have something to tell me.'

For the next hour, the four of them had fun completing the clues for the Easter egg hunt and putting suggestions forward to Stephen about what to put in his Easter sermon. The hour extended further into the afternoon and, before they knew it, the Merryweathers two boys, Mark and Luke, were running in with news of their school day.

'I came third in the spelling test,' Mark said proudly and listed a number of words that had been in the test. 'And Mr

Chrichton started reading *The Wind in the Willows* to us.'

'He's reading *Peter Pan* to us,' Luke said, adding that he would like to be able to fly like the boy in the story.

Anne straightened their ties, bemoaning the fact that they always looked so smart when they went out in the morning yet arrived back looking like a couple of scarecrows.

Mark fought himself out of Anne's reach and took his tie off. 'It's silly having a uniform anyway. The teachers always send us out at break time and you can't stay clean if you're playing football.'

Luke, in the habit of copying everything his brother did, shrugged his jacket off. 'Can we go out and play?'

'Go and change out of those clothes before you do that.'

The boys raced upstairs.

James and Beth agreed that they'd had the same issue with their twins, Harry and Oliver, when they were boys.

'Boys are always so untidy,' Beth added. 'And I notice they all still go poking around by the river once those

54

school gates open.'

James smiled. It always amazed him how many everyday things became tradition. It could be recipes passed down through the generations, a hobby passed from father to son, dress-making skills taught by a mother to her daughter, games played by the children today that were probably played by their grandparents; hop-scotch, skipping, hide and seek and conkers. He wondered when he became a grandfather, if he'd be handing down his own family traditions but then realised that he'd already begun doing so. These traditions were passed on from the moment the new generation was born and he could imagine Harry and Oliver doing the same with their children.

After some time, the mantel clock chimed a gentle reminder that it was now six o'clock. James apologised for keeping their friends so long and they made their excuses to leave.

Anne insisted they stay for dinner. 'We're cooking sausages and I have plenty so do say you'll stay. You're always inviting us for a meal and it's nice to return the hospitality.'

James made his excuses. He wasn't over-hungry and he knew George would be waiting for him. Beth accepted the invitation and asked James to pick her up once he'd finished. Between them, she and Anne could write up the clues and that would be the egg hunt task finished.

'All we'll need to do,' she said, 'is place them along the route the day before the hunt.'

James left the ladies to their writing and strolled across the village green to the pub. It was a dry evening and a thin layer of cloud made the moon appear like an apparition. Although it was dusk, a few of the older children were playing cricket and, by the sound of things, entering into a competitive game.

The chatter inside the Half Moon promised a busy evening for Donovan and Kate, and James acknowledged a number of farmers and villagers as he made his way to the bar. He could almost taste the beer from the smell of hops and malt that greeted him. Kate Delaney stood with her hands on her hips, wearing a welcoming smile.

'George is in the corner waiting for you,' she said.

Through the crowds, James glimpsed the top of his friend's head. 'Right you are. I'll have a pint of . . . I say, have you had the Easter ale delivered?'

Kate tapped the end pump. 'Easter Amber. Donovan's given it the taste test.'

Donovan sidled up next to his wife, wiping a pint glass with a tea towel. 'You'll be wanting that — 'tis a beautiful ale, mild and full of flavour.'

James placed his order and Kate carefully drew the ale and put the full dimpled pint jug on the bar. He supped the first half inch. 'That *is* mild, isn't it? Splendid.' With pint in hand, he manoeuvred his way through a group of farmers to sit opposite George who was filling his pipe with tobacco.

George concentrated on getting some puff before acknowledging him. Finally, he sat forward and said: 'We know who Jonathan Dunhelm is.'

James' shoulders fell in relief. 'Well, hurrah for that.' He went through the numerous telephone calls he'd made and how he and Fiona were sure the name was familiar. 'Come on, George, put me out of my misery.'

'He's a property man. His father was a big developer and, when he died, Jonathan took over the family business.'

James frowned. 'In Cavendish?'

'No, no. They're now based in Crawley. He was part of the group that put in to build the New Town although they live outside of the town.'

James closed his eyes in realisation. 'Of course, yes, yes, of course.'

'You know him?'

'Not him, no, but I'm sure father used to play golf with a Mr Dunhelm. Must have been Jonathan's father.'

George explained that this would have been Ernest Dunhelm. 'He died some years ago.'

'If my memory serves me well,' said James, 'I recall Ernest being a wealthy man who seemed to have the Midas touch where the building trade was concerned. But I didn't think his business was based around here.'

'It wasn't originally. The company headquarters was based just outside North London. Then it moved down to Surrey but when Dunhelm Snr died, Jonathan moved everything to the industrial estate in Crawley.'

James rapped the table. 'Ah yes, it's all coming back to me now. Beth and I attended a function at the Dunhelm house. It was to do with the New Town. Must have been around twelve years ago. Now where on earth was that?' He sat up with a start. 'Yes, I remember, they owned a huge house in Rusper. I think Ernest had died by then. I don't remember him being there. Perhaps this Jonathan was there and I didn't realise. Well, the New Town business would have been a goldmine for anyone in the building trade. Probably still is.'

Crawley was originally a village that was designated to become a New Town after the war. The idea was to build semi-rural and modern developments and get people away from the bomb-damaged streets of London. This particular village was the second in a list of around twenty

59

towns to be built. As far as James could make out, it had been a relative success, with new schools, roads, shops and the recently refurbished Gatwick Airport. He did recall some strong protests from the locals and he completely understood their anger. He'd be the first to debate such extensive building proposals if they ever came to Cavendish.

He twirled a damp beer mat in his hand. 'Do you have any information about why he could have been killed?'

'Preliminary enquiries with Ernest Dunhelm's old business partner suggests Jonathan wasn't liked. The partner refused to work with Jonathan.' George cradled his glass. 'He walked out and started up his own business and left Jonathan to find another partner.'

'Interesting. There's money in building, George, that could be your motive.'

'Mmm, I thought that. There's something else too.'

James waited.

'The blow to the skull. According to Maurice, it wasn't accidental. He thinks that was a fatal blow.'

4

Preparations for Maundy Thursday were well under way. Stephen had originally intended to host an outdoor event; but the expected high pressure front from the Azores had failed to arrive so the hive of activity remained in the church hall. People appeared to come out of the woodwork at Easter, as if emerging from their winter hibernation and all hands were on deck where this event was concerned.

James helped the men set up tables and chairs. Beth, Anne and other members of the WI followed behind to arrange tablecloths and napkins along with an assortment of cutlery and plates loaned by those attending. The WI ladies had made beautiful posies of daffodils and tulips to lend colour and Kate Delaney had found some bright yellow ribbon that she wrapped around the bases of vases and the handles of serving spoons.

Graham and Sarah Porter delivered sliced ham and sausage rolls, Philip Jackson arrived with several bowls of salad and Elsie Taylor pulled up in a car full of freshly baked bread. Bob Tanner, who had friends at the Merrydown vineyard, had managed to strike a deal on several bottles of blackberry wine and Miss Withers, from the newsagents, delivered lemonade and Tizer for the children. Dorothy Forbes dashed to her car to retrieve bowls of potato salad that she'd almost forgotten. And Professor Wilkins, a man not known for socialising or attending these kinds of functions, had surprised James by not only making an appearance but by handing over a dozen large pork pies.

Within an hour, the hall had been transformed to a colourful and welcoming gathering place. Anne and Helen covered the food and motioned for everyone to make their way to the church for what Stephen described as a quick community service. Anne had spent the morning decorating the church and given it an Easter feel. Four vases of daffodils stood at the front of the church and at the end of each pew, she had pinned yellow ribbons crafted into bows. A number of tall yellow and cream candles flickered making the church warmly atmospheric.

Beth congratulated her. 'It's surprising what a difference a little colour makes. And those candles are gorgeous.'

'And,' said Anne, 'it's lovely to see bright colours after such a dreary winter.'

James and Beth took their normal spaces in the front row alongside Philip and Helen and sat back to enjoy the spectacle. Every year, twelve regular church-goers were chosen at random to be part of the Maundy Thursday ritual. This year several farmers, James' childhood fishing tutor, Mr Bennett, Rose and Lilac Crumb and Mr Chapman, the bank manager, took their place in this centuries-old tradition.

Stephen knelt with a bowl of water and gently dowsed the feet of his twelve villagers and reminded them they represented the twelve disciples at the Last Supper. They each balanced their feet over the bowl as he loaded his sponge and squeezed water over them while emphasising the need to serve and respect one another. Anne followed behind with a small towel.

Once the chosen disciples had returned to their pews, James and Beth handed Stephen a pile of envelopes for their pensioners, each containing half a crown. Stephen distributed the envelopes and Graham and Sarah followed close behind to hand out the promised lamb chops. The pensioners smiled their thanks and a few nearby joked that it would soon be their turn to receive these gifts.

Returning to the pulpit, Stephen asked that everyone should bow their head in prayer. 'Our a-act here today represents humility and grace; an act of love and friendship. It shows that w-we are all equal and that th-those with power must learn how to serve and give back. Teach us to be good people, Lord, and embrace the love you gave us and show us how to give that l-love to others. Amen.'

The back door of the church cannoned open and the congregation turned as one to see Bert Briggs holding up a hand in embarrassment. 'Sorry, vicar, I meant to come in quietly.'

James suppressed a grin as Stephen beckoned him in. His old Cockney friend slipped in the pew beside him with shrug. ''ow was I to know the door would open that quick?'

Stephen shushed him and continued with two more prayers. A few children shuffled impatiently, which prompted him to ask God to give children the patience to wait, causing the villagers to chuckle. With a final 'Amen', Anne swept the doors open and the villagers made their way next door to the church hall.

James likened their Maundy Thursday celebration to the huge street party they'd had during the Queen's coronation. He estimated there were at least one hundred residents waiting to eat. With so many people present, the chatting and laughter soon began as the elderly were helped to their seats and parents organised their children.

Everyone had brought their own chair or stool and he couldn't help but smile at the comical scene in front of him. Mr Bennett had opted for a deckchair which, when he sat in it, made his nose level with the table, while Rose and Lilac Crumb had settled on kitchen stools that made them tower over their neighbours.

A few people dashed into their respective homes around the green and retrieved cushions for those needing more comfort. Stephen returned to the church and brought out several kneeling cushions to help those needing a little more height. Young children tugged their parents' sleeves, demanding to know when they could start eating.

Fortunately Stephen had a large hand-bell with him as it was the only way to gain some attention. He rang it loudly and cut through the noise until a hush descended. Much to the children's annoyance, he asked everyone to bow their heads and say grace.

As one, the villagers spoke: 'For what we are about to receive, may the Lord make us truly thankful.'

With the formalities over, the joy of tucking into a communal feast began. The seriousness of Stephen's sermon gave way to banter and catching up with one another's news. The solicitor, Mr

Bateson, dressed in a suit with a daffodil buttonhole, rose to sing with Bob Tanner.

> Now a day before Easter the morn bright and clear,
> The sun it shone brightly and keen blew the air.
> I went up in the forest to gather fine flowers,
> But the forest won't yield me no roses.

As the men continued singing, James helped himself to some salad, a bread roll and two slices of ham. The roll was soft, still warm and he guessed that Elsie must be using the oven in the tiny kitchen at the back of the hall. The smell of fresh dough set his taste-buds dancing as he added a dollop of butter and allowed it to melt.

Further along, Beth nattered with GJ, Catherine, Dorothy Forbes and Kate Delaney. Bert sat alongside him to the right and to the left were Philip and Helen Jackson and their young daughter, Natasha. Opposite were Professor Wilkins and Charlie Hawkins with his two children, Tommy and Susan. They spent a pleasant hour passing the time of day and enjoying the first of many activities relating to the season.

Bert reached across for a pork pie. 'What's all this I 'ear about you finding a skeleton?'

James took a sip of the sweet blackberry wine before going over the events of the last couple of days along with George's findings the previous evening.

His friend nudged his flat cap up from his forehead. 'Dunhelm — 'e's the building bloke, isn't he?'

'You've heard of him?'

'Yeah, in passing.' Bert referred to third-hand accounts of families who had been forced out of their homes to make way for development. 'I'm sure that's the Dun'elm lot. Got quite a bad name a few years ago. Not 'eard much about 'em recently.'

'Ties in with what George was saying. Was this in Crawley — for the New Town?'

'Nah mate. I think this was up around

London somewhere. But I 'eard that if they can make some money, they'll make it, by fair means or foul.'

Philip chipped in that Jonathan must have overstepped the line if he forced people away from where they lived. 'An Englishman's home is his castle, as they say. You start turfing people out of their homes, eventually someone will take exception.'

'It seems awfully extreme to resort to foul play though, don't you think?' James put in.

Elsie appeared behind them with a new batch of freshly baked rolls. She placed them on the table and numerous hands reached out to grab one, including James.

He peeled the roll apart and loaded his knife with butter. 'I say, Elsie, you've been busy. Have you closed the café?'

Elsie was a plump woman in her late thirties, with long wiry blonde hair always tied back in a pony-tail. Her passions were simple: running the café and baking, so she'd set up the cafe to fulfil her dream. Her home-made cakes brought customers in from far and wide and she'd recently begun using some of Grandma Harrington's recipes. James was always quick to recommend her cosy establishment to his own guests.

She explained to James that she'd brought in extra staff. 'I've a friend helping me here and my regular waitresses are holding the fort back at the café. I could do it the other way around but this is such a lovely day that I wanted to enjoy it myself.' She made her excuses and carried on plonking bowls of bread on the tables.

James decided to stretch his legs and wandered around the hall chatting to residents and exchanging Easter greetings. He was relieved to hear the discovery of the skeleton in the forest was not yet common knowledge and was keen to keep it that way. But there was no escaping the Snoop Sisters, his nickname for Rose and Lilac Crumb. Judging by the way they made a beeline for him they had clearly overheard something. If that was the case, it wouldn't be long before the whole community heard. They scurried up to him.

'What's this we hear?' asked Rose, licking crumbs from her lips.

'A body at Harrington's,' added Lilac.

'Is it someone we know?'

'Was it a man or a woman?'

'Are they local?'

James stopped them. 'Ladies, I have absolutely no idea about any of it. If you wish to find out more, I suggest you chat to Detective Chief Inspector Lane, he'll update you.'

The two ladies huffed and wandered away with their normal mutterings that accused James of knowing things and assuming that they weren't good enough for him to share that knowledge with them.

Beth sought him out. She wore a flattering navy pencil dress with a red cardigan draped over her shoulders.

'So,' she said, 'what did the Snoop Sisters want? Although I'd hazard a guess they're after snippets of information about our skeleton.'

'I chose not to divulge anything.' He slipped his hands in his pockets. 'Although they are the sort of people who know things. D'you think they will have heard of the Dunhelms?'

'They may do. I know they spent their early years outside the county but they spent most of their adult life in Sussex and Surrey. Perhaps you should ask them. If anyone picks up gossip, those ladies do. Word will be out soon about the discovery anyway.' She folded her arms. 'You've already started investigating this so you may as well see what they have to say. You *are* investigating, aren't you?'

He raised an eyebrow and smiled. 'It would be churlish not to. And anyway, it's an old case, so the killer is probably long gone.'

James watched as Rose and Lilac began saying goodbye to the villagers and making their way out of the hall. Beth was right. It would soon be common knowledge. As much as he hated the tittle-tattle of gossip, these sisters might have some useful hearsay for him.

'I'll go and ask.'

He found Rose and Lilac unlocking the door to their vintage Citroën. James wondered how on earth it still ran. It was a relic of a bygone age, with wide running boards and huge headlights. He held a hand up to attract their attention and was a little spooked by the way they stood and fixed their eyes on him. It was as if they had built-in radar. Their expressions were of morbid expectation.

'Ladies, I do remember something about the skeleton. I think George said his name was Dunhelm. Does that mean anything to you?'

The sisters stood in reflective silence. Finally, Rose stared at Lilac. 'Ernest Dunhelm. Do you remember him?'

'Yes, yes I do.'

James tried to hide his surprise. They explained that Ernest Dunhelm had been responsible for building a factory on a site near their grandparents' home in Romford, on the outskirts of London.

'Is that the man in the ground?' said Lilac.

'Was he murdered then?' added Rose.

'Who'd want to murder him? He seemed a nice man.'

'Although perhaps a little ruthless.'

'Oh yes, father said he was focussed

solely on business — business-minded and no thought for feelings.'

James stopped them. He put a foot on the running board and leaned on the car. 'I don't think it's Ernest but are you saying that you knew Ernest Dunhelm well?'

'No, no. Father mentioned him,' said Rose. 'Father dealt with all things business although he never did business with Mr Dunhelm. Father helped some friends of our grandfather, an elderly couple, wasn't it Lilac dear?'

'That's right, although I don't recall the details.'

'These friends, was their home affected?' asked James.

'Not directly, no . . . '

The sisters nattered between themselves while he tried to make sense of their ramblings.

'No, not directly, but do you remember, Lilac, that there was that Mr and Mrs Fuller, a younger couple. They were upset about having to move. They were on the estate affected by most of the upheaval.'

'Ooh, yes, not happy at all. They were moved somewhere of a much lower standard.'

'Mmm, yes, much lower standard although Father was sure that the Fullers protested.'

'Along with many other families.'

'Yes, many others. But was that Ernest, dear?'

'I thought it was, but didn't he have a brother or a son working with him?'

James asked if they knew where these families had been moved to and learned that many of them had relocated toward London, in particular to Eltham, south of the River Thames.

'When was this, ladies?'

The sisters paused and mentally counted back, reminding each other of different events and when they occurred.

Lilac announced that it would have been just after the war. 'Clearing bomb-sites they were, but not making a good job of it.'

Rose added that some of the houses were prefabs.

'Are you saying that these families were

moved into prefabs?' asked James.

'Some were, yes, although it may have been short term.'

Prefabs were small post-war bungalows with a garden plot; they had only been intended to last a few years, nine or ten at the most. They provided temporary accommodation for those people whose properties had been bombed out. He asked if the Fuller family were eventually moved to more permanent accommodation.

'Couldn't say.'

'Lost touch once they'd moved. We never really had much to do with them.'

'And we were living elsewhere. We got all of this from the people who lived nearby.'

Rose opened the boot of the car to load their stools into it. The smell of oil and petrol drifted up.

'Ladies, before you go, do you remember the Fullers' full names?'

'Ooh, yes. Eoin Fuller. E.O.I.N. Remember that because it was an unusual name. Irish, I think it is.'

'His wife's name was Lottie. Had a

little boy they did. He'll be nearly grown up by now.'

James opened the passenger door for Lilac as Rose climbed into the driver's seat. The old car spluttered to a start and he winced as she crunched the gear stick into first. Eventually, the ancient vehicle began its journey and James waved it off.

He puffed out his cheeks. Well, that had certainly been a worthwhile conversation. If Jonathan was as ruthless as his father, it wouldn't be surprising if someone had decided to put an end to things. If the Fullers and their neighbours were still in prefab housing after all these years, the list of people wanting to exact revenge would be long, particularly if they'd been forced to leave a good neighbourhood. But, again, the thought that someone would kill over such a matter nagged at him.

He returned to Beth and the Merryweathers and recounted his chat with the sisters. Stephen was horrified to learn how these families had been treated; effectively pushed out of their home for no apparent reason.

'Th-these prefabs were for people re-housed from w-war damaged properties. Why would this Dunhelm man move people from perfectly g-good properties into those earmarked for the homeless? A-are you sure Rose and L-Lilac have their f-facts straight?'

Anne made it clear she'd be livid if someone moved her to a prefab from a perfectly sound house. 'They couldn't have known, could they?'

'How d'you mean?' asked James.

'Surely they wouldn't have agreed to that. You wouldn't give up a perfectly good home for a prefab, would you? I know I wouldn't, unless the home I was in was of poor quality. If they felt they'd been swindled they would seek some recompense, wouldn't they?'

Beth agreed with the sentiment. 'Perhaps Jonathan was as ruthless as his father with the business. But his body's been found on our estate so it must be something more local than Eltham, don't you think? I know it's not the other side of the world but it seems awfully strange to bring a body here when you could put it in the Thames. This has to be something that Jonathan was involved in.'

'You're right, darling, but Jonathan may have been involved in this Eltham affair. It wouldn't hurt to track Eoin Fuller down. He can give us a good idea about what happened and how they felt about it. It'll shed some light on Jonathan's personality too. Learn about the victim and you learn about the motive.'

'W-well you know who'll do th-that for you, don't you?'

James smiled. Yes indeed, Bert Briggs. His old friend had an uncanny knack for tracking down contacts and finding out information; especially if it centred on London. Bert was a true Cockney, born within the sound of the Bow church bells. He grew up in the East End and knew the place like the back of his hand. If he were to be led round the streets blindfolded he'd be able to pinpoint exactly where he was by the sounds and accents around him. He'd recently spent a lot more time around the Bethnal Green area where he'd rekindled an old friendship with a lovely lady named Gladys, who ran the

East End mission. Although Bert played down any possible romance, even James could see the man was smitten with her.

He excused himself and, after topping his glass up with wine, caught up with Bert who was accepting a paper bag from Helen.

'Oi, oi, Jimmy boy. Nice start to the Easter weekend.' He held the bag up. 'Graham and Sarah know a thing or two about making sausage rolls. The pastry's that flaky it goes everywhere. I've nabbed some for my bus ride home.'

James made a mental note to grab one before they all disappeared. 'Bert, I wonder if you could put a few feelers out.'

His friend gave him an expectant look. 'Is that you off again, hindering the police with their enquiries?'

'Humour me, please.'

Bert listened as he outlined his conversation with the Snoop sisters. 'Would you be able to track down this Eoin Fuller chap?'

'I'll give it a shot. I know a few people in Eltham. The prefabs are still there, I know that much, so they may be in the same place. Leave it with me 'coz I've gotta get going. My bus is due any minute now and I don't wanna miss it.' He shouted a farewell to everyone with a promise to James that he would let him have an update as soon as possible.

Beth sidled up to James. 'Penny for your thoughts.'

'I believe we have a good excuse to call on Mrs Dunhelm tomorrow. We said we wanted to watch the marbles and it's the championships in Crawley. Rusper is only a couple of miles up the road so we could try and glean some information about her son.'

'George won't thank you for butting in.'

'My visit is purely compassionate. After all, her son was found on our land and we have met before, albeit some time ago.'

'Shall we invite Stephen and Anne in their official capacity?'

He smiled. That was certainly an excellent idea and gave more credibility to their stopping by. 'Let's invite them. Stephen has his riverbank reflection session in the afternoon but we can make sure he's back for that. I'm sure Luke and Mark would love to see the marbles.'

With the Maundy Thursday celebrations coming to a close, they all dug in to help put furniture back and pack up the items they'd brought with them. In less than an hour, the church hall had been cleared and the floor brushed clean of crumbs. Tomorrow was Good Friday, the start of the marbles world championships and a visit to the victim's mother.

He and Beth made their way back to the car. 'I'll telephone Mrs Dunhelm when we get home. I say, did you get the ingredients for the simnel cake?'

'Yes,' said Beth, 'fortunately, I remembered to stop by the grocery store. I've also reminded the WI that we need sponge cakes for the races.'

'Good girl.' James had forgotten all about that. Thank goodness she was organised. He opened the passenger door for her. 'Shall we bake a couple of simnel cakes tonight and take one to Mrs Dunhelm?'

'Charmer!'

He grinned as he fired the engine up.

The now familiar buzz flashed through him. A mystery to solve; a new jigsaw to complete. He hoped he could find all the pieces and establish what on earth had taken place all those years ago that warranted placing Jonathan Dunhelm in a shallow grave.

5

In order to find a good vantage point, they'd arrived early for the marbles championships but the Greyhound pub at Tinsley Green was already heaving with people. The pub itself was an impressive building with a wonderful rounded entrance complete with a semi-circular balustrade balcony on which a handful of visitors stood while, below them, around two hundred people had gathered for the annual competition. Discarded bicycles leaned against walls and hedges; parked further up the road were half a dozen cars, including James' Jaguar.

The marbles playing arena was cordoned off with rope. It was a large area with a six foot wide playing surface in the centre. Five yards back on either side were two wooden benches where the opposing teams were seated. Two teams were already in play; the Rusper Rockets and the Horley Hurricanes. The Horley team sported jumpers with their team motif embroidered on the front. They consisted of middle-aged men in twill trousers, smoking pipes and studying the clay marbles in front of them. The Rusper Rockets were a much younger group of men in jeans and high-top suede boots. Their hair was combed back with the new fashionable quiff at the front. Although they were fans of the new rock and roll music and American fashions, like the older group, they took their marbles seriously and the concentration on their faces was clear to see.

The large group of onlookers looked on in respectful silence as the players paced around the circle and thought about their moves and strategy. There were occasional nods of approval as the teams competed.

Luke and Mark, along with many other children, sat cross-legged just in front of the barrier. Mark was the older by two years but they were similar in looks with shiny black hair and brown eyes. Both had a few freckles over their cheeks. With Anne's firm instructions ringing in their ears, they held Radley's lead tight.

'I don't want to see that dog chasing marbles,' she said.

Stephen arrived with a tray of soft drinks and packets of crisps. There were sixteen teams competing and the referee, an elderly man in a duffle coat, studied proceedings closely and jotted notes down as the game went on.

Beth sipped her drink. 'I don't think I've ever played marbles.'

Mark twisted round and glared at her. 'How could you *never* have played marbles?'

'I've been playing all my life,' added Luke who, at nine years old, spoke as if he was well into his fifties.

She shrugged an apology.

James explained that the game had taken place in this area since the sixteenth century. 'The pub wasn't here of course but marble-playing origins are historic in this area. Two men apparently played to decide who was to wed a local maiden.'

'G-goodness, I didn't kn-know that.'

'Officially, it's been here since the early thirties.' He turned to Beth. 'They play a version called Ring-Taw here. I believe it's called Ringer in your part of the world.'

Beth, who originated from Boston, reiterated that she'd never played but the name of the game did sound familiar. She ruffled the boys' hair. 'Perhaps you could teach me how to play.'

Luke and Mark were quick to say they would before returning their attention to the action.

There was a cheer from one of the players and a round of applause broke out as the Horley Hurricanes triumphed over the Rusper Rockers. The teams shook hands, picked up their pints and vacated the playing area for the next competing sides. James scanned the crowds and his eyes settled on 'Pop' Maynard who was now synonymous with the championships. He never seemed to change. He wore his customary tatty suit and had a straggly grey beard. A flat cap perched jauntily on his head. He held audience with a number of youngsters, showing them how to flick a marble effectively. Alongside Pop was another elderly man whom James recognised; a Crawley man who was here long before the New Town.

'That looks like Ted Cote over there.'

Beth followed his gaze. 'Isn't he one of the original Crawley people?'

James said he was and decided to pop over and have a chat. He threaded through the crowds and tapped Ted on the shoulder. The man turned. In his early seventies, he could have been Pop Maynard's twin, dressed in a similar suit and cap, his eyes twinkling in recognition.

'Lord Harrington,' he said in a soft Sussex burr. 'Well, I'll be jiggered.'

James reached out a hand and made a mental note to pay attention. Cote was 'old' Crawley and used a number of traditional Sussex words. It was a bit like having to translate some of the traditional Cockney phrases from the East End.

'We thought we'd take in the championships this year and I spotted you in the crowd. Ted, I wonder if I could pick your brains.'

Ted chuckled. 'I'm a bit adle-headed these days but go on with yer.'

'You were one of the people against the

New Town, weren't you?'

A firm nod established that he was. James offered the name of Jonathan Dunhelm and asked Ted if he knew him.

'Not from round here, ruddy furriner.'

James was keen not to get into a debate. 'What d'you remember about him?'

'He had pull about him, people listened, people followed him, had their heads turned.'

In the next five minutes, as James translated some of the dialect in his head, it was clear that Ted Cote had done his best to stop the New Town development from happening. He, along with many of the residents, had put in objection after objection but finally accepted that, inevitably, the proposal would go ahead. Building had begun in the late 1940s. The idea was to have several suburbs within Crawley, each with its own shopping parade, school and church. In the centre was the hub of the town, with a large selection of shops and a department store, along with the bus and train station. The new town had attracted a number of London factory-owners to move to the area and many of their employees along with their families made the short journey south with the promise of new, modern housing in the region of the old village. With the Sussex countryside right on the doorstep, it had been an easy decision for many.

James had driven around Crawley on a number of occasions and found it to be a clean, modern town. If Jonathan Dunhelm was mixed up in something dodgy, he didn't think it had been anything to do with inferior housing.

'I say, Ted, do you know if Jonathan was mixed up in anything untoward?'

He watched as the old man brought out his pipe and filled the bowl with tobacco. 'All I can tell you is that I heard he was a codger and a spruser. Don't know much else.'

James thanked him and made his way back to Beth. A codger — a miser; a spruser — someone who deceives. Money was the driving force for the Dunhelm men. If the murder was down to business, George needed to be investigating Dunhelm's property deals, he was certain of that.

An hour into the tournament, Stephen announced they ought to make a move. 'I-I've a busy schedule with the contemplation this afternoon and watching m-marbles wasn't on my list. If you want me as your vicar, you n-need to make use of me now.'

★   ★   ★

Twenty minutes later, James pulled up on the road outside a large detached house surrounded by a few acres of land. They were on the outskirts of Rusper, a small village between the two towns of Crawley and Horsham and around half an hour from Cavendish. Similar to Cavendish, there had been a settlement here for centuries but it was now a beautiful hamlet with pubs, a church and a vibrant community. The Dunhelm house stood back from the road about a mile from the main street.

Beth, who was sitting on the back seat with Anne and the children, suggested that just he and Stephen call in. 'Taking the children would be inappropriate and I think it'll be too much for all of us to descend on her.'

James agreed. 'I hadn't mentioned the Merryweathers when I telephoned yesterday so I think that would be wise.'

'Can we go and watch the cricket?' said Luke. 'I saw them playing on the field next to the church.'

Mark turned to Anne. 'Can we Mum?'

Anne collected her bag and coat. 'Why don't we walk toward the village and watch the game?'

James checked his watch and assured Stephen he was mindful that he needed to get back for the reflective hour. It was getting close to midday. George had said that he would be visiting Mrs Dunhelm first thing that morning. He hoped that he had, as it would help to pave the way for their visit. 'We shouldn't be too long. I don't want to outstay our welcome. You go and watch the cricket and we'll pick you up on the way home.'

Anne and the boys scrambled out of the car.

Beth handed James a cake tin. 'Don't forget this.'

Stephen pulled down the sun-visor with the small mirror attached, adjusted his dog-collar and smoothed his hair back. 'D-do you want me to make introductions, seeing as I'm s-supposed to be here officially?'

'No. I met her once before at this house so we are vaguely acquainted. I'll kick off and we'll go from there.' He put the car in gear and turned onto the drive. 'Come along; let's see what we can find out.'

6

Those meeting Celia Dunhelm for the first time would say that she had a fierce expression, an unfortunate look that could intimidate. But, beneath that expression, they would then remark that her manner was kind, charming and gracious. James put her at around sixty years old. She had pure white styled hair and unlike many of her vintage, she'd kept her figure, striking an elegant pose in a calf-length black dress, a dainty silver necklace and matching earrings. She wore chic spectacles and James detected a splash of Chanel No. 5.

When her housekeeper had announced their arrival, she'd come straight into the hall to greet James, saying how kind it was for him to take the time to pay his respects. James didn't need to put on any pretence. Now he'd seen her, he remembered her from the event he'd attended all of those years ago. She'd been charming then and she was charming now.

He introduced Stephen. 'I know this must be a difficult time for you, Mrs Dunhelm, and my friend here is a tremendous support in such circumstances.' He suddenly remembered the tin in his hand. 'Oh, and my wife and I were doing some baking last night. We thought a nice simnel cake would be appreciated.'

'How thoughtful and, please, do call me Celia.' She gave them an appreciative smile and ushered them through to the lounge. A young maid followed them in and took Celia's request for tea. She gave her the tin and told the girl to serve the cake along with it.

'I could certainly do with something sweet and tasty,' she said.

The room was large, immaculate and tastefully decorated. A grand piano took up one corner and a huge stone inglenook fireplace dominated the far wall. The recently-lit fire had begun to spit as the flames took hold. The dark blue sofas had a silky texture to them and the lined curtains that framed the window were tied back with beautiful cream tassels. He knew the house had around six bedrooms and, if his memory served him right, there was also a similar sized room to this for dining with a study and billiards room off to one side. The Dunhelms had wealth and he wondered if there had been some improvements as the property appeared a little different to how he remembered it.

'Has this house been extended? I know I've only visited once before but it looks bigger.'

'A new building, yes. When Ernest died I did think about moving somewhere smaller. There were too many memories here and, you may know that we entertained considerably before the war. Your mother and father attended some of our functions.'

'Yes, I'm beginning to recollect the occasional visit.'

'And you were here many years ago with your delightful wife.'

'That's right, something to do with the New Town as I remember. I did struggle to recall the name Dunhelm but it's very clear now.'

'Jonathan took the east wing of the

house for his own accommodation and had that enormous barn built to the side of the house for his collection.'

'Collection?'

'Cars, Lord Harrington. He couldn't get enough of them. Not the modern ones we have today; old, ancient things from bygone days.'

'H–how lovely,' said Stephen, adding that he enjoyed being a spectator at the Veteran Car Run between London and Brighton.

'Ah, yes, he entered a car in 1938, a year before the war started.' She sat up proudly. 'I was his passenger. We dressed for the period and it poured with rain.' With a clap of the hands, she let out a poignant laugh that almost led to tears.

James observed her. She was putting on a brave face. To have a son she held dear missing for so long only to be found under such dreadful circumstances must have been difficult. Fortunately, Stephen had come armed with clean handkerchiefs. He moved across to sit next to her on the sofa.

'Mrs Dunhelm, Celia, i–it is always

better to allow your grief to show. Y-you are among friends here and we will c-comfort you in any way we can.'

She dabbed her eyes and thanked them. The maid entered with a silver tray and placed it on the table. An older lady, who James assumed to be a cook, followed with a cake stand holding several slices of simnel cake. As they closed the door behind them, Celia clasped her hands together.

'I find it all so baffling, Lord Harrington. What was Jonathan doing on your estate?'

James scratched his head. 'Celia, I wish I knew. Did he have friends in Cavendish?'

Her reaction surprised him.

'Friends,' she mumbled gazing out of the window. 'The word 'friends' conjured up a different meaning to Jonathan than for everyone else. I'm not sure he had friends, more like acquaintances. They seemed to come and go on a frequent basis.'

Stephen prepared the tea. 'A gentleman normally h-has one or two confidants.'

She rose from her chair and retrieved a photograph from the top of the piano. James accepted it from her and examined it. It showed two men in their mid twenties — both debonair and carefree.

'Jonathan is on the right. The man with him is Pip Logan, his school friend. He was the one person, apart from me, whom he confided in.'

The man staring back at James wore a flying jacket. He was a stunningly handsome man with blond hair flopping over his forehead and an easy grin. He passed the frame across to Stephen and asked what he felt was an obvious question.

'No girlfriend?'

'He was courting a young lady, Natalie Kershaw, about the same age and terribly pretty. For some reason, Jonathan called it off with her. That was a few months before he went missing.'

James made a mental note of the name. 'When did he go missing?'

'Oh I know that. It's etched in my memory. April 9th, 1950. Easter Sunday. That's the day I contacted the police.'

'Did Natalie have any thoughts about what happened to your son?'

'I believe the break-up was quite acrimonious, Lord Harrington. When I reported Jonathan missing, the police did speak with her but her comments were quite inappropriate. She seemed to relish the disappearance.'

James raised his eyebrows. After a pause he commented that Jonathan was a handsome chap who had probably had women falling at his feet.

Celia chose a piece of cake from the stand and put it on her plate. Using a small fork, she cut into it and toyed with the sponge before speaking. 'My son had everything. Looks, money, health, power . . . Unfortunately, the latter he inherited from Ernest.'

'W-was that to the d-detriment of everything else?'

She complimented Stephen on his insight. 'I make no bones about it, Jonathan used people. I loved him dearly; he was my son, my beautiful boy who loved me as much as I did him. He included me in his adventures and took me travelling with him but it pains me to say that he was a ruthless man who ran roughshod over others. His father was the same.'

She'd spoken those words in a matter-of-fact way and James was getting a sense of things here. She loved her family but the men clearly had an unpleasant streak about them and she put up with it or turned a blind eye. He asked if they were different when relaxing at home.

'Oh yes,' she said with some poignancy. 'The men in my life almost worshipped me. Ernest swept me off my feet when we first met and he couldn't do enough for me. Whatever I wanted, I had. I adored him and I never really became involved in his business dealings. I was the wife at home who entertained his colleagues and associates when it was required. I must have learned, at some point early on, that it was not my business to interfere.'

'And that continued with Jonathan after your husband died?'

'Oh no. Jonathan never entertained clients here. He never included me in any business dealings or even discussed them with me. I knew he'd become more ruthless than his father.' Her steely eye met his. 'He was not always a nice man, Lord Harrington. But he was gracious and loving with me.'

'Are you saying that what's happened doesn't surprise you?'

She allowed herself a few seconds before answering. 'If you are ruthless in business, you upset people. The higher your position, the more powerful the people are that you upset.' She stirred her tea. 'I never thought that Jonathan had disappeared. He wouldn't do that, not without leaving word. He never took anything with him. I've left his rooms exactly as he left them because I always thought he would come back. That he would return. At least now I can lay him to rest.'

'A-and you have no i-idea who would want to h-hurt him?'

Celia explained that DCI Lane had asked the same question. 'I will speak the truth to you as I did to him. I think it would be easier to ask who *wouldn't* want to hurt him. His business partner didn't like him. Ernest's partner left the company two years after my husband's death because he couldn't work with Jonathan. I told the Inspector to speak to the people he did business with.'

'I say, Celia, was Jonathan in the RAF? I notice he has a flying jacket on in this photo and I couldn't help notice the watch that he was found with.'

'Ernest and I gave him the watch. He joined as soon as war broke out. He flew Spitfires.'

'Where was he based?'

'Biggin Hill.'

James started. 'Good Lord. They were in the front line for a few missions, weren't they?'

'They were, Lord Harrington. He was in 74 squadron and, for a few months, served alongside 242 squadron.'

James and Stephen exchanged an impressed look.

'Th-that was Douglas Bader's u-unit.'

James couldn't believe it. He'd have moved heaven and earth to serve alongside Bader — a man who carried on flying after losing both legs, although he understood he wasn't always easy to get along with. But, Bader had managed on false legs and, when losing a prosthetic leg after having to parachute out of his aircraft, the Germans had offered to guarantee safety to an aircraft carrying a spare leg. If memory served James right, the British refused and, instead, dropped off the leg during a bombing raid. This would have amused Bader no end who had made it his mission to be, in his words, a 'bloody nuisance' to the enemy.

Celia explained that Jonathan's service to his country was a proud memory for their family and one that she clung to. 'I have his medals displayed in the hall.'

James couldn't help but admire some aspects of Jonathan Dunhelm. Yes, he'd been ruthless and apparently distant with people. It was clear that Celia disliked many aspects of her son's character and behaviour yet the man had volunteered to join up and put his life on the line like so many other young men.

'D-did he keep in touch with h-his squadron?'

They received a stony expression to the question.

'He only kept in touch with people who were of use to him.'

Goodness, James thought, a telling insight. He finished his tea and sat forward. 'Celia, may I be presumptuous?'

She tilted her head.

'Would you permit me to see his room? I've done some successful sleuthing these past few years and DCI Lane will attest to that. I'd like to try to find out what happened to your son if I may. Would you allow that?'

She considered his question for some time. Finally, she placed her teacup on the tray, reached for a small bell by her side and rang it. The young maid entered.

'Diana, show Lord Harrington and the Reverend Merryweather to Jonathan's room.' She turned to James. 'Please leave everything as you find it. And, if you do stumble on something promising, you must tell me and the Chief Inspector.'

'Of course.'

They followed Diana up a sweeping staircase and onto a spacious, carpeted landing with views across the landscaped gardens. The wooden banister had been recently polished, leaving a strong smell of beeswax.

The young girl unlocked a door that led to a long, wide corridor. 'Mr Dunhelm had this wing to himself, your Lordship.' She showed them a button on the wall. 'Press this when you're ready to leave and I'll come and lock up.'

James asked if Mrs Dunhelm ever visited this part of the house at all.

'Occasionally. Always around the anniversary of when he went missing and if she's feeling that way inclined.'

'Were any of the household here when he disappeared?'

'The gardener was. He'll be about somewhere if you need to speak to him.'

She half-curtseyed and closed the door behind them. James opened a couple of doors along the corridor that turned out to be cupboards housing overcoats and footwear. Stephen led the way into the lounge which looked over the front of the property across the fields toward Rusper. It was decorated tastefully, reflecting the style the time he went missing although it was not old-fashioned by any means. The first couple of feet of wall area were covered in cream wood panelling. Above the dado, the walls were painted mint green. The furniture, James guessed, was either original Gio Ponti or an excellent copy. It was expensive and the design carefully thought out. There was a level of functionality yet practicality about everything. He had to admit, it wasn't to his taste although the 1930s armchair in the corner was an exception.

'A-a very modern y-young man, James,' Stephen observed.

James moved over to a bureau, slid a few drawers open and leafed through some papers. There was nothing of any significance here. The police must have taken relevant documents when he was reported missing. He scanned the walls. There were two shelves of books mainly to do with business and architecture. Half a dozen on the end caught his eye — detective fiction and a couple of factual books about investigating crime.

Further along were photographs of

Dunhelm and his mother on various travels: Egypt, Rome, Paris. He studied them for some time and began thinking about this relationship. Jonathan must have been in his early twenties. At that age, he would have expected him to be going away with his friends or his girlfriend, Natalie. Perhaps he did and chose not to display the photographs. Turning, James spotted a sheet of loose paper on the coffee table. It seemed out of place in such a tidy environment. He picked it up and turned it over; a hand-written score for the song, 'Daisy'. He replaced it and squatted down to flick through the record collection. All jazz-inspired: Peggy Lee, Ella Fitzgerald, Tommy Dorsey, Louis Armstrong.

They moved on to the bedroom, a huge room overlooking the rear of the property.

'G-gracious, this is bigger than th-the whole of our ground floor put together!' exclaimed Stephen.

It certainly was immense and, again, modern to the eye, even nine years on. The walls were painted in light terracotta and low chairs were scattered about.

There was a step up to where a double bed was positioned on a dais to allow a view of the gardens.

James opened the bedside table drawer. 'Aha.'

'W-what?'

He brought out a framed photograph and held it up. 'D'you think this is Natalie Kershaw?'

The lady in the frame was demure, almost aloof, in her pose. She wore a white shirt waister with the collar up and had short wavy hair. She was certainly a beautiful lady but James couldn't help but think she would be difficult to get to know. There was no warmth about her.

Stephen remarked the same. 'P-perhaps, knowing Jonathan a little more n-now, she was a good hostess and outlived her value to h-him.'

An RCA record player was on a cabinet to one side of the bed. James opened the lid and studied the record on the turntable. The 'Hallelujah Chorus' by Handel. He wondered why the record player was in here and not in the living room. And Jonathan's collection was solely jazz so what was the relevance of this classical piece? The record-sleeve lay on the bed. He closed the lid and opened the wardrobe door. A smell of stale aftershave drifted out. Inside hung a number of suits; checking the labels, he discovered they were all from the same tailor in Savile Row. On the shelf above were several felt hats. The flying jacket that Jonathan had worn in the photograph was here. He checked the pockets but found them empty.

Stephen waved another framed photograph. 'Another one of his parents. D-don't you think it strange that th-there are no photograph albums or pictures of friends?'

James agreed but reminded Stephen of Celia's comments. He didn't appear to have friends in the same sense that others did. 'My guess would be that he features in a good many photographs taken by other people.'

'Mmm, th-the sort of person who oozed nectar and people flock to be n-near.'

'Absolutely. I would imagine this chap having some presence, some gravitas. People wanted to be with him, be seen with him, so he probably features in a good many albums, just not his own.'

'And he mixed with them o-only because they served a p-purpose.'

James picked up a second stray piece of paper and read the contents. 'Down in old Mexico, where a child will slap your face, Down in old Mexico, where a child will slap your face, They make a bread with cayenne pepper, drink gunpowder to kill the taste.' He stared at Stephen. 'What on earth does that mean?'

His friend shrugged and suggested that perhaps Jonathan was a poet although not a very good one.

'It seems so out of place.' He motioned to the record player. 'And that choice of music on the turntable contradicts every other record in his collection.'

In the corridor he rang the bell, frustrated that the rooms had revealed little about Jonathan apart from his taste in decor. They returned to Celia and thanked her for her hospitality. Stephen gave her his card and reminded her he was happy to pop by if she would like some company. She expressed gratitude and promised that she would call.

She turned to James. 'Lord Harrington, you seem genuinely interested in what happened to my son. If you do uncover anything about him, I want you to tell me — no matter how painful it may be.'

At the door, James asked if Jonathan had attended the church in Rusper.

She tilted her head and let out a sigh. 'I was the moral compass of the Dunhelm family. I forced Ernest and Jonathan to church every Sunday. I said grace during mealtimes and, where I could, it was me that steered them towards being compassionate and caring people. Ernest went along with my insisting on these things because he loved me. Jonathan loved me but when he became an adult, asked me to forgive him for not attending.' She shrugged. 'By then he was a grown man, I couldn't force him. And how the two of them behaved as businessmen was beyond my sphere of influence.'

They stepped outside but, before Celia closed the front door, James made one last observation. 'His rooms are exceptionally tidy, Celia, everything in its place.'

She invited him to continue.

'There were three things that seemed out of kilter; the sheet music, the classical record and that odd poem.'

'Yes, I agree. I've thought about that over the years. It's not the sort of music he liked or listened to. Perhaps it belonged to Pip; he's quite musical, listened to all sorts and tried to get Jonathan to appreciate it. But I don't recall Pip mentioning having recommended such selections.'

She closed the door and they trotted down the steps onto the drive where James pulled Stephen back. 'Hold on, old chap, I think that's the gardener over there. Let's have a quick word.'

He held a hand up to attract the man's attention. The gardener, dressed in ragged corduroys, a moth-eaten sweater and a well-worn cap, put his wheelbarrow down and rubbed his nose. His hands were covered in peat and his hobnail boots were caked in mud.

James introduced them simply as acquaintances of Celia Dunhelm and asked if he remembered Jonathan.

The man shifted on his feet and pulled

a face. 'I never knew him well.'

James saw the signs and was surprised to hear Stephen be so forthright when he said, 'Y-you mean you didn't l-like him.'

The man paused before answering but then admitted that he had had no time for him or his father. 'I do this garden for three reasons. One, I get paid. Two, I like gardening and three, I respect Mrs Dunhelm and always have done. She's one in a million that one, treats everyone with dignity and grace.'

'Are you saying,' said James, 'that Ernest and Jonathan treated you as a servant or something less?'

'I've been in service since I was fourteen, always in the garden, and I know the difference. I know what you're talking about. In service you expect to be servile, to be invisible, but you are generally appreciated. But they were different. Had no time for you; no little thank you presents at Christmas, no recognition of how lovely the garden was. Mrs Dunhelm always did that, still does. She walks around here nearly every day and takes an interest in what I've done and what I've planted.

114

Always gives me and the family a little treat for Christmas Day.'

'You know Jonathan's skeleton was found, don't you?'

'I do.' He grabbed the handles of the wheelbarrow. 'Good riddance. That's what I say.'

James and Stephen watched as he marched past them toward a large greenhouse.

'I w-wonder if we'll find anyone who has a g-good word to say about Jonathan.'

'Yes, that man had the world at his feet. I don't understand why he would take advantage of it in such an unsavoury way.'

The gravel crunched beneath their feet as they strolled toward the car. James thought George had his work cut out. Jonathan's business associates and, indeed, Dunhelm senior's partner appeared to dislike the man. Natalie Kershaw's broken heart was, according to Celia, steeped in bad feeling and now the gardener had confessed that he was glad to see the back of him. All of these people might have had a motive for killing Dunhelm Jnr. He wondered if George was getting any further insight.

His curiosity was getting the better of him so when he returned home, he added George to their dinner reservation.

7

The Silk Brothers, four siblings from London, performed a wonderful repertoiré in the dining room at Harrington's. James and Beth had booked them on several occasions after being impressed by their variety of songs as well as their appealing looks. They took their lead from many quartets of the time by incorporating a pianist, a double-bass player, a drummer and a jazz guitarist. Between them, they sang ballads, popular songs and jazz and, if they saw couples waiting for a dinner course to arrive, invited them onto the dance floor.

Watching them in their grey lounge suits, their hair Brylcreemed back, James thought there was always something unique about family members singing together. They had the same timbre to their voices and synchronised together like no random individuals could.

A few couples took to the dance floor

and moved slowly in time with the music. Other guests enjoyed the Easter menu and the ambience within the room.

The dining room had undergone a facelift over the winter months with a complete refresh of the paintwork and curtains. Beth had decided to replace the carpet and they'd laid a new wooden dance floor in the centre. In spring, she'd insisted on napkins and tablecloths of yellow and cream. It brightened the room nicely, especially with the fresh spring flowers displayed on the tables.

Adam held a chair out for Beth and took her coat to store away. James and George unbuttoned their jackets and seated themselves. The band played 'Moonglow' as the young waiter jotted down their order. Without hesitation Beth opted for the roast leg of lamb and James and George were quick to do the same.

'New potatoes or roast, your ladyship? We had a delivery of Jersey new potatoes if that helps.'

'Mmm, you've made my mind up. Jersey potatoes it is.'

One of Adam's colleagues brought the

requested sherries for James and Beth and a half-pint of cider for George. James asked how his visit to Celia Dunhelm had gone.

His friend loosened his tie. 'It was enlightening. The family were close but only because of her, I think. If she'd have died instead of Ernest I think we'd be looking at two suspicious deaths.'

'They do seem to have been pretty ruthless, don't they? Did you take a look at his rooms?'

'Yes, didn't give up much. Tidy man for someone that age. Some of that furniture was, according to my sergeant, expensive stuff. How he'd know about it I don't know. What did you think?'

James went over his thoughts about the designers he'd seen and that he thought they were all original pieces. 'It shouldn't be of any surprise though, he can afford it. You don't live in a house like that and fill it with rubbish.'

Beth sipped her sherry and asked George if he knew how much Jonathan was worth.

'As an individual, he's a millionaire.

We're checking the company records now but everything seems to be in order and in the black. They were making a fair bit when Jonathan was in charge, especially with the contract they had in Crawley. That part of the investigation will take a while though. We need to sift through a lot of archived accounts.'

'Have you spoken with Jonathan's business partner?'

'The current one? Not yet, no.' He put his elbows on the table and steepled his fingers. 'I'm on a skeleton staff, 'scuse the pun. A lot of our officers are on the canal path murders and I'm part of that group.'

James grimaced at Beth who returned a similar look. He didn't want to dwell on this, a grisly series of murders along a towpath near Chichester. It had made headlines in the previous day's nationals and a number of high-ranking police were putting their heads together to solve it. It didn't surprise James that his friend had been summoned and it was right that resources went there first. A body buried nine years ago would not take priority.

'I got some more information from

Maurice, though,' said George.

James pulled his seat closer.

'Healthy male, five foot ten inches tall, no damage to bones except for one cracked rib. The blow to the skull would have killed him.'

'Is that all you've found out?'

Adam arrived with their meals and placed a gravy boat in the centre of the table, along with a bowl of fresh mint sauce. They took turns to help themselves to the various condiments and, before George took his first mouthful, he turned to James.

'I assume, from that comment, you've something to tell me.'

James nodded as he bit into a tender slice of lamb topped with the tart mint in vinegar. Didier always worked miracles in the kitchen and even an ordinary piece of lamb was elevated to something wonderful once he'd got his hands on it. There was a hint of rosemary through the meat and sprigs of the same herb in the gravy. Very similar to what his grandmother had cooked. He wondered if Didier had been flicking through Granny's recipe book.

They always had it to hand when they discussed the menus. George took a swig of cider and waited; James appreciated his friend's patience as it gave him time to consider his thoughts before speaking. But the timing was inappropriate.

'I feel that a good meal could be spoiled by the subject of murder. Can I propose we chat about something else while we have dinner?'

* * *

After a convivial twenty minutes of chat and laughter, there was a natural lull in the conversation during which they spent time watching the guests dancing.

James reached for his sherry. 'Turning to the business in hand, George, my musing may be nothing but there were some items in Jonathan's rooms that I feel may be significant.' He settled back in his chair. 'Only two people appear to be in Jonathan's true circle of friends: his mother and his school friend Pip Logan. I get the impression from Celia that her son used people when he needed something and then dropped them once they'd served their purpose.'

'How rude,' said Beth. 'That's bad-mannered and thoroughly discourteous.'

James agreed. 'The ex-girlfriend may be worth chatting to. Natalie Kershaw. According to Celia, they parted on bad terms and she was far from distraught when he went missing. The gardener also expressed a similar view. 'Good riddance' was the term he used.' He loaded his fork with the last morsel of lamb and swirled it in the gravy. 'The father's business partner wanted nothing to do with Jonathan once Ernest had died. The current business partner was not his biggest fan.'

'He sounds boorish,' Beth put in.

George admitted the same. 'I'll get around to speaking to these people.'

'You're on the canal murders you say? Full time?'

'Unfortunately, yes. My superior thinks this is less important.'

James frowned. 'But there's still a murderer out there.'

His friend shrugged and finished his meal.

'Sweetie, tell George what you thought about his rooms.'

James pushed his plate away and dabbed his lips with a napkin. 'You remarked yourself that the flat was tidy beyond belief. Jonathan was clearly a chap who liked everything just so but there were a couple of things that struck me as odd.'

George reached for his cider. 'Oh? And what's that?'

'The music.' James paused to allow Adam to collect their plates and they put in an order for three sherry trifles. 'First thing is the sheet music, 'Daisy'. He doesn't play the piano and Celia said it wasn't his sort of song.'

George pulled a face. 'That doesn't really tell me anything.'

'And also the record on the turntable. Handel it was. The rest of his collection was jazz. Then there was that odd poem lying on the sofa.'

'I don't see what you're getting at.'

James sighed. 'Well, neither do I but something is nagging me about those things because they are so out of place.'

124

'George,' Beth said, 'James and I could always make a few enquiries if you're busy with that awful canal business.'

George set his pipe on the table and gave Beth the sort of look a father would give an errant daughter. 'You're normally the sensible one in this relationship and now you're egging him on to go asking questions.' He brought a photograph out of his wallet. 'I'm popping into some more of the local newspaper offices over the next couple of days. They're publishing this to see if we come up with anything. The *Argus* has placed it in this evening's edition. It's on the cards that the nationals will pick it up tomorrow; the Dunhelms are a wealthy family after all and a body in the woods brings the readers in.'

'Oh lord,' James groaned, 'we're not going to have the newspapers here are we?'

'I hope not. We've supplied this photograph and emphasised that the case is nine years old and that there's nothing to see. And anyway, the canal murders are taking up the columns so I don't think you need to worry.'

'I hope so. I'd best warn Paul that he may receive some phone calls.'

Beth took the photograph from George and caught her breath. 'Is this Jonathan Dunhelm?'

James wondered, from that reaction, if she'd known him.

'No, I don't but, my goodness, he's like a matinée idol. I can't believe a man this handsome could be so horrible.'

'Well he was, darling, take his mother's word for it.' He turned to George. 'Beth's right, I can ask a few questions here and there. Whatever I find out, I'll pass on.'

George lit his pipe and wafted the nutty aroma of tobacco toward the ceiling. He grumbled at James for getting too involved. 'Why you can't keep your nose out of it, I don't know,' he said.

James smiled. 'The man was found on my land, George. I think I have a right to ask some questions.'

Paul, the maître'd, approached their table. 'Your Lordship, Mr Briggs is on the telephone.'

James raised an eyebrow and followed

Paul through to reception. 'Bert? Everything all right?'

'I've found your fella, Eoin Fuller.'

'My word, that was quick.'

'He 'asn't moved, mate. A few questions on the estate was all it took. He's off tomorrow if you want to 'ave a chat with him.'

James mentally went through his diary and said he could pop up in the morning. 'Will you be there too?'

'I can be if you want me to be.'

'Confirm it with him.' James jotted down the address and asked Bert not to mention anything to the man about the reason for his visit.

'I 'ad to tell him something, Jimmy boy, but only that you had a few questions about the Dunhelm family.'

'What was his reaction?'

'He said a few choice words that I won't repeat.'

James thanked him and manoeuvred his way through the dancers and back to the table where he updated George and Beth on his plans for the morning.

Beth looked put out. 'I have a hair

appointment tomorrow morning.'

George said he'd come along. 'I don't have to be in Chichester until the afternoon. If you're going to stick your nose in, I may as well keep you in line if I'm free. We can go on and have a chat with Natalie Kershaw after.'

'The ex-girlfriend?'

George told them that he had her contact details. Adam placed three sherry trifles on the table. The smell of alcohol reached James before he even dipped his spoon into the dessert. This must be Granny's recipe — she always insisted on being rather generous when a recipe included alcohol.

He heaved a satisfied sigh. The next day would, he was sure, be an enlightening one.

8

The next day saw James and George in Eltham and, on seeing Bert, George blustered that this was too unprofessional.

Bert baulked. 'Oi, I found the bloke and set up the meeting, that's all. I'm just making sure you find it all right and I'm their sort of person. It ain't easy 'aving a copper and a toff land on your doorstep. Strewth, George, a bit o' thanks wouldn't go amiss.'

James settled his two friends down as Bert led them to the prefab belonging to Eoin Fuller. A few young children on scooters raced by and two neighbours further down the road chatted over the garden fence. The estate was a large one and although these temporary residences were now over ten years old, the people living there had kept them in good order. The gardens were well tended, with flowers, vegetable plots and fruit trees. Mr

Fuller and his family lived in the dwelling on the corner.

The buildings all looked the same, each a bungalow with two windows to one side of the front door and one window to the other. George rapped the knocker. After a couple of minutes, a woman in her early-forties appeared. She was plain, with shoulder-length hair and wearing a floral apron. She wiped her hands on a towel as a lad of around fifteen rushed into the hall to see who their visitors were.

George held up his warrant card and introduced James and Bert. She acknowledged them and opened the door wider.

'I'm Lottie, Eoin's wife. He's just in the back garden. Go through and make yourself comfortable. Do you want tea?'

She shooed her son out and caught Eoin's attention through the window. Entering the lounge, they took their seats on a long well-worn sofa. The room also served as a dining area and there was a foldaway table by the far wall. The kitchen door was open and James saw that Lottie must have been preparing lunch. Potatoes were on the kitchen table ready to peel and an onion was half cut on the chopping board.

Through the rear window, Eoin planted his garden fork in the earth and strode into the kitchen to wash his hands. James had a good view of him from where he was sitting. He stood around six foot tall with short hair and a 'lived-in' face. He would have put him down as a military man by the way he carried himself; upright with his shoulders back. The man grabbed the biscuit barrel and followed his wife through to the lounge where he greeted them. The smell of earth entered with him. He appeared bemused at having such an assortment of people in his house and, as he plonked himself down in his armchair, he rolled up his sleeves before questioning their reason for visiting.

'I know from Mr Briggs that this is about the Dunhelm family. What 'ave they done now?' He pulled his shoulders back. 'Blimey, they've not done you over, have they?'

James afforded him a quick smile and

assured him that no, they hadn't *done him over*. He sought George's approval to expand on the reason for their visit. George asked permission to smoke and gestured for James to continue.

'Mr Fuller, the skeleton of Jonathan Dunhelm was dug up on my land in Cavendish.'

Eoin jolted with a silent 'Oh'; Lottie sat down on the arm of his chair, wearing an equally alarmed expression.

'Well that's the last thing I was expecting,' Eoin said with some concern. 'I'm assuming he weren't in a family graveyard or anything?'

'He wasn't.' James gave him a bite-size version of the events leading to the discovery.

Lottie shifted into the chair next to her husband and spoke to George. 'Are you saying he was murdered?'

'Most definitely, Mrs Fuller.'

A hint of a snarl appeared on Eoin's face. ''ere, you're not accusing me of killing 'im, are you? I'm a respectable bloke, I mean, I didn't like 'im and he was . . . '

Bert told him to hold his horses. 'No one's accusing you of anything, mate. The Inspector here is just trying to get a picture of what this geezer was like.'

'I'll tell you what he was like,' Eoin said, leaning forward. 'A money-grabbing toe rag who turfed me and my family out of a perfectly good house to put us here. A prefab that was supposed to go to people who'd been bombed out.'

James struggled to comprehend what had happened. 'But why? I mean what was he doing? How did he get away with it?'

Eoin rubbed his thumb and forefinger together. 'Money, weren't it? He'd dreamt some scheme up to get us out of there. Had friends high up in the council that he palmed off with a bribe to turn the other cheek. Six families he evicted and we all ended up here. And we're still here.'

George asked what was built on the site they vacated.

'A load of flats. He replaced half a dozen houses with thirty flats. More money, see.'

'He was all charm when he sat down

with us,' said Lottie. 'Told us we'd 'ave a new place with a garden and schools. It sounded wonderful, didn't it, love? He showed us the plans and everything.'

'Didn't tell us it was a prefab though. I mean, these are all right. A lot of people jumped at the chance of living in these 'cos they'd have a garden and indoor privy. But we had that.'

James couldn't quite believe what he was hearing. 'So you signed on the dotted line on the strength of what Jonathan Dunhelm told you?'

'We all did.' Eoin's expression began to show signs of anger. 'He had us round his little finger.' He glanced at Lottie. 'You tell him, love.'

Lottie went on to explain how they'd been summoned to the Dunhelm head office where Jonathan had constructed a model village of where they were moving to and how it would appear. 'It looked really nice. Bungalows, a school down the road, a garden. It was gonna be a bit further for Eoin to get to work but we didn't mind, we thought we'd landed on our feet. A brand new house. And that Mr

Dunhelm was so lovely. He was good with the kids, bent over backwards to answer all our questions — he seemed like a proper gent.'

James asked Eoin what it was he did for a living.

'I'm a senior foreman at an engineering plant. Been there since I was fourteen except for a few years out in the army.'

George jotted a few things down in his notebook. 'So you signed a contract and then the move went through.'

'Took about three months.' Eoin explained how they'd said goodbye to friends in neighbouring streets and how much they'd been looking forward to moving into a new house. 'Dunhelm covered all our moving costs.'

James was wary about asking his next question. 'And when you came here?'

Eoin let out a sarcastic laugh. 'Well, you see for yourself. We swapped bricks and mortar for glorified hardboard and nails. We didn't 'ave a leg to stand on.'

'But couldn't you have contested the agreement?'

'None of us could afford to challenge

him. The way the contract was worded, it would have been a risk I couldn't take. None of us could afford a solicitor; not to fight Dunhelm Developments.'

George asked if Eoin had confronted Jonathan Dunhelm about it.

The man bristled. 'Too right, I did. Me and the others. We planted ourselves on his doorstep every chance we had.'

'And?'

'He came out once and went through the agreement we'd signed. After that, he never came out and faced us. He'd moved offices. His staff were closing down the one we'd been to. Told us he'd moved further south. Obviously done what he wanted to do and was off to fleece more families.'

James assumed this was when Dunhelm was getting his tenders in for Crawley New Town. 'This was around the late 1940s?'

'That's right,' said Eoin. '1947. These were only s'posed to be here for a few years. The other families on the estate were housed 'ere like they should've been. They'd been bombed out, didn't 'ave anywhere to go, but us — well we were fine. We had no reason to move.' He gritted his teeth. 'Put us in an awkward position when people found out where we'd moved from. They wanted to know why these 'adn't been given to those who needed 'em.'

George scanned the room and tried to lighten the mood by saying they'd made it a home.

Lottie smiled her thanks and explained that she and Eoin had put a lot of effort into making it nice and that everyone here had done their best to make the neighbourhood respectable. She didn't know if they would ever be moved on. 'We'll be sure to check the smallest detail if we're ever asked again.'

'When was the last time you saw Jonathan Dunhelm?' asked James.

Lottie's gaze fell to the carpet and Eoin broke eye contact.

George held his pipe. 'If you haven't done anything, you've nothing to be afraid of.'

'I saw him in a car showroom. I'd taken my boy to London Zoo and we was having an ice cream on a park bench. I was looking around at who was about and spotted a bloke coming back from testing out a new car. Brand new Rolls Royce it was. I was just admiring it and telling the kid what sort of motor it was when I saw who got out of it.'

James stole a quick look at George. 'And what did you do?'

Eoin clasped his hands together. 'Me brother was with me. I told him to look after the boy and I went over there.' He pursed his lips and James could see a vein of anger beat in his temple as he relived the moment. 'I poked him in the chest and told him he was a double-crossing bastard.' Eoin let out a 'Pah' of disbelief. 'He couldn't even remember who I was but I told him. I told him good and proper and he just shrugged. You signed the paperwork, he said. You could've checked it out. You could've visited the site but you didn't. I didn't lie to you. Pompous little . . . ' He stopped himself.

James watched the man clench his fist and realised that Jonathan had been an absolute bounder. He had deliberately misled them and had failed to provide the full picture.

Eoin slammed the arm of his chair. 'When he shrugged at me again I had to do something so I punched him — square on the jaw. I told him that one day he'd get what was coming to him.'

George raised his eyebrows. 'And what did you mean by that?'

Lottie reached across and held Eoin's hand. 'He meant that he'd get his comeuppance one day. If you believe in God then he'll put it right. If not down 'ere then when he meets his Maker.'

Eoin reiterated that he had no part in the death of Jonathan Dunhelm. 'I had good reason to kill him but I've a wife and boy to look after. I'm no use to them at the end of a rope.'

George asked if there had been anyone else with reason for killing Dunhelm. Eoin told him to ask anyone who ever had dealings with him.

'Can you remember where you were around Easter in 1950?'

'That's easy answered. Up until they died a couple of years ago, we spent every

Easter with Lottie's family in Croydon. We went down Good Friday and we came back Easter Monday. My father-in-law always came to pick us up. Our factory's like a lot of others, closes down for the Easter weekend. Is that when he was killed?'

James said that this was when he had been reported missing.

'Well, I ain't your man, your Lordship. I'm sorry he's brought you some trouble on your estate. He can't help himself, can he? Even upsets people from beyond the grave.'

George thanked them for their time and asked for permission to return if he had further questions.

Eoin invited him back whenever he wanted. 'I've nothing to hide. You can search the place, check my papers, speak to my boss, do whatever you 'ave to do but I ain't your man.'

Outside, James lit a cigarette and watched the smoke dissipate. 'What d'you think?'

George put his trilby on and flicked through his notes. 'He sounds genuine enough but that could be an act. He's had nine years to perfect an alibi. And Croydon isn't more than an hour from Cavendish. He could easily have made a detour over that weekend. And the parents are dead so I can't corroborate what he's told me. He still has motive and opportunity in my mind.'

'He's certainly big enough to hold his own in a fight.' He turned to Bert. 'Bert, you've been unusually quiet through this. What's on your mind?'

'Nothin' mate. I just hope he didn't have anything to do with it. They seem a nice family; settled. They've made the best of a bad deal. I think you're looking at the wrong bloke. He's got a nice wife, a lovely kid . . . ' He trailed off.

James studied his normally chirpy friend. This was nothing to do with the investigation; this was Bert Briggs regretting a life he didn't have and perhaps missing that side of things: a loving wife and family. Something inside him wanted to reach out but he wasn't entirely sure how to go about it. Beth was far better at this sort of thing but instinct told him to enquire after his lady friend, Gladys.

'She's all right, thanks. I'm popping over to the mission tonight to have fish and chips with her.'

'Why don't you come to ours for dinner one evening? It'd be nice to see her again.'

His face brightened. 'I'd like that. She would too. Yeah, that'd be great, thanks.' He checked his watch. 'The 56 bus is due soon. That takes me into Bethnal Green so I'll 'ave a chat with Gladys about that meal.'

James watched Bert saunter toward the main road. How lovely it would have been if Bert and Gladys had forged a bond when they first knew each other. Bert had always struck him as a positive man who never suffered with nostalgia; but today he'd seen a twinge of regret.

An aircraft roared over their heads. He shielded the sun from his eyes to see a Comet making its way to London Airport. 'Goodness, that's a sound to wake the dead.'

George checked his own watch. 'Right, James, I want to call in to see Natalie

Kershaw. You coming?'

'Of course.' He unlocked his car. 'Jump in; let's hear why young Natalie was so unhappy with her beau.'

9

James parked the Jaguar outside a large, converted stable; a low-level building that sprawled across a manicured lawn. Its short gravel drive faced a road that led to the small village of Newdigate. A Standard Vanguard saloon was parked by the front door. A postman waved hello as he wheeled his bicycle away. As they approached the building, the door opened and James couldn't help but stare at the vision in front of him.

If this was Natalie Kershaw, he could understand why Jonathan Dunhelm had been attracted to her. She wore a lemon calf-length dress and black stilettos. Her hair was short, wavy and cut in a chic style. She oozed elegance and sex appeal as she placed the post on a side table and held out a slender hand to welcome them.

'I can hazard a guess as to who is the detective,' she purred as George took off his trilby. She turned to James. 'And you must be Lord Harrington. Delighted.'

James allowed her a brief smile. There was a hint of sarcasm behind the 'delighted' comment. Despite her beauty, there was something a little false about her. He preferred ladies who were natural with their charm; women who just by their presence made you feel welcome. Natalie gave him the impression that she was opening her house to the public and they could quickly become a nuisance. George had picked up on this too as he overheard him somewhat abruptly ask if she was Natalie Kershaw.

'How rude of me,' she said ushering them in. 'Please go through to the left and make yourself comfortable.'

She followed them through to a large double-aspect room with modern furniture and abstract prints on the walls that were not to James' taste. It reminded him a little of Jonathan's decor. Heading straight for a glass cocktail cabinet, she mixed herself a Martini.

'Drinks?'

George emphasised that he was on duty and he didn't want anything. James took a seat as he bit back a grin — his friend had already decided he didn't like this woman. Natalie pouted. He thought back to their twins pulling the same expression when they were young children unable to get their way. To keep the peace, James requested a whisky and soda with plenty of the latter. He sat back and scanned the room. There was a photograph on the wall of two young girls in school uniform sitting with Natalie Kershaw, a professional portrait that seemed too posed. He wondered how much love there was in this family. He gestured at the image.

'Your daughters?'

'My darling girls,' gushed Natalie as she prepared the drinks. The crystal tumblers chinked and he frowned as he watched her pour the measures. His idea of a small whisky was lost on her.

'They board, of course,' she continued. 'I see them during the term breaks but this week they're on holiday with a friend's family in Brittany.'

James hid his feelings of disapproval as he accepted the drink from her. He couldn't have comprehended sending his children away for weeks at a time. And to miss seeing them during the holidays too! He and Beth had decided when Harry and Oliver were born that they would dedicate their lives to making them independent but ensure they were, at the end of the school day, cocooned in family life. His own mother and father had done the same and he felt a better person for it.

George used the stem of his pipe to point at the portrait. 'No pictures of your husband?'

'No.'

'Are you still together?'

She sipped her Martini and James noted her flushed complexion. This wasn't her first drink of the day and it was barely lunchtime. And stilettos inside the house — who was she trying to impress?

'He works in Copenhagen and he's rich.' She laughed. 'He's much older than me. I don't have his photograph on the wall. He's not an attractive man. That's my choice, he's hardly here anyway. I have what I want.'

James shifted in his chair, quickly beginning to dislike the woman. 'Is that something you hoped you'd get from Jonathan Dunhelm?'

The comment almost rattled her but she managed a quick smile. 'It wasn't a serious relationship. He was just a bit of fun.'

George pushed himself up from his seat and wandered around the room glancing at table tops and paintings. 'That's not what his mother told us. We understood you were in a relationship with him for two years. That's more than just a bit of fun, isn't it?'

Natalie stared out of the window across the rose garden. James watched as George put a finger to his lips. Remain quiet. They waited for some time before she turned on her heels with a thunderous expression.

'He ruined two years of my life. Stringing me along, telling me I was his one true love and how happy we'd be together. He did everything but propose; promised me the earth, a beautiful home, beautiful children. He was going to buy a yacht and we were gonna sail to Monte Carlo.'

Aha! James detected a slip; a London accent beneath the eloquence. George had picked up on it too. He studied his notebook.

'You're from Woolwich, I understand.'

James' jaw dropped. Woolwich? That was a working class area near the London docks.

George continued. 'Quite a poor start in life, so I understand.'

Natalie regained her composure and opened a cigarette case. 'You certainly do your homework, don't you?' She placed the cigarette in a holder and lit it. 'A girl can do well, Inspector, if she makes something of herself. I learned how to behave like a lady. I'm a beautiful woman and beautiful women attract handsome men.

'And,' she continued after a brief pause. 'Jonathan was certainly a handsome man.'

James restrained the words he'd like to have said. Learned to be a lady? Her behaviour here was far removed from what he termed being a lady. He wondered how she'd ended up with an unattractive husband. *Beautiful women attract handsome men.* If she was so shallow as to choose someone on looks only, why had she married an ugly man? Had she run out of money? He sipped his drink. 'Where did you meet Jonathan?'

'At Wimbledon — the tennis. It was a beautiful, warm day. He was drinking Pimms and bumped into me. I could tell he was smitten. He was my type; outrageous and charming at the same time and, my God, women drooled over him. But he chose me. To him I was beautiful and dangerous. Jonathan loved dangerous.'

'And what happened? asked James, ignoring the ego.

'Two things, Lord Harrington. I suspected another woman. I should have known that a man like that can't stay faithful.'

'And the second?'

'His true self came to the surface.'

'And that was?'

'There was a cruelty about Jonathan. I had a school friend, Judy. She was a plain girl but one of the best friends I could ever have had. I introduced them one day when Judy was visiting and his sarcasm about her looks and figure shocked even me. I'm no angel, Lord Harrington, and I'm happy to pass comment on people's appearance with the best of them but this was something more. It was cruel. It upset me.'

She rammed her recently-lit cigarette into an ashtray and went into a tirade about what was wrong with Jonathan Dunhelm. Here was a man who had played with her with no intention of marrying; a man who spent time with her only when it suited him; a man who would not allow her to meet any of his friends or business associates unless there was a reason for doing so.

'In short, Lord Harrington, I was a fool. He was arrogant. I make no bones about my own situation. I wanted to marry into money and I wanted to do it with love. I've managed the former but will never experience that first feeling of love I had with Jonny. But when I saw that side of him, I began to hate him. Oh, it wasn't just that. I was having to wait

151

until he had the time to see me. I got to the point where I almost had to make an appointment. When he went missing, I was over the moon. I actually wished him dead.'

James didn't know what to think about this woman. She'd obtained her dream; to marry a rich husband, live in a big house and have two beautiful children. But was she happy? Absolutely not. This lady was lost in a wilderness, detached from her roots. No sense of belonging to the class she aspired to and distancing herself from the one she'd left. Her children were at boarding school and she spent her days alone, drinking.

George rolled his hat in his hands. 'Miss Kershaw, Jonathan Dunhelm's remains were found on Lord Harrington's estate.'

Natalie caught her breath. She rushed to the sideboard, pulled open a drawer and frantically rummaged through paperwork until she'd found what she wanted. 'My poor, beautiful Jonathan.'

James joined her, took a large colour photograph of Jonathan from her grasp and turned it toward George. He returned it to Natalie.

'You're still in love with him, aren't you?'

Natalie straightened her shoulders, threw the photograph in the drawer and slammed it shut. 'I've told you. He was a cruel, horrible man. He was like an iceberg, beautiful and pure on the surface but dangerous and a mass of unknowns underneath. Anyone sailing too close to Jonny was broken in two.'

She turned her back on them. James gave George a helpless look. Should they go? Had they got what they needed from her? For the life of him, he couldn't fathom this lady out.

George appeared unmoved by all of the emotion. 'Where were you during Easter of 1950?'

James saw her hand go to her face. Was she wiping a tear away? Was this an act? He clenched his jaw. This blasted woman was the most difficult person to make out. One minute she was detached and aloof, then she appeared over-dramatic and now she was upset; or perhaps stalling to think of an alibi. And why were there no photographs of her husband? Surely if he was so repulsive, she wouldn't have married him; those children in the picture were beautiful. He wondered if Natalie had embarked on an affair. Did those children have another father?

She began tidying magazines that were already perfectly straight and slid a newspaper under the pile. 'Mending a broken heart.'

'When he went missing, what did you think?'

'That he was a coward who didn't have the guts to tell me to my face that he'd found someone else.'

'But surely,' said James, 'his business was nearby, he couldn't just up and leave.'

She shrugged, perhaps realising her suggestion was a poor one. She lit another cigarette. 'I didn't care about what had happened. But if you're asking me if I had something to do with his death, you are knocking on the wrong door.'

George repeated his question about her whereabouts.

She spread her arms. 'I would have been with my parents, in Woolwich. They live here in Newdigate now but they won't remember. They can't recall what they had for dinner last week. They're elderly and their memories are buried in the past.'

He thanked her for her time and informed her that he might have further questions as the investigation went on. James followed him to the front door.

'Goodbye Miss,' said George. He put his hat on and walked toward the car.

Natalie tugged James' sleeve. 'Did he suffer?'

James swallowed hard. He had no idea. For all he knew the man might have been buried alive. He patted her hand. 'No. I'm pretty certain it was very quick.'

The door gently closed.

He joined George in the car. 'What do you think, old chap?'

'I think that love is a powerful emotion.'

'And hate,' James put in. 'And I believe Natalie Kershaw has experienced both to the extreme.' He offered George a cigarette but he opted to stay with his pipe. James lit the tip of his own cigarette and wound down the window to blow smoke out. 'Easter 1950, she's admitted she was recovering from a broken heart but not, I would imagine, in a distressed way. I would say she was a bubbling volcano waiting to erupt.' He turned in his seat. 'And she seemed shocked to learn of the discovery of Jonathan's remains. Surely she must have seen that paper.'

'You spotted that, did you?'

They'd both seen a copy of the *Argus* on the table before she'd tucked it under the magazines. Jonathan's photograph had been on the front page. 'I think she knew. She could hardly have missed it. I believe she walks around that house drinking Martini all day. She blows hot and cold where temperament is concerned. She's an unstable woman.'

'She certainly struck me as someone I wouldn't want to upset.' He loaded his pipe and blew out the first few puffs of tobacco-smoke. 'She's not a happy woman is she?'

James went over his thoughts about her motives and how being rich appeared to be her driving force. It reminded him of Olivia, a woman who had been poisoned at Harrington's over Christmas, and her goal to be famous at the cost of everything else. What a shame these girls were so motivated like this. All the money and success in the world could not burn a candle of happiness in their heart. He thought about Bert, a man from the poorest part of London's East End, a man who rarely had more than a couple of pounds in his pocket, who had no savings for a rainy day; yet, a predominantly chirpy individual who lifted everyone around him with his happy-go-lucky attitude.

The colourful flash of a jay caught his eye as it flew onto a branch. 'She seemed melodramatic, don't you think? And why not have a photograph of your husband on display? I can't imagine her marrying simply for money. A woman like that is vain and would surely land not only a rich man but a handsome one too. Can she despise him that much? I mean, she answers to her maiden name! Is she definitely married? Those girls weren't born out of wedlock were they?'

George didn't have the answers but confirmed that she was listed under her married name of Sturgis but when he telephoned she'd said she preferred the name Kershaw. 'What we do have is a lady spumed by Jonathan in an ungracious way. She was in Woolwich when he went missing — not a million miles away. She had every reason to want to bludgeon him to death. They could have had a massive row during which she picked up something hard and whacked him over the head.' He opened his own window. 'Interesting she prefers her maiden name, don't you think? Perhaps the grief of losing her one true love stops her from using her married name, especially if she doesn't care for him. In her mind, she is still devoted to Jonathan. Husband's away a lot; d'you think she has another man in tow?'

'I wouldn't put it past her. The children are away. She doesn't strike me as someone who gets involved in the community. She stroked my hand when she gave me my whisky as if I might be her next conquest.' He heard George chuckle. 'D'you think the husband is alive?'

'I'll get my people to check up on that when I get back.'

James reached for the ignition and pushed the starter button. 'I'd check quite a bit. The woman is flawed. That's not the first drink of this morning. Her make-up hides a drinker's complexion. She's gone from loathing Jonathan for everything he stands for to loving him unconditionally. She's kept that photograph of him all these years and I'm sure if you searched the house, you'd find plenty more. She fell back in love with him and probably now hates her husband. She will, unfortunately, never be truly happy.'

'So is her emotion grief or guilt?'

He put the car in gear. 'Difficult to say. If she did kill him it would explain why she feels like she does. Perhaps your other suspects will throw something into the ring.' As he pulled out from the drive, he mentioned Jonathan's alleged affair. 'She was pretty certain about that and from what we know about Jonathan, it's probably something he'd do. Does Mrs Dunhelm recollect any other women apart from Natalie?'

'Didn't mention it, no.'

'I wonder if he was seeing his secretary.'

'She's on my list of people to speak with but I'm having to put this on hold for a couple of days. It's Easter and the businesses are closed and we've got a few leads on these canal murders. I was going down to Chichester this afternoon but I've got to interview someone.'

James pulled over. 'I've an idea.' He reached out of the car window to extend the aerial and turned the radio on.

His friend closed his eyes in despair. 'You're going to go and chat with the secretary aren't you?'

'I've got the afternoon free. You must have her address, I could drop in, get the lie of the land and all that.'

George mumbled something about James always doing this to him. He brought out his notebook and copied an address down. 'Her name's Felicity Pemberton. She lives in Crawley. Number 13 Mole River Close.' He tore off a slip of paper and gave it to him. 'Don't you let on that I've given you this information. If she asks, you got it from somewhere else.'

James pulled away. 'I'll pick Beth up, have a chat with Felicity and we'll continue on to Elsie's for some tea and cake.'

After dropping George off, he stopped at a telephone box. On getting through to Beth, she leapt at the chance to help and said she'd be ready by the time he arrived home. He smiled as he replaced the receiver. Once upon a time, she would have been ordering him to leave things alone; now she was happy to join in with his sleuthing activities although he was pleased that she tempered that with a good deal of common sense. Perhaps he should introduce themselves as Paul and Steve Temple. He chuckled to himself. No, that would be going a bit too far.

10

On the way to Crawley, Beth told him about the remaining Easter activities. 'Charlie and Anne have planted all the clues for the Easter egg hunt. They've done a marvellous job with pictures of rabbits and deer showing them which way to go; the rhymes are challenging but the children should be able to work them out.'

'As long as the adults can work them out too. I always get a little bamboozled by riddles.' He reminded her of his efforts to solve the riddle when they investigated the death of Delphine Brooks-Hunter. It had taken half a dozen of them to get to the bottom of things.

'Mr Chrichton will keep an eye on everything,' Beth continued. 'He's organising who's bringing up the rear to make sure everyone solves the riddle and gets to the next clue.'

'Do we have enough eggs?'

'Oh yes. Stephen popped into Haywards Heath this morning and bought fifty eggs so every child will get one.'

'Fifty!'

'I know, it's getting bigger and bigger. We only have thirty three children but we bought a few more just in case. It's all come out of the event funding and I added a few pounds so they're not too short for the May Day festival.' She sat up in her seat. 'Oh, and we've added another event once Easter's been and gone.'

He groaned. 'Haven't we enough things going on around Easter?'

'Graham suggested a fundraiser. He's going to cook his famous hog-roast and Bob Tanner and a few of the folk club regulars will sing songs on request. Everyone has to pay for their food and bid to have a song sung. We'll also have some stalls selling crafts and food. It'll help replenish the pot for future events.'

James turned into Mole River Close. 'That actually sounds like a good idea. The funds always run a bit low over the Easter period. When is this taking place? We could perhaps hold it in the field we use on Guy Fawkes night.'

'A couple of weeks after Easter,' she replied, adding a comment about the lack of a river in Mole River Close.

'Yes, I know. The river runs further toward Gatwick but there are a few tributaries nearby that run into it. The Mole may have been here but I believe they diverted it when they built the New Town.' He parked alongside a Morris Minor. The circular close consisted of around twenty semi-detached houses, each with a garage attached. In the centre was a small green with three trees.

A few children played football on the grass where two of the trees provided ready-made goalposts. The other goalposts were made up of discarded jumpers. Two boys whizzed by them on a go-kart and young girl was taking her first precarious steps on roller skates.

The estate had been built around ten years previously and, James thought, to a high standard. He understood that these houses were part of a private build and wondered if they were anything to do with Dunhelm Developments.

They approached Number 13 and rapped on the knocker.

A tall woman with shoulder-length hair and horn-rimmed glasses answered. She had the natural demeanour of a professional secretary, even though she was clearly in the middle of some decorating as she wore old dungarees and held a paintbrush in her hand. She looked at them expectantly.

Using his full title, James made the introductions and apologised for interrupting her. Her brow knitted and she asked how she could help them. He reminded her of the news in the papers. 'Perhaps you haven't heard.'

Recognition flashed across her face. 'Oh goodness, Lord Harrington, of course. Mr Dunhelm was found on your estate.' She flung the door open. 'Do come in and excuse the mess, I'm just repainting some of the woodwork in the lounge.' She welcomed them in to a large square hallway and then into a bright lounge that overlooked the back garden. An apple tree was beginning to blossom by the back fence, surrounded by a thriving vegetable plot. A dust sheet covered part of the carpet. 'Can I offer you some tea?'

They declined, knowing they would be visiting Elsie's immediately after. They made themselves comfortable on the sofa while Felicity perched on the edge of an old wooden chair and carried on painting. The windows were open but the smell of paint lingered. 'I'll carry on because I don't want the brush to dry out. I've only this last little bit to do. I couldn't believe it when I saw the news in the paper.'

The *Argus* lay face up on a small occasional table. Jonathan's handsome features stared out from the front page.

Felicity heaved a sigh. 'Such a wonderful man, a delight to work for and so generous too.'

James had briefed Beth on all of the conversations to date and how the man didn't seem to have any positive attributes to speak of. Felicity clearly felt otherwise and she had picked up on his confusion.

'Oh I knew there was a side to him that annoyed people, but I never gave him cause to be like that with me. I am a professional and do my job well. He appreciated that.' She carefully dragged her brush to the end of the dado rail.

'Can I ask, Felicity,' said Beth, waiting until she'd finished painting, 'were you fond of him?'

James shot Beth a look of astonishment. Goodness, that was a little more forthright than he was expecting but it certainly did the trick. Felicity faltered. She stared at the newspaper, took her glasses off and rubbed her forehead.

'If you mean, was I in love with him then, yes, I was. But he never knew. I knew I wasn't his sort of girl so I did nothing to encourage him. He was in a relationship and I am, if nothing else, a professional. But that love meant me always going one step further to please him. I arranged his diary, his meetings, read through his contracts and shielded him from business that wasn't pressing, refused visits from staff who I knew would waste his time. I was doing my job in that respect but I suppose I always hoped that he might notice me as more than just his secretary.'

167

James assumed that, as a result, she was paid well. 'You said he was generous.'

'He appreciated my dedication and, I believe, my professionalism.' She reached across for a jar of turpentine, plunged the brush in and swept it around. The clear liquid turned cream. 'My Christmas bonus far exceeded my weekly wage.'

'And you still work there?'

She smiled fondly, wiping her hands with an old rag. 'Oh yes, when Jonathan left it was difficult to begin with. There was a lot of unfinished work and when he went missing, we didn't know what to do. Was he going to come back? Had he been in an accident? I remember the police checking with hospitals and going through his diary but there was nothing. When he didn't contact the office, we had to fulfil contracts and obligations so we all carried on.'

'In spite of your feelings for him, Mrs Pemberton, I assume you were aware of his ruthlessness.'

She studied her hands and picked at some dried paint. 'I'm a professional secretary, Lord Harrington. I've worked for a good many company directors and most, I'm afraid, are ruthless in business. But I believe Jonathan had that nature about him personally. He didn't seem to have many friends. He rarely spoke about people who were not connected to business. I recall a school friend . . . '

'Pip?'

'Yes, that's him. Pip Logan. I never met him.'

'Did you meet his girlfriend?'

'Once.' As she rolled up the dust sheet, she went on to describe a business function and the arrival of Jonathan with Natalie Kershaw. 'When they arrived, the room hushed. They were like a Hollywood couple attending the Oscars. He had an air about him. When he walked into the room, you couldn't help but notice him.'

Beth agreed. 'I've only seen photographs but he was an attractive man. Awful that he had a side to him which might have prompted murder.'

Felicity turned her attention to the garden. 'He had everything. But that drive for business, power and making money turned an attractive man into an extremely unattractive one. After two years of working for him, even I saw beyond his looks.'

'Do you know who would have wanted to kill him?'

'I was his secretary but not his confidant. I'm sure there were plenty of people he upset. My husband for one, although I can assure you he is no killer.'

'Your husband?'

'Mr Pemberton. Jack. Jonathan's business partner.'

James and Beth exchanged a look of surprise and shock.

Felicity smiled. She transferred the paint tin and turpentine to a piece of folded newspaper on the table. 'I got to know Jack far better once Jonathan had gone. We worked closely to get the business back onto a secure footing to ensure we didn't let anyone down. We grew close and I realised I loved this man.' Her eyes led them to a photograph. 'Our wedding day.'

Jack Pemberton was about ten years older than Felicity; a stocky, balding man.

James found it difficult to see the two together. She seemed so upright, fashionable, and fastidious. Jack Pemberton cut a figure that no suit would do justice to and wore a pained expression.

She hinted that Jack hated wearing suits. 'He's more at home in the garden. I had a suit tailored for him a few years ago and it hung on him like a bed-sheet.' She laughed.

'Is Mr Pemberton here?'

'He should be here at any moment. He's been at the allotment but he said he'd be back around this time.' She paused. 'I'm surprised the police haven't visited.'

James explained that DCI Lane would be calling on them but that he was intrigued as to why this chap Jonathan had pitched up buried on his estate. 'You say you met his girlfriend, but did you know if he was seeing anyone else?'

'A man like Jonathan Dunhelm does as he pleases, Lord Harrington. As I say, I wasn't privy to his private life but it wouldn't surprise me if he'd had two or three women dangling on his arm.' She held a finger up. 'I do remember a man bursting into the office and threatening him.'

'Oh?'

She described a bulky man with short hair who'd accused Jonathan of misleading him over a property deal. 'I'm sure if he'd had a knife with him, he would have stabbed him there and then. I don't think I've ever seen anyone so annoyed. He did have two other men with him, from the same estate.'

'Do you remember his name?'

Her brow knitted together. 'It was an odd name; not his surname but certainly his first name. The spelling was awkward.'

'Eoin? Eoin Fuller?'

She stared at him. 'Yes. Yes, that was it.'

'He came to the offices here, in Crawley?'

'Yes. We'd just moved our headquarters here. He wasn't the only one though. There were several unhappy people who wrote threatening letters.'

Beth asked if they had reported it to the police. Felicity said they never did. 'Jonathan waved the whole thing away and laughed at it. He always said *They signed a contract, I haven't broken the law.*'

James frowned. Why did Eoin not mention this? The front door opened and James saw the rotund figure of Jack Pemberton. He took off his wellingtons and left them on the front step. His face reminded James of a potato and his small grey eyes questioned the guests.

Felicity got up with a smile. 'Jack, this is Lord and Lady Harrington; it was on their land that Jonathan was found.'

Jack winced. 'Goodness, that must have been a shock. I thought he'd turn up somewhere but not in a grave on the Harrington estate.'

Beth went through how he was found. 'You say you thought he'd turn up. Did you think he'd simply left the business?'

He shrugged his tatty gardening jacket off. Felicity took it from him. 'I didn't know what to think at first; he said his business was his life so when he didn't come back, I thought he'd been in an accident. He liked cars and motorbikes so I was expecting Mrs Dunhelm to come and tell me he'd been killed in an accident.'

He noticed the fresh paintwork. 'That looks nice, love.' Easing himself down in his armchair, he gestured at the newspaper. 'Murdered, so it says there.'

'Does that surprise you?' asked James.

'Not the in the least. I'm sure when the police come calling, I'll be one more person on an endless list of suspects.' Jack went on to recount tales of dirty tricks, bribery and emotional blackmail to secure a good business deal. 'He had his finger in all types of property deals, new builds, regeneration, renting, leasing commercial properties — you name it, he had something going on.' He shook his head. 'I didn't like it, Lord Harrington, it weren't right. I mean, we all want a good deal and we had a business that we wanted to be profitable but not at the expense of people's livelihoods and emotions. I never signed the papers that related to deals he had. My business dealings were all above board.'

Felicity brought in a cup of tea and had caught the tail-end of their discussion.

'Jack had a heart attack about six months before Jonathan went missing.'

'Brought on by Jonathan, I'm sure of it,' Jack put in. 'I got that annoyed with the way he treated people I could feel myself getting more anxious by the day.'

James asked why he didn't say anything.

'You didn't know Jonathan Dunhelm. I was his partner and on a good wage. If I'd have crossed him, he'd have got rid of me somehow. I turned a blind eye but it affected me. I keeled over at work and was in hospital for three weeks.' He sipped his tea. 'I must say, when he went missing, you could have knocked me down with a feather. The business was doing well and he just upped and left. In the end I thought someone was after him, that he'd gone too far with one of his business proposals.'

'And had he?'

'No more than normal. But you're dealing with different personalities aren't you. One person may take it all and not be bothered, another may erupt.'

Like Natalie Kershaw, James thought. 'You run the business now?'

He sat up with a proud expression. 'I do and it's all legal and above board. We don't have anything underhand going on and we've turned it into a respected and trustworthy business.' He smiled at Felicity. 'Me and Felicity got married. We've not been blessed with children but we've a wonderful young lodger who's become part of the family. Life couldn't be more perfect.'

James struggled with his next question. 'Please excuse me for asking. It's just that I associate company directors living away from their working environment.'

Jack chuckled. 'I know what you're getting at, Lord Harrington. On my wage, I should be in a larger house out of town and not having to rely on a lodger. Truth is, when Jonathan left, we had people to pay off. I wanted the business run as it should be and that meant negotiating different deals, reimbursing some funds and paying out for cancelled contracts. It was a tight few years so me and Felicity settled for this semi. But it suits us. I'm from a working class family and this place is somewhere that I would have aspired to as a youngster. The lodger helps with the rent and we don't need that extra income any more but he's part of the family. Having said that, he's looking for a place of his own now, so we'll have the house to ourselves.'

James apologised if his question had been too intrusive. Beth suggested to James that they ought to leave Felicity and Jack to enjoy the rest of their day.

Felicity commented on the location of Jonathan's remains. 'Who on earth would have thought to put Jonathan there? It must have been awful to find it like that.'

'It was actually the vicar's dog that found it,' said James. 'And a skeleton is not quite as gruesome as a complete body but it's a shock nonetheless. DCI Lane I'm sure will be in touch, but thank you for seeing us.'

She followed them out to the hall and opened the front door. 'He was such a handsome man. It was easy to be swayed by him and the girls in the office all fell for him. He was the typical model for all women, tall, masculine, fair and hand-some.'

James turned with a frown. Felicity Pemberton stood in her slippers at around five foot eight inches. 'Tall?'

She tucked her hair behind her ears. 'Yes, that's why he had such a presence. He must have been around six foot three, maybe taller.'

He did a double-take with Beth then returned his attention to Felicity. 'Six foot three?'

She appeared guarded. 'Yes, why?'

James dismissed the question, claiming a personal assumption that Jonathan had been shorter. They said their goodbyes and walked briskly to the car where Beth pulled James round to face him. 'Didn't that examiner say that skeleton was five foot odd?'

'Perhaps we misheard.'

They stared at each other for a few seconds.

James unlocked the door. 'Let's telephone George and see if he can meet us at Elsie's. Hopefully, he'll put us right.'

11

James complimented Elsie on the seasonal decorations in the café. She and her regular waitress had given it an Easter theme and the senses were bombarded with bright colours and enticing aromas. Every table had a vase of freshly cut daffodils on it, bright green napkins and small fluffy ducks were placed between the salt and pepper pots. Brightly painted wooden eggs stood to attention along the shelf of the French dresser behind the counter and the menu board was crafted into the shape of a huge Easter egg.

The smell of hot cross buns filled the room with a mixture of orange peel and cinnamon scents.

Elsie delivered a tray of tea, three hot cross buns and a sample slice of Grandma Harrington's layer cake. 'Fresh made this morning — I hope it lives up to expectations and thank you so much for the recipe. I'm up to my eyes baking hot cross buns so it made a change to have something different to make.'

'I'm sure it'll be perfect,' said James eyeing up the sample of thin layers of sponge with dollops of butter cream throughout.

'It looks delicious,' exclaimed Beth with delight. 'And you've put a knob of butter on top of the toasted buns. How lovely.'

George let out a satisfied sigh. 'Indigestion, here I come.'

Beth prepared the cups and saucers and agitated the tea in the Brown Betty teapot. James poured a dash of milk into each cup as George undid his jacket to make himself more comfortable. He loaded his fork with some layer cake and took a mouthful.

'That's a smashing bit of cake.'

James took a forkful and agreed. 'Elsie always sticks rigidly to the recipe so I know it'll be just like Grandma's.'

He moved on to his toasted bun, scooped some butter onto his knife and bit into the crisp surface of the hot cross bun. He grabbed a napkin as butter drizzled down his chin. The mixture Elsie made was not dissimilar to his grand-mother's recipe, using a generous helping of cinnamon. What a shame these buns were only available at Easter. He told Beth they ought to have them year round.

'That wouldn't be right, James. These are specifically for Easter. If you wanted something similar, you could have a teacake.'

'But teacakes don't have the peel and spice. We could do the mixture but not put the cross on top.'

George said this was all very well but he hadn't got all day to sit talking about buns and cakes. 'I've quite a bit on at the moment and I'm not getting very far with any of it. It's one step forward, two steps back.'

'Are you talking about the canal murders or our chap Jonathan Dunhelm?'

'Both.' He'd brought with him a buff folder which lay on the table, under the sugar bowl.

James was itching to know what was inside it and asked that George reveal all. 'I mean to say, you wouldn't put it in plain view if it wasn't for our eyes.'

'Before I do that, I want to know how you got on with Felicity Pemberton. You telephoned me for a reason and she's the only person you've seen since I left this morning.'

Beth poured the tea into dainty china cups. 'Well, for a start, did you know that Pemberton is the name of Jonathan's business partner? She married him.'

George said that he did and gestured for her to continue. She did so and, after a short while, their friend was completely up to date.

'The trouble,' James said, 'is motive and opportunity. Felicity, like most of the women around Jonathan, appeared to be quite infatuated with him at one time. But, as she got to know him, she began to see him for what he was, although she always remained professional. Never made her feelings known, or so she said. If that's the case, I'm not sure she would be in the frame.'

'But,' Beth put in, 'Jack had benefited quite nicely out of Jonathan's disappearance. He's now running the business except on a more legal basis and he's married the secretary. They have a lodger but we didn't meet him.' She explained the state of the business when Jack took over and the cost of putting it onto a more professional footing. 'I think Jack could have easily killed Jonathan. He hated his business methods, could see a way of getting his hands on the business and rid himself of Dunhelm. Although it cost him initially, he's nicely off now.' She turned to James. 'They said themselves they don't need to have a lodger now, although it sounds like he may be moving out. Felicity could be an accessory.'

James agreed and studied his friend who had continued to enjoy his bun and slurp his tea. They'd been here about fifteen minutes now and he hadn't jotted a single thing down in his notebook. He knew George was busy with the canal atrocity but he seemed singularly unimpressed with anything he or Beth had to say. He put the last morsel of bun down on his plate.

'I say, George, you strike me as someone who either has too much going on at work or the information we've given you is already known. Which is it?'

George dabbed his lips with his napkin. 'A bit of both.' He waved Elsie across and ordered another batch of hot cross buns. 'Your message to me earlier indicated that you had something a little more than you've provided so far. I got the impression you'd come across something significant.' He pulled the buff folder toward him and flicked it open. 'We stumbled across something significant too.'

James and Beth edged in.

'Jonathan Dunhelm fractured his leg when he was about eighteen. This skeleton shows no sign of a fracture.'

Beth turned to James. 'Well that proves it.'

George let out a mumble of frustration. 'Don't tell me you already know that. How on earth did you find that out?'

James told him what had happened when they'd been saying goodbye to Felicity. 'I mean, she's only a couple of inches shorter than me and when she said he was tall, well, I had to ask.'

'She said Jonathan stood at around six

184

foot three,' Beth said, glimpsing a black and white photograph of the skeleton in the folder. 'We thought Maurice said he was shorter than that but we wondered if we'd misheard.'

'Height of this skeleton would put the body at five foot ten at the most,' said George. 'We'll need more than Felicity Pemberton's description but the broken leg is evidence enough. We've been investigating the wrong man.'

There was a long silence as they absorbed this new turn of events.

Elsie returned with a fresh batch of buns. George immediately reached for one and added more butter. James topped up the teacups.

Beth frowned, clearly trying to make out what had happened. 'The man buried on our estate was not Jonathan but made to look like him.'

'Whoever did that missed out a detail,' said George as he stirred his tea. 'I couldn't understand why there were no keys on the remains. If you go out, you take your keys with you. If this is someone made to look like Jonathan, where are his keys?'

James settled back in his chair. 'Do you have any idea about who it is we dug up?'

His friend was none the wiser but said that whoever it was must still be linked to Jonathan Dunhelm. 'There's been a deliberate change of identity here so whoever did this, well, they must have known the victim.'

James noticed Beth's eyes had glazed over. 'Darling, what is it?'

She opened her palms wide. 'Surely Jonathan is now a suspect. If that's not Jonathan in the ground, then where is he? And why has he disappeared?' She gave him a resigned look. 'He must have been the killer.'

George discreetly held a hand up. 'Now don't go making assumptions, Beth. We've got to start again which is a pain in the neck because I'm up to my eyes in a current murder.'

James helped himself to a second bun. 'We could help. Let us call in on Mrs Dunhelm again and see if we can glean something that'll lead us in the right direction.'

Beth suggested they should also speak to Pip Logan. 'He's Jonathan's oldest friend. He may know something or have heard Jonathan discuss someone who threatened him.'

'Good idea, darling. George, do you have Pip's address?'

George's reaction was swift. 'I'm not that happy about you poking your nose in, James. You're seeing far too many people and this is, after all, police business. I shouldn't be giving out names and addresses willy-nilly for you to go out and pester possible suspects.'

James gave him a 'Why do you have to be so awkward' look and reminded him that he'd been happy to hand over Felicity's address earlier. 'But, listen, I don't want to put you in a difficult position, so don't worry about breaking your regulations. We'll call in on Mrs Dunhelm; I'm sure she'll let us have the details we need and that means you don't get into trouble.'

George gritted his teeth. 'I'm not being awkward, James, but you know the position I'm in. I can't keep handing information over to you. But promise me that you'll let me know anything you find out — no matter how trivial.'

The chatter in the café faded as James drifted into his thoughts. In some respects it was a shame that it wasn't Jonathan's body they'd dug up. There were so many people with motive and opportunity to want him dead he'd been certain they were well on the way to narrowing down who the killer was.

But if it wasn't Jonathan Dunhelm in that grave, who on earth had Radley dug up and why did he have Jonathan's things on him?

12

Anne's jaw dropped as she slid a new hymn number onto the board in the church, ready to mount it on the wall by the pulpit. 'So it's not Jonathan Dunhelm?'

Stephen was in the pulpit helping her secure the board. 'So you've no idea who the b-body is?'

Beth, who asked if there were any daffodils and tulips left after helping to arrange several displays in the church, then added, 'We're visiting Mrs Dunhelm after the service to see if we can find anything else out.'

Anne questioned how she would know. 'After all, it's not her son in the ground, what could she tell you?'

James studied the stained glass window at the end of the church, depicting Mary and the baby Jesus. 'We presumed they must be linked. I mean, you'd have to have Jonathan's personal things to put on the body. This wasn't just an item of clothing; there were specific documents, the shoes and that engraved watch.'

Stephen joined him. 'D-do you think someone is t-trying to frame Jonathan?'

'Could be,' said Beth checking with James.

He shrugged. It was certainly an idea. Jonathan had upset so many people from all walks of life that he wouldn't put it past anyone to frame the man for a crime. But he imagined Jonathan to be careful in his conduct and unlikely to allow himself to be compromised. He turned to Anne. 'Judging by what we know, the missing Jonathan would have people on his payroll doing the dirty business. He's the sort of chap who'd take a step back from anything majorly untoward, don't you think?'

She suggested that Jonathan was the murderer. 'That's the most logical conclusion. Someone upset him, they came to blows, Jonathan kills the man and swaps identities. He sounds selfish enough to do that.'

'But why? Why go to all of that trouble?'

'I-I would say there is more to Jonathan

Dunhelm than m-meets the eye.'

'I do too,' said Beth, giving her thoughts about the missing house keys. 'If Jonathan is a murderer and did swap identities he would have wanted to return to the home of his victim.'

'That's right,' said Anne, looking inspired. 'If he did change identities, he would need items that the dead man had owned.'

The church door opened and Anne hastened to the entrance to welcome their parishioners in. As James and Beth took their seats, Stephen squeezed James' arm. 'L-let's catch up later; today is rather hectic.'

A chuckle behind them broke James' train of thought. Over his shoulder, he nodded a hello to Philip and Helen and their pretty daughter, Natasha. Further along the pew were Graham and Sarah with their two children, Thomas and Georgina. Across the aisle the Snoop Sisters took the front row with Professor Wilkins and Mr Chrichton alongside. Their cleaner, Mrs Jepson, smiled at him. Mr Bennett and his dog, Blackie, took their place toward the back of the church and Charlie Hawkins was doing his best to stop his children from being too noisy. Stephen happily welcomed boisterous children as he thought they brought a bit of life into the church but a stern stare quietened them down if they became over-excited. Everyone, apart from the sick and infirm, appeared to be here.

Stephen's Easter Sunday service was delivered, as usual, with humour and celebration; a celebration that the Saviour had risen from the dead. As was his habit, Stephen said prayers from the pulpit but also wandered round the church when speaking to his flock. James remembered him saying, a few months ago, that it kept his audience from falling asleep. His brief time as an army chaplain had sharpened his wit and when he'd first arrived in Cavendish, the older residents had taken a little while to adapt to his less formal approach. But, with Anne's unquestioning support, the village had taken them to their hearts. To James, it felt as if the Merryweathers had been here far longer than a couple of years.

Stephen returned to the front of the church to go through more prayers and, with a nod to the organist, Mr Bishop, everyone stood to sing the joyful 'Christ the Lord is Risen Today'. Stephen sang out loud and encouraged his congregation to sing to the rafters. A few hand signals to turn up the volume worked its magic and, with contributions from Bob Tanner and the singers from the folk club in the congregation, the harmonies sent goose bumps along James' arms.

He received an elbow in the ribs from Beth as she jerked her head, inviting him to look toward the back of the church. He did so and smiled. Dressed in their Sunday best were Bert and Gladys. He grinned at Beth and felt a gentle flow of happiness. How wonderful to see the two of them together; an old friendship rekindled after many years.

Beth whispered in his ear. 'I've invited them for dinner.'

'Today?'

Her eyes sparkled. 'It'll be nice to get to know Gladys. I also invited Professor Wilkins.'

The look he gave her was a quizzical one. The Professor was, like Philip Jackson, attractive to the women in the village but, whereas Philip had the manners and decorum to match, Wilkins was both abrupt and aloof.

But Beth had fun trying to bring him out of himself even though, most of the time, her efforts failed. 'He spends too much time on his own in that museum. Anyway, he said he can't come; gave me an excuse, I'm sure.'

James grinned and tentatively asked if there were any other ad-hoc invitations. She assured him the only guests were Bert and Gladys. He reminded her they were visiting Mrs Dunhelm after the service.

'I know. I've told them we have a prior engagement so they won't be arriving until five o'clock.'

Anne leaned in to speak to Beth and Helen. 'Can you help me with the tea?'

The three women discreetly disappeared into the small kitchen at the back of the church. Mr Bishop hammered out the last chords of the hymn and Stephen returned to the pulpit. 'A reminder th-that we have the Easter egg hunt tomorrow.' The children chattered between them. 'We're to meet at the back entrance of Harrington's at ten o'clock. Mr Chr–Chrichton and Mr Hawkins will be there to make sure everything runs s-smoothly.' He focussed on as many children as possible. 'My wife, Lord and Lady Harrington and Mr Hawkins have planned an adventurous route for you all.'

The children sought out one another; their excitement was almost tangible.

'B–but for now, we have tea and fresh hot cross b-buns baked by Elsie and Mrs Keates.'

The congregation filed out of the pews and drifted toward the front of the church where Anne had wheeled out a trolley holding a large tea urn, jugs of milk and bowls of sugar. Beth and Helen followed behind with the hot cross buns, butter and knives. Various members of the Women's Institute dashed forward to lend a helping hand.

James watched Gladys drag Bert toward him. 'Oh your Lordship,' she said, 'wha' a lov'ly thing to do, inviting us to dinner. You sure that's all right? I mean we're not yer average guest are we? I don't wanna show you up.'

He delivered his most welcoming smile. 'I would much rather have you and Bert here for dinner than a pompous Duke and Duchess.' He slapped Bert on the back. 'Bert is one of my oldest and dearest friends and if I can't break bread with him, it would be a travesty.'

Beth held Gladys' hand. 'I'm so looking forward to catching up with you. We've never really had a chance to speak and you've had such an influence on things around here.'

How true that was, thought James. Gladys had come into their lives during the previous spring when they'd stumbled across GJ in the barn at Harrington's. Their lengthy investigation took Beth and Bert to the East End mission where Bert realised he knew the lady running the soup kitchen. He'd grown up with Gladys and had always had a soft spot for her. Over the years, they'd drifted apart as Bert spent less time in the East End. But, with their friendship renewed, there was a suggestion of romance in the air. James couldn't remember the last time Bert had made such an effort to attend church in a suit. He normally pitched up in his normal 'togs' as he called them.

Although Gladys had come to GJ's wedding, they'd never got the chance to actually sit down and chat. He had a full day ahead of him that day but was quietly pleased that Beth had made the dinner arrangements.

The Easter service slowly turned into a social event and, over the next hour, neighbours caught up with one another's news and the talk of the body at Harrington's surfaced, courtesy of Rose and Lilac Crumb. James and Beth gave each other a knowing look. Here they were gossiping about the body of Jonathan Dunhelm and, for once, the Snoop Sisters were way off the mark.

'D'you think we should tell them?' asked Beth.

'Absolutely not.' He steered her toward the cakes. 'Come on, I don't want to miss out on these.'

Beth tutted and told him he should mind his waistline. 'And we're bound to be offered some of your simnel cake if Mrs Dunhelm hasn't eaten it all.'

He grabbed a plate and helped himself to an Easter bun. At that moment, he wasn't too bothered about simnel cake. What he did hope for was that Celia would provide something . . . *anything* . . . to point them in the right direction; a direction that would help them identify the skeleton they'd dug up.

★   ★   ★

Celia opened the front door personally and James sensed a difference in her. The severe features had softened and although she'd been a considerate and amiable hostess during their last meeting, today she appeared more animated. She wore a flattering emerald green dress and black court shoes. They accepted her invitation to go straight through to the lounge where tea had been served.

'I knew you'd be on time. Guests of stature always are so I asked Diana to go ahead and prepare tea. You've come straight from church?'

James and Beth went through the morning's activities and described the various events they had planned for the rest of the Easter week.

She clasped her hands together. 'You certainly have a close-knit community there, don't you?'

The comment didn't surprise James. How often had he heard this from various individuals over the years? Community didn't create itself and the village worked hard to keep its folklore and traditions alive. Sometimes it seemed a chore but the rewards at the end of it outweighed any inconvenience or cost. Easter was a particularly hectic time and combining the religious aspect of it with the more modern games and pastimes meant relying on more villagers than ever to help. And now, this year, Graham had added a fundraiser. Although he'd groaned at yet another Easter tradition, the kitty for the village events was running a little low, so the idea to top up the pot was a good one.

Beth helped Celia with the tea. 'You must be so pleased to hear the news about your son.'

The lady paused, reached across and rubbed Beth's hand. 'Thank you my dear,

I am relieved to know that my son is still walking this earth but,' she tapped her chest, 'I loathe the thoughts that enter my head without invitation.'

James asked what thoughts they were. He received a look of despair.

She spread her hands. 'Where is he? Why hasn't he been in touch?' She poured the tea while Beth distributed slices of simnel cake. 'I thought our relationship was good, Lord Harrington. Why hasn't he been in touch? Just a note to let me know! But I've received no word; no word whatsoever. What am I to think? Is he lying in a different grave? My instinct tells me no. But, then, where is he? My thoughts veer to the same answer.'

With a strained smile, she accepted some cake from Beth.

'I'm afraid that Jonathan killed that man and left the country. But why didn't he confide in me? Why didn't he come home and tell me? It might have been self-defence. Oh, goodness, I know he had enemies, I know he upset plenty of people, I'm not naive, but I simply can't see Jonathan *killing* someone — not intentionally. I don't see him as a killer.'

She stared at the patterned carpet while Beth did her best to reassure her. James could always rely on his wife to say the right thing. She had obviously taken note of everything he'd told her about this woman; her character, her state of mind, her acceptance of her son's failings. And, she had an uncanny knack of identifying the positive traits in an individual, even someone as ruthless as Jonathan Dunhelm. She emphasised the need for her to think back on how wonderful her relationship had been with her son and the importance of remembering the good times and his kind and generous nature toward her. It took some time, but Beth managed to perk Celia up.

'And you must always remember,' Beth said, 'that DCI Lane is an astute policeman who doesn't make assumptions. He keeps all options open.' She shot a sideways look to James who continued.

'Jonathan may have a good reason for staying away. Perhaps he witnessed something that he can't put right; perhaps he's covering up for someone and the best way to do that is to stay away.'

'You're both kind and thoughtful people but that still doesn't answer the question as to why he hasn't contacted me. A letter, a telephone call, a message passed on just to let me know he is alive, even if it is to say I must do or say nothing.'

James straightened the crease in his trousers. Yes, that was an odd one and he didn't have a definitive answer for her because he didn't understand that himself. The photographs and anecdotes provided by Celia reinforced the sense of a wonderful rapport between mother and son. He likened it to the relationship Beth had with their twins, Harry and Oliver. Now in their early twenties, they were more like friends and the four of them were comfortable chatting about all manner of topics and spending time together.

A photograph of Celia and Jonathan stood on the table next to him. The pair of them were roaring with laughter — it was a natural, carefree moment captured in time. He felt incredible sympathy for her and wondered how many emotions she'd experienced over the past few days; a mixture of highs and lows. Delight, now, to hear that her son was probably alive, yet despair that the boy she loved so much had not contacted her and could possibly be a murderer.

'I say, Celia, is there anything about Jonathan that might shed some light on things. The watch that was found, he didn't give that away to anyone.'

'Goodness no. That was his pride and joy. He cherished that watch. No, no, there's nothing.'

'What about hobbies? Did he have any?'

'Only his cars but that was a solitary thing. He didn't belong to any clubs or anything. He'd polish those cars until they gleamed and on high days and holidays, he'd take them out for a spin around the country lanes. He has a beautiful 1949 Jaguar 2-seater roadster in the garage. He used to let me drive that one. I still do,' she added with a cheeky smile.

'You still have all the cars?'

'I have always said that I wouldn't part with anything until I knew what had happened to Jonathan. I was preparing for a funeral and thinking about auctioning the cars. Now, in a way, I'm back to where I was before — not knowing.'

Beth asked her about Pip Logan. 'Perhaps Jonathan confided in him. Best friends can keep secrets. Would you like us to speak with him to see if he has some idea?'

'He always maintained to me that he knew nothing. He was as shocked as I was when Jonathan disappeared. He searched every day, checking the roads where he drove, asking at hospitals, calling in on every person he could find who had some link with Jonathan. I doubt he'd know.'

James suggested that people often remembered something many years later. 'It may seem trivial to them at the time but Jonathan may have mentioned something, a woman he'd taken a shine to, a new interest. What about the music? You said he didn't care for the music we saw left out in his room. Do you think he'd changed his tastes?'

She made a face and apologised for being so unhelpful.

'What about the arts, films, theatre, books, that sort of thing?'

The question alerted her. 'He was interested in detective work.'

James remembered the books he'd seen upstairs. 'In an active way?'

She rubbed her forehead, struggling to recollect anything of relevance. 'He wanted to do private investigation work but I'm not sure that he started anything.' Her eyes focussed on them. A memory had risen to the surface. 'I do remember . . . now what was it . . . he told me something about having to follow a man to see what he got up to. It all sounded horribly common and I told him I didn't want to know about it and I wanted no part of it. It was the briefest of conversations. Funny that I suddenly recollect it like that.'

Beth asked if he'd kept any paperwork concerning that. 'Do you know if he was paid?'

'I wouldn't have thought so. I don't even know if he started. It would have been a game for Jonathan, a lark. It wouldn't have lasted. He never mentioned it again.'

James asked if they could have Pip Logan's address. 'Now you've remembered that, it may be that Pip will know a little more. Whatever we find out, we'll pass on to Inspector Lane.'

She gave a keen nod. Knowing that so many people were trying to get to the truth was, she said, humbling. She reached for her address book and took out a card. 'You're welcome to take this.'

James accepted Pip Logan's business card and raised his eyebrows. 'A landscape gardener?'

'Yes, Pip was always an outdoors man. No one could ever imagine him in a suit or sitting in an office. He helps my gardener maintain the grounds here and works on a number of the estates outside Horsham. We're always in touch. He's my link to Jonathan, a reminder of happier times.'

They thanked her for her hospitality and made their way out to the hall where she emphasised her need to know, once and for all, so that she could learn to live with the truth, whatever it was.'

Beth assured her they would keep her appraised with any news.

In the car, James handed Pip's business card to Beth. 'He lives in Horsham. Have we time to drive over? I can't imagine he'll be working on a Sunday.'

'Providing we're home by four o'clock for me to put dinner on, that should be fine.'

James pulled away and wondered if he had a sixth sense. When he'd accepted the business card from Celia he had a good feeling about it — as if, at last, something was going to fall into place. He hoped this Pip chap would come up trumps.

13

Pip Logan lived in a two-up, two-down tumbledown cottage on the outskirts of Horsham, a market-town about twenty minutes from Cavendish. Given that he was a landscape gardener, it was no surprise that his front garden was immaculate, with a variety of coloured blossoms and shrubs. Beth stepped out of the car with a look of wonder.

'Oh how beautiful.'

James had to admit it was a sight to behold — a tiny cottage garden in a blaze of purples, yellows, peaches and pinks. A rose bush had been trained to frame the wooden trellis built around the front door. The wooden side gate was open and a man in his mid-thirties strolled out with a garden fork resting on his shoulder. His sleeves were rolled up and he wore muddy wellingtons and faded corduroy trousers. When he saw them, he stopped in his tracks.

'Ah, hello. Can I help?'

'Pip Logan?'

A warm smile lit up his face; the same handsome face that James had seen in the photograph with Jonathan. It was clear the man spent his whole life outside. He had a healthy walnut complexion, clear blue eyes and scruffy blond hair that he swept back from his forehead with muddy hands.

'That's me. How can I help?'

When James introduced himself and Beth, Pip immediately jammed the fork into the ground and wiped his hands on his shirt. 'Of course, Celia told me you'd visited to see her about Jonathan. Bloody awful business.' He pulled a face. 'Sorry, didn't mean to swear.'

For some reason, the man was so likeable that neither of them was too concerned about it.

'That's quite all right,' said James. 'Do you have a few moments to spare?'

'Of course. Follow me — but you'll have to mind the mess. My beautiful wife has taken our two children to visit her mother in Cumbria so I've reverted to bachelor mode.' He held the door open.

Beth asked about his family and how long he'd been married. He led them into a small pantry where he lit the gas under a dented kettle and popped a couple of scoops of tea into the teapot. All the while he spoke non-stop about his wife, Amelia, and their two children Connor and Cameron. Amelia's parents were originally from Ireland, he said, and had now settled in Cumbria. He'd met Amelia when he was in the air force and she worked for the Air Transport Auxiliary, delivering aircraft.

'You both flew?' asked James.

Pip grinned, held a finger up and dashed into the next room. In a couple of seconds he was back with a framed photograph of Amelia dressed in overalls, standing by a Lancaster bomber.

Beth's jaw dropped. 'She flew this?'

Pip continued organising tea. 'Delivered it. That's what those girls did. She flew Spitfires, Hurricanes, Lancasters, Wellingtons — if it was in service with the RAF, she could fly it. Amazing woman and loves speed. Got a bit of oomph about her. My type of girl. I thought Jonathan might have nabbed her, especially with his collection of cars, but she only had eyes for me.'

James studied the photograph. Having been in the RAF himself, he had seen at close quarters the expertise and courage of these women, delivering aircraft to bases all over the country. He remembered one of them telling him she could fly thirty six types of aircraft. Many of them had been champing at the bit to fly in combat and extremely disappointed they weren't permitted to do so. Amelia was clearly a spirited lady and it was obvious that Pip was as proud as punch. He placed the frame on the kitchen dresser.

'You served with Jonathan?'

Pip loaded everything onto a tray and asked them to follow him through to the lounge. He kicked a leather football off the sofa and asked Beth if she would mind clearing the comics from the coffee table. She held them until he suggested she simply put them on the floor. He put the tray down.

'I'm so sorry about the mess; yes, we

joined up together. Take a seat — shove anything on the floor. Shame you didn't pop in later in the week. Amelia's back then and I'd have had the place spotless.'

Beth offered to pour tea. James, who felt he would look like a pot of tea by the end of the day, waited for Pip to expand.

'We went to school together. I met Jonny when we were four years old at prep school, Ardingly.'

James started. 'That's where I went.'

Pip's eyes opened wide. 'Well, hurrah for that. All the best men went to Ardingly.'

They did, James said, recalling that the school was the best grounding for life that he could ever have wanted. He was warming more and more to this young man. He had an easy way about him, a comfortable and welcoming manner. The ramshackle home, where nothing matched, suited him and James had a sense that he would be good company over a pint in the local pub. If Jonathan Dunhelm had possessed the same magnetism, he could quite understand how friends and strangers alike would latch onto them, wanting to be part of their circle.

Pip helped Beth with the drinks. 'We loved Ardingly, particularly the sports. Jonny and I were in all the teams, rugby, cricket, athletics, football, archery, the whole kit and caboodle. We went our separate ways at university but then the war kicked in and we didn't need asking twice.'

'Any reason why you chose the RAF?'

Pip grinned. 'Vanity. We had a good discussion about it. Jonny said the army sounded too muddy and the uniforms were a disgusting colour.' He roared with laughter. 'We quite liked the sound of the navy but didn't want to end up cooped up in a submarine. The RAF was glamorous. Nice uniform, get to fly a plane and it seemed like the service for us. All the nice girls love a sailor, so they say, but a RAF pilot got a little bit of hero worship.'

Beth gave James a mischievous grin. 'So,' she said, 'you joined because of fashion and status.'

He reached across to a wooden barrel full of biscuits and invited them to help themselves. 'That's right,' he said in a matter-of-fact way. 'In all honesty, we didn't think we'd see the war out so we thought we might as well sign up and meet our maker while wearing a smart uniform. We saw a good many flight crew shot down or badly injured; it seemed just a matter of time before it was our turn.'

'Commendable,' said James. 'But you managed to avoid the man with the scythe.'

'We certainly did. Came out unscathed but a little more mature about things.' He munched on a biscuit. Crumbs fell on the floor. He scooped them up and dropped them in an ashtray. 'Meeting Amelia and having the children settled me down and my job is a mile away from the violence of those days.'

Beth remarked that it must be lovely to spend whole days working with nature. Pip agreed and spoke about his work with great enthusiasm. 'I wouldn't do anything else. It doesn't pay that much but I'm not from the poorest of backgrounds so I can't complain.' He motioned to the back garden. 'And I'm beginning to get known as the man who not only turns out a good garden but provides excellent groceries.'

James went to the window to see that every inch of outside space was utilised for something. By the house was a small play area for the children but further back there were neat rows of vegetables and fruit trees. At the far end was a huge greenhouse, inside which a tall gentleman with a beard, around a similar age to Pip, was fixing long canes into place, presumably for tomatoes.

Pip continued. 'That's Jerzy in the greenhouse. He was in the Polish air force. Had nothing to go back to after the war and comes from a farming background so he's helping me out here. Knows his vegetables too. Thanks to him that side of the business is going into profit.'

'Do you supply shops?'

'Shops, restaurants, whoever wants to buy it.'

James made a mental note to let Didier know. His chef was always on the lookout for new suppliers. 'And Jonathan? He didn't fancy the outdoor life?' He watched Jerzy tidy away spades and pots.

The man shrugged a jacket on and left by a gate at the far end of the garden. A few seconds later, James heard the roar of a motorbike as it sped off.

'Not for all the tea in China. Once the victory parade was finished he began planning his future. Once he'd inherited Dunhelm Developments, he was off like a whirlwind, making deals, building houses, renting, buying, selling. I told him to take it easy, that he was becoming more like his dad every day but he wouldn't listen to me.'

'More like his dad?'

'There was a side to Jonathan, always had been; Celia must have told you; a ruthless, stubborn streak. It served him well on the sports field and certainly in the RAF. Having Jonny alongside you in a life or death situation was an enormous comfort but, in the powerful world of business, I know that more people loathed him than liked him.'

Beth frowned. 'How did you feel about that; being his closest friend?'

Pip's head motioned left to right as if to say that it was a fine balance. 'I tried to get him to be more diplomatic and consider people's feelings, especially if he was getting them out of their homes. I didn't agree with the way he did things. At times he treated people like commodities and didn't understand the emotional side of things.' He reached across for another biscuit. 'I took a step back in the end. I didn't want to spoil our friendship — he'd been nothing but the best of mates to me and how he went about things at work had nothing to do with me but it was a side I didn't like.'

'And what about his girlfriend?'

The young man raised an eyebrow.

'Girlfriends, I think you should be asking. I believe you spoke to Natalie Kershaw.' James expressed surprise and Pip explained that Mrs Dunhelm had telephoned to let him know what James was doing. 'Well, she thought she was the sole partner but he really played the field. If I'm being honest, the war never changed Jonathan. It made me grow up and want to experience what my parents had, you know, marry, have children. But for Jonny, well, a part of him didn't grow up, he still wanted to sow his oats and damn the consequences.' He suddenly sat forward. 'There was one girl, though, who had really got to him.'

James asked for permission to smoke. 'Not Natalie Kershaw?'

'No, no, he strung Natalie along. No this was someone he became infatuated with. I never met her and he only began mentioning her a few months before he went missing.'

'Do you have a name?'

'Belle or Bella, something like that. That's the only thing I remember. Short for Elizabeth I suppose or Isabelle. He'd been doing something odd, aside from his normal business dealings.'

'Are you talking about the private investigating?'

'You know about that?'

James outlined what Mrs Dunhelm had told him. 'She didn't seem to know much about it at all; indeed, I believe she told him that it all sounded a little seedy and that he was to stop.'

A quick smile. 'Jonathan loved his mother but didn't take a lot of notice of her. He did what he wanted to and he thought having a shot at being a private eye would be fun. Too many of those awful commercial paperbacks he read. Never admitted that, of course, he'd get them from the library. Fancied himself as a Philip Marlowe or whatever his name was.'

'You know what he was working on?'

'No, only that it was a woman and she was from a wealthy family.' He ruffled his hair. 'I can't tell you much more except that I was annoyed when he went missing and he never told me where he was going. Typical of Jonny, not thinking about the few people who were close to him. So I went searching.'

He repeated everything that Mrs Dunhelm had told James and Beth; visiting hospitals, telephoning every contact number in his address book, retracing routes taken and checking ditches but to no avail.

'After six months, I decided he was dead, that he'd had an accident but for some reason he couldn't be identified. It didn't dawn on me that he might have ended up in a grave.' He sat up. 'But then he didn't, did he? Celia said the remains weren't Jonathan's.'

'That's right.'

'So where is he?'

Beth linked her fingers. 'That's what we'd all like to know. And what about the music that Jonathan had in his rooms?'

Pip frowned. 'Music?'

James described the sheet music, the poem and the record on the turntable.

Pip made a face and shrugged. 'I've no idea. I'm a piano player but those pieces are not my sort of thing and I can take or leave Handel. Can't help you there I'm afraid.'

'And,' said James, 'you have no idea where this Belle girl lived?'

'I'd say local, only because his business was around here and he never went away overnight or anything like that.'

They finished their visit off with some small talk and made their excuses to leave, with apologies for calling in on a Sunday. Pip invited them to call again at any time.

He stood at the front door. 'I'd love to

know where Jonny is. If he's done something awful, I'll have to accept that, but he'll always be my friend. I'll always be there for him.'

The drive home was a thoughtful one, with each of them putting questions to the other, not expecting an answer. James had hoped Pip would shed some light on things and felt a little let down by their lack of progress. He wondered if they would ever discover who Belle was and, more importantly, the identity of the chap in the grave.

When they arrived home, the telephone rang. He picked up the receiver. 'Cavendish 261. Ah George, how the devil are you? What's that? Really! Well, that is interesting, where's he from?' He listened and scribbled on the notepad, before delivering their own news about their visit to Mrs Dunhelm and Pip Logan. 'This private eye escapade may be a line worth following don't you think?'

After a few minutes, he made a promise to stay in touch and sought Beth out in the kitchen where she had begun preparing individual loins of lamb. Taking her instructions from Didier, she'd chopped some fresh rosemary, mixed it with crushed garlic and was rubbing the mixture over the meat.

'George had one of his men check the names of anyone who disappeared the same time as Jonathan Dunhelm. He had two in the frame and one of them is from Crawley. The other one lives in Portsmouth. The local constabulary down there made some enquiries and that chap is alive and well and still living in Portsmouth.'

'Well that's good news for him. Who's the local man?'

'Terry Hyde. Worked as a driver on the buses in the town and rented a room just off the high street. I thought about taking a run over there and chatting to the landlady. According to George, she's still there.'

Beth glared at him. 'George won't thank you for interfering.'

'I'll take the chance and cross my fingers that I don't upset him.'

'Well you can't go now. We have dinner guests in an hour.' She placed the lamb on a baking tray and put it in the oven.

James did a double-take at the clock. Where had the time gone? And what an eventful day it had turned out to be. In some respects he hadn't felt they'd gone any further forward but in fact they had. Jonathan Dunhelm was dabbling as a private eye. Had his dabbling got him into trouble? And who was this Belle girl he was so enamoured with? It was likely they now had a name for the man in the grave. They were moving in the right direction. Now it was a case of making sense of it all.

14

Gladys and Bert proved to be entertaining guests on all counts. James couldn't remember the last time he'd laughed so much. The pair of them had anecdotes going back to their childhood in the East End of London and although the poverty there had been extreme, they had clearly made the best of a bad thing.

Bert covered everything from being a small boy waving dog pooh on sticks at other children to his continued passion for the East End favourite, jellied eels, a dish that prompted James to wince in disgust. He'd never tried the dish so wasn't qualified to make a judgement, but just the look of it made him queasy.

Gladys recounted days of hopscotch, leapfrog, swinging on lamppost cross-bars and juggling balls against walls. 'And I remember the smell of wet washing on wash-days. Always a smell of damp in the air.'

James discovered that Gladys had never left the East End and never visited anywhere 'exo'ic'. Exotic to James and Beth meant visiting the French Riviera or the Caribbean or gliding down a canal in Venice. Gladys' exotic was anywhere outside a twenty mile radius of London. She'd visited Brighton for the first time with Bert last summer.

'Cor strewth, it were marvellous. Two piers and one 'ad a theatre on it, an' all those beach huts — ooh it were wonderful.'

Beth told her she should visit more often. 'Brighton railway station is more or less in the centre of the town. You could take a day trip from Victoria and you don't have to change.'

'I told yer,' said Bert, cutting into his lamb. 'Get out of the smoke a bit more and see the world. You've other people who can 'elp out at the mission.'

'You can talk, Ber' Briggs, you ain't much more travelled than I am.'

Bert baulked. 'I made it down to Cornwall.' He sought James out for backup. 'Didn't I Jimmy boy?'

James spooned some mint sauce onto his plate. Their holiday in Cornwall with the Merryweathers had turned into quite an adventure. During it he had been delighted to catch up with Bert who had travelled to the West Country for the horse-racing.

Bert prodded his chest with pride. 'I'm well read, Gladys. I may not be well-travelled but I know fings.'

Beth told Gladys that he certainly did know things and was keen to commend the knowledge he'd shown during the many mysteries James had been involved in. 'I remember when James was investigating the death of a farmer a couple of winters ago; we were all staring at one another wondering what on earth a Gollum was and Bert looked at us as if we'd all gone mad.'

James added that Bert had provided all sorts of information and knowledge that he thought he'd only find in the library.

'Go on with yer,' said Gladys, her rosy cheeks glowing with undeniable pride.

She was a large lady who wore garish colours but, in a peculiar way, they suited her. James couldn't imagine her in any tailored costume; instead, she chose flowery dresses from the market or they were hand-me-downs from family and friends. And, to his delight, she had no qualms about it. *If someone don't want it anymore, why let it go to waste?'* was her motto.

Over dinner they discussed a variety of topics before Bert asked James how his investigation was going. 'I 'eard the bloke in the ground isn't who you thought it was. Not Jonathan Dunhelm?'

James and Beth went through what had happened over the previous couple of days.

'Quite honestly,' said Beth, 'it surprised me completely. I mean, so many people had reason to want Jonathan Dunhelm dead.'

'And wha' about this private eye palaver. D'you think he was poking his nose in where it didn't belong?'

James sliced into his new potato. 'I wondered that, although it could be a business associate that we don't yet know about. George is getting in touch with the business partner, Jack Pemberton to see if the name Terry Hyde resonates with him.' He poured another helping of gravy over his lamb. 'I'm still unsure about the music.'

Beth quizzed him on why that was so interesting. 'Perhaps someone lent the music to him — recommended the songs.'

Bert asked if there were any more peas; Gladys told him off for being so rude. Bert shrugged. 'I like peas.'

Beth smiled and went through to the kitchen, calling back as she went. 'Gladys, there is one thing I love about Bert. I know when he comes to dinner, he'll eat everything I put in front of him. It's a pleasure to cook for guests like that.'

'Well, you've got a luverly kitchen to cook in, that's for sure.'

James explained that the whole thing was only a few months old. 'That's why we went to Cornwall; to get away from all the building work.'

'Enough about kitchens,' Bert said, accepting a dish of peas from Beth and spooning them onto his plate. 'What music was it?'

'The song 'Daisy' and Handel's 'Hallelujah Chorus'.'

Bert frowned and muttered a few lines from Daisy. 'And what's the name of this mystery woman?'

'Belle or Bella.'

His friend sat back and appeared to go into a trance. Finally he asked James if he had an encyclopaedia. James said he did and excused himself. He popped through to the study and shouted out. 'What subject?'

'Whatever you fink Handel's Hallelujah comes under.'

James returned with a large reference book and handed it to Bert. 'This is probably more relevant. It's a music encyclopaedia.'

Bert thumbed through it.

'What are you searching for?'

'Information on that bit of music.' He heaved the book to a more comfortable position.

Beth reminded them that the piece was entitled Handel's *Messiah* and that the 'Hallelujah Chorus' was just a part of it.

Bert poked the open pages. ''ere you are, Handel.' He scanned through the text.

While he was doing that, James refreshed everyone's drinks. 'I'm not entirely sure what you're hoping to find, Bert.'

Gladys joked that he was tapping into his wealth of knowledge, for which she received a *tut* from Bert. He manoeuvred the heavy book across to James who asked what he was supposed to be looking at.

'That bit there about 'andel's *Messiah*.'

James studied the text. 'The Easter section . . . ' He stabbed the page. 'I thought this was a Christmas piece.' He returned to the book. 'Part two highlights news of the resurrection.' He scanned through reams of text. 'There's something here about Christ rising from the dead. It ends with the glorious 'Hallelujah Chorus celebrating the resurrection.' His finger followed the text down. 'Part three returns to the theme of resurrection.'

He closed the book.

'Bert, all this is telling me is that this piece of music is an Easter performance, not a Christmas one.'

'Look at the clues, mate,' he replied with a hint of frustration. 'You're going on about these odd bits of music lying around. 'Daisy' is a song about a man's love for one particular woman. You know the lyrics?'

James recited them:

'Daisy, Daisy, give me your answer do,
I'm half crazy all for the love of you,
It won't be a stylish marriage, I can't
    afford . . . '

He turned to Bert. 'What is this supposed to be telling me?'

'The song ain't called 'Daisy'. It's 'Daisy Bell'.'

Beth put her knife and fork down. 'Belle! Jonathan's mystery woman.'

'It's not spelt the same but it sounds the same don't it?' Bert sat forward. 'That Jonathan bloke went missing over Easter. The *Messiah* is a bit of Easter music about the resurrection. What's the resurrection?'

James closed his eyes, embarrassed that he hadn't made the connection. 'Returning from the dead.' He sat upright. 'Celia was upset because Jonathan never left a message for her; absolutely beside herself that he disappeared with no word. Well, this is his message to her. That music must mean something to her.'

Beth frowned. 'But how would she have made that connection? It seems very tenuous.'

'But, darling, it explains the odd selection of music. I wonder if Celia knows Belle. Jonathan wouldn't leave music scattered about that didn't mean anything, not when everything else in his rooms was so tidy.'

Gladys pushed her plate away. 'It all sounds a bit 'igh-brow to me. If 'e wanted his mum to know he weren't dead, why not leave a note.'

'Because' James said, 'Jonathan doesn't want to be found. He wants people to think he's dead. He left the clues there hoping that his mother would eventually understand. She's a strict church-goer. If nothing else, the *Messiah* would mean something to her.'

Bert returned to finishing off his dinner. 'You know what you've gotta do? You've gotta 'ave a chat with Terry Hyde's workmates at the bus depot. And get down to his landlady. You've got a few leads to go on there and one of 'em might lead to Jonathan.'

'Mmm.'

'And I'll tell you what, Jimmy boy, it's looking more and more like this bloke Jonathan killed Terry Hyde and is on the run somewhere.'

James caught Beth's look of concern. She didn't want Jonathan to be a murderer. They'd discussed this earlier and their feelings were solely for his mother, Celia Dunhelm. What would she be feeling?

The next day was Easter Monday. James had to be present for the egg hunt and, later in the day, the races on the green. He tucked into the last morsels of his dinner. First thing tomorrow morning, he would make appointments to visit Mrs Dunhelm, call in on Terry Hyde's landlady and, on Tuesday, visit the bus depot. A crime of passion might well be the reason behind all this cloak and dagger business. He didn't like to wish his life away but Easter Monday couldn't come round soon enough.

15

At the back of Harrington's, Mr Chrichton clapped his hands and shouted for the children to pay attention. They scrambled together, pushing for places close to the front, jostling to stand by their friends and siblings. James stood to one side with Beth, thankful that the rain had stayed away. Although it was a chilly day, the sun peeked through the scudding clouds. But the forest floor was still damp and muddy and they'd given everyone notice to dress appropriately. Most wore wellingtons and raincoats and a few parents had brought umbrellas.

Mr Chrichton held a twelve foot high wooden pole in his hand; tied to the top was a large Union Jack. 'Now, first things first. Try not to stray off the path. I'll have this flag with me the whole time so if you do get a bit lost, start looking out for this. Me, Lord Harrington and Mr Hawkins will lead the way. Lady Harrington and

Mrs Merryweather will bring up the rear.' He turned to Anne. 'Have you got the first clue?'

Anne gripped the paper with an excited grin. She told the children to gather round as she read the first clue aloud:

'Rabbits bounce around the fields
    but live beside the trees,
You'll have to follow paw-prints to
    the pile of fallen leaves,
They live inside a burrow, all snug
    and warm inside,
Your clue is by their open door, so be
    sure to stay quite quiet.'

For a few seconds the children mumbled amongst themselves until Tommy Hawkins stuck a hand up. 'Mrs Merryweather, could you read it again please?'

Anne did so, then handed the paper to Tommy with instructions to put it safe and not to drop litter. Tommy, to James' surprise, took charge of the group.

'It says to follow paw-prints so look for tracks. There must be some around here.'

Mark Merryweather held his hand up.

'I know what rabbit tracks look like.'

His brother, Luke, sidled up to him. 'Me too.'

'No you don't, you're just saying that because I said it.'

James grinned as, one by one, the village children and those belonging to their hotel guests pitched in to boast that they could follow tracks and knew what to look out for. A guest's son said he had a book with pictures of animal tracks in it and that he was happy to go and get it. Tommy insisted it wasn't necessary. Meanwhile, his sister, Susan, had wandered away from the main crowd and shouted across. It took some time for her peers to take any notice but finally her voice was heard.

She'd picked up a large cardboard paw-print. 'They're pretend prints.' She pointed to the trees. 'Going that way.'

James chuckled as the gang of children raced toward her. Within a minute, they had picked up several prints and were heading toward the edge of the forest. He nudged Mr Chrichton and caught Charlie's eye.

'We'd better get going, we're supposed to be in front.'

They marched off with the Union Jack flapping in the breeze above them. Beth and Anne wandered slowly toward the children.

James, Charlie and Mr Chrichton strolled ahead of the next clue and stood by the river. In the distance, they heard the children's high pitched shouting about the pile of leaves. This was closely followed by a reminder from Beth and Anne to remain quiet because the rabbits might be sleeping. James felt a tinge of poignancy. Their twins, Harry and Oliver, had followed the same traditions and customs as they were following now. Every year, for decades, the Easter egg hunt and races had taken place in Cavendish on the Bank Holiday Monday and now his sons were grown men themselves. It was a shame that neither of them could be here this year. Although they were no longer children, they always took great delight in walking the route with the youngsters and encouraging plenty of enthusiasm.

Both of them were now doing their

National Service. Unlike many, they were actually enjoying their time and he wondered if either of them would sign up full-time. He hoped not, for purely selfish reasons. Oliver seemed intent on becoming a teacher and, as far as he knew, nothing had swayed him to the contrary. Harry, although keen to become involved in the family business, had a hankering for adventure. He was young and, at that age, James had been racing cars and having some adventures of his own. Perhaps it would be good for him to get that out of his system before joining him full-time at Harrington's.

A few yards away, the children whooped in delight. They'd found the next clue. Georgina, Graham Porter's daughter, read it aloud. James and his companions moved on.

It took a good couple of hours for the children to find all the clues and the men waited close to the final marker for the crowd to catch up with them. They stood by a fallen oak tree where Philip and Helen's daughter, Natasha, read the final clue.

'Chickens,' she said with a frown.

James couldn't help but smile. The group fell silent then quizzed one another, repeating the word 'chickens' as if by doing so a wizard would appear and show them the way.

One of the guests' children piped up. 'Chickens lay eggs.'

Charlie tutted at his son and met James' gaze. 'Look at the state of him.'

Tommy had entered the forest looking smart in grey shorts, long socks and a jacket and now resembled a scarecrow, with bits of twig in his hair and mud up his sleeve.

'That's it,' said Tommy. 'They keep chickens at the far field for their eggs. There're loads of hutches there. Come on!'

The group went tearing off across the field yelling encouragement and challenging one another to a race. Beth and Anne caught up with James, Charlie and Mr Chrichton.

Mr Chrichton expressed concern about the chickens as they began to make their way back across the field. 'They'll be laying eggs out of fright with that mob running toward them.'

Beth told him not to worry. 'Didier moved them to the far hutches this morning and Adam built a makeshift coop to store our chocolate eggs. But, yes, you're right, we also thought the chickens would keel over with all of the commotion.'

The commotion began soon after, with screams that the eggs had been found. Some of the smaller children jumped up and down in glee and the guests' children peered in hoping there were enough eggs for everyone. Susan told everyone to queue up so that she could give the eggs out.

James turned to Charlie. 'I say, your two are very organised. I notice Tommy took control of things back at the house and Susan is certainly one to make sure everyone's included.'

'Tommy gets the organisation from me and Susan takes after her mum when it comes to making people feel welcome.'

Anne insisted that that particular trait had also come from Charlie as he was one of the first to make her and Stephen feel so welcome in the village. Charlie thanked her and said he always tried his best. It had been a hard few years for the librarian; he'd lost his wife to an illness when the children were still quite small. But, James thought, he was an amazing father who, no matter what, was always there for Tommy and Susan and, being a librarian, had become a teacher to them as well. Just recently, Charlie and Tommy had joined him to fish on the estate's river. James was an astute fisherman who studied the river and fished according to its flow and the seasons. He'd gained that knowledge from old Mr Bennett and had passed it on to Harry and Oliver. He felt good about doing the same for the next generation.

They continued toward Harrington's where they saw a few of the WI ladies giving out soft drinks. Charlie pulled him to one side and asked him about the investigation. 'I hear George is pretty wrapped up in that business with the canal murders. I saw his photograph in the local paper yesterday. I suppose he hasn't got many resources to help out on an old case.'

'He is somewhat preoccupied,' said James. 'But, I'm popping over to visit Mrs Dunhelm in about half an hour; see if I can jog her memory about the music.'

'Has this Terry Hyde got a wife or a mum or dad?'

'Yes, apparently he has a father living in Crawley. I'm going to look him up and see what he has to say.'

'Interesting what Bert came up with about that music. But you don't know what that poem relates to?'

James pulled a face. 'No. It means nothing to me — it sounds like something he made up.'

Charlie shouted across to Bob Tanner and waved him over. 'Bob, have a listen to this and tell us if it means anything?' He turned to James. 'It's just that it sounds like a song, it's got that sort of flow to it. More like a lyric than a poem.'

'Yes, I suppose you're right.' James turned to Bob. 'It's easy to remember because it repeats itself so much. '*Down in old Mexico, where a child will slap*

242

your face, Down in old Mexico, where a child will slap your face, They make a bread with cayenne pepper, drink gun powder to kill the taste'.' He tilted his head. 'Does that mean anything to you?'

Bob raised an eyebrow and appeared a little incredulous. 'Yeah, yeah it does. I haven't heard that in a long while — it's an old blues song.'

'Really!'

'Yeah, not a popular one but when I first started playing the guitar, I used to like the blues songs. Couldn't get many records over here when I was younger but I managed to get quite a few from a shop four or five years ago and that song was on a couple of 'em. It was written back in the thirties. It's called 'I've Got the Blues for Murder Only'.'

16

James had arranged to meet Celia at midday and this time he was shown into the study opposite the lounge where they'd met before. She appeared strained, admitting that the realisation of what had happened was beginning to dawn on her.

'Lord Harrington, it is likely that my son is mixed up in this business in a way that I don't wish to dwell on. And, if he is, he must take responsibility and admit to his involvement. If he's alive, he needs to be found and I want you to find him.'

He started to speak but she held a hand up. 'Please don't advise me to speak to the police. That Inspector man is very thorough and gracious but you and I know his priority is that awful business by the canal.' Her eyes pleaded with him. 'Please will you find my son?'

There was a knock on the door and Diana entered with a coffee pot and two large cups. 'I'm sorry, ma'am, but we've run out of simnel cake so I put some chocolate biscuits out for you.'

Celia thanked her. While James poured the steaming coffee, she placed two biscuits on a plate for him. 'I've a very good cook, Lord Harrington. I don't think you'll be disappointed with these.'

'I'm sure I won't,' said James, going on to tell her about his grandmother and her baking skills. 'I am a little unusual, for a man, in that I enjoy cooking. There's something rather therapeutic about gathering ingredients and turning them into something tasty. Who'd have thought that plain old flour, butter and sugar could turn into a delicious sponge?'

She smiled and agreed that she, too, liked to try her hand. 'I'm not as proficient as my cook here but I do love to make bread. As you say, it's terribly therapeutic.' She sipped her coffee. 'Now, Lord Harrington, have you changed the subject purposely or are you happy to assist me?'

'I'm more than happy to help; indeed, I've a good contact to make those enquiries with.' He thought, straight away, of

Gerald Crabtree. He'd met Gerald originally when investigating the murder of Delphine Brooks-Hunter and had asked him to help a couple of times since. He worked at Somerset House, the building where records of all births, deaths and marriages were stored. Although Gerald was employed in a different part of the building, he did have access to a number of areas and James thought this would be a good place to start. He made a mental note to telephone him.

He placed his plate on a side table and sipped his coffee. It had a mellow flavour as it had been made with hot milk. 'I'm presuming there's a reason we're in the study and not the lounge.'

His hostess reached across to a large notebook. 'After your last visit, I began to have a bit of a search. If Jonathan was foolhardy enough to start playing detective, he must have had something somewhere. I found nothing to begin with but then came across this.' She handed it to James.

James opened the book at the back, flicked through the pages and found the majority were blank. It was only when he arrived at the first two or three that Jonathan's scribbles emerged. Two pages were titled 'Terry Hyde' and 'Belle'. Underneath Terry's name were details of the bus depot where he worked, his position and further names:

Danny Just, Conductor, Crawley Bus Station.

Shirley Sands, ex-girlfriend and Conductor, Crawley Bus Station.

Mrs Wilkes, landlady, Ifield Road.

Reg Hyde, Father.

On the opposite page, under the name 'Belle' was one word — 'Goddess'.

The fact that there were hardly any notes here was evidence that this had been a new adventure for Jonathan but one to which he didn't seem particularly dedicated. He closed the book and asked if he could hold onto it. 'I'd like to have a chat with the people listed here if I may and I'm sure DCI Lane would be interested. Celia, does the name Belle mean anything to you?'

'Yes, yes, it does and it didn't come to me until recently, when I found this book.

It was when he started getting involved in all this investigation nonsense. He came home one day full of the joys of spring. He always had a smile for me, Lord Harrington, but this one day his smile lifted my heart. It was as if something wonderful had happened and when I asked him, all he said was, 'My Belle, my beautiful Belle'.' She turned to him. 'He was terribly secretive and said he'd tell me more in the next couple of weeks.' Her gaze sank to the floor. 'Of course, that time never came.'

'Has DCI Lane been in touch about the music? I'm not sure whether he would have had time yet.'

'He said he'd try to call in later but I know you had concerns about it.'

'It's just that we believe Jonathan may have left a message for you after all.'

She caught her breath and put her hand on her heart. 'Oh I knew he would. Was I being an ignorant old fool not to have noticed them?' She stared at him. 'When you say 'we believe' who do you mean?'

James mentioned the help he'd had

from a close friend. 'Let me try and explain.' He went on to speak about Handel's *Messiah* and the information Bert had discovered about the theme of the resurrection in it and it being an Easter piece. 'I have to say I didn't put two and two together. Beth thought it a tenuous link but when you put all of the music together, it does provide a message.'

Recognition flashed across her face. 'Of course! He wasn't a lover of classical music, but it didn't dawn on me that he was trying to tell me something. I knew it was a seasonal piece — our church often performs this during the Easter festivities — and Jonathan went missing at Easter — that was his way of telling me he wasn't dead — that if they found remains, it wasn't him. The Resurrection — oh my goodness!' She swallowed hard. 'That's a little blasphemous of Jonathan to liken himself to Jesus like that.'

James couldn't help but grin and assured her he didn't feel that that had been Jonathan's intention.

'But what about the other music? I don't understand how Dais . . . oh, yes, it's 'Daisy Bell', isn't it? *I'm half crazy all for the love of you.* He'd found someone to love, hadn't he?' She pulled a handkerchief from her sleeve, dabbed her eyes and then gave James a look of confusion. 'But that odd poem, what on earth does that mean? He hasn't gone to Mexico, has he?'

'I hope not. I struggled with that until I spoke with the man who runs our folk club. He knew exactly what it was.' He told her the name of the old blues song and waited for a reaction.

She paled. 'Oh dear, it's like he's telling me what happened and why, don't you think?'

'I certainly believe this is more about the love of a woman than any business dealings. But please don't jump to conclusions. Assumptions can be a bad thing, Celia.'

She sat upright and placed her hands on her lap, poised to say something that was hard for her to convey. 'I must acknowledge that my son may be responsible for the death of this Terry Hyde.'

James tried to stop her but she gestured for him to remain quiet.

'It would be naive of me to think otherwise, Lord Harrington. You must be thinking this yourself. He is a free man and if that was my son you'd found — and we thought it was to begin with — I would want to see his killer brought to justice.' She wagged a finger at the notebook. 'You speak with those people listed there. You talk to his father and tell him that you will bring my son to justice.' She took a deep breath. 'There, now, that's said.'

James allowed the silence to lengthen a little as he prepared a second cup of coffee each. In all honesty, he didn't know what to say to this woman after such a bold statement. To accept that your son could be a murderer was something so incomprehensible to him, he simply couldn't fathom it. Finally, he rested his elbows on his knees and assured her of his commitment to find her son.

'I'll do everything I can, Celia, but could I say one thing? If I do find him, I will have to tell the police. And, if I do find him, is there something that you wish me to convey, a message from you?'

'I would want to see him, Lord

251

Harrington. I cannot think of the words at this moment in time — my emotions are all over the place. One minute I want to disown him, another minute I want to hold him in my arms and shield him from the horrors he'll face. You may tell him that you were working for me and that I wanted you to find him. But tell him that I must speak with him, face to face, mother to son.'

James nodded his understanding and asked to change the subject. 'I think we've finalised the details here. Why don't we move to a lighter subject?'

For the next twenty minutes, they spoke about the garden, the English country-side, the weather — the topic that dominated all dialogue in England — and Jonathan's collection of cars. James explained that he was also a car enthusiast and told her about his brief spell as a racing and rally driver.

She invited him to visit one afternoon to view the vehicles. 'Bring your wife too and we could have lunch in the conservatory.'

He accepted the invitation but warned

her that he would probably behave like a child in a sweet shop. She laughed and explained that Jonathan had been the same where cars were concerned. She spoke fondly of her son's passion and James kept half an ear on the conversation while planning what to do next.

He decided that his first job would be to telephone Gerald Crabtree. Then there were the Easter races on the village green to attend. Tomorrow, he'd call in and see the people listed in Jonathan's notebook. Hopefully, at the end of it all, he might have more of an idea about the whereabouts of Jonathan Dunhelm.

He wondered where his enquiries would lead him. Was Jonathan still in the area? Had he moved abroad? What if he had gone to Mexico? More importantly, could one of these people at the bus garage give him an idea of who the mysterious Belle was?

★ ★ ★

Gerald Crabtree expressed his delight on hearing from James. 'Absolutely ruddy marvellous! How's your Easter going? I expect you've all sorts of customs and traditions going on, knowing Cavendish.'

James went through the busy itinerary and how Stephen and Graham had introduced a couple of new things into the festivities. After ten minutes, he passed the receiver to Beth who insisted on having a quick chat. She'd warmed to Gerald the first day they'd met and with the promise that she would sort out a day for them all to meet, she handed the telephone back to James and returned to the kitchen.

'Now, James, I can't believe you're telephoning me just to wish me happy Easter. I suspect you have something you need me to find out, yes?'

James sat at the foot of the stairs and recounted recent events to Gerald, explaining that he now wanted to establish the whereabouts of Jonathan Dunhelm. Beth reappeared, wiping her hands on a towel.

'Thing is, old chap, his mother is insisting that I find him. George is up to his eyes in a current murder investigation and this matter appears to be on the back burner. Whatever you can dig up, excuse the pun, would be a help.'

As Gerald responded, Beth gave him an urgent wave.

'Gerald, could you hold on for a second?' He covered the mouthpiece. 'What is it?'

'Don't forget he swapped identities. See if he can find out about Terry Hyde.'

'Oh yes,' James said squeezing her hand in thanks. 'Gerald, Beth has just reminded me of an important matter.'

'I think I can guess. You want me to trace the name of the man in the ground.'

James agreed that this was exactly what he wanted and, checking Jonathan's notebook, provided him with his name, lodging address and the address of his father, Reg Hyde. 'How soon d'you think you can get back to me?'

'I'm back at work tomorrow and it shouldn't be hard to find this out. Why don't you and Beth pop up in the afternoon for some preliminary socialising before we arrange a formal dinner date? I've an invitation to an event at the

Houses of Parliament that isn't going to last all morning. Are you familiar with that restaurant nearby, on the river?'

'The Moorings?'

'That's the one.'

'Splendid.' It'd been some time since they'd eaten there. He could make all his visits in the morning and keep the afternoon free. With arrangements in hand, he told Beth about meeting Gerald. She expressed her delight but was quick to remind him that the Easter races were due to start in the next hour.

James decided to get changed and opted for a country look: dark brown flannels, an open-neck Tattersall shirt and a tweed jacket. Beth had chosen sailor-style bell-bottoms with a polka-dot blouse and cardigan. She slipped on a pair of plimsolls, telling James that she had entered the women's race and needed all the help she could get.

They arrived to see a large number of villagers surrounding the green and, to James' delight, Donovan and Kate had set up a temporary bar outside the Half Moon, where they were serving the most popular drinks. Graham and Sarah had also supplied a batch of small sausage rolls which were placed on a table alongside.

He was thrilled to see that so many people had turned out. Many had brought deck-chairs and blankets to sit on and a few dogs, including Radley, were pulling on their leads, wanting to be involved. They caught up with Stephen and Anne by the edge of the green. The green itself had been roped off where a temporary running track had been marked out with white paint.

Anne sipped a small sherry and asked how the investigation was going. Beth gave her an update, explaining how James had been asked to find Jonathan.

'That poor woman,' said Anne. 'First she thought it was her son in the ground and now it's likely he's alive but could be a murderer. I'm not sure which is better.'

'N-neither,' said Stephen. 'I think it w-would be good for us to pop round to Mrs Dunhelm and offer some c-comfort.'

'Good idea. Shall I telephone her after the races?'

James added that he thought it would be timely to do it that very day. 'I'm pretty certain the woman could do with company after my visit this morning.'

'D-do you need any more help with your en-enquiries?'

He rubbed his hands together. 'Stephen Merryweather, are you asking me if you can get involved with this investigation?'

Their wives chuckled as Stephen backtracked. 'N-not at all, although I must admit, our little m-mystery adventure in Cornwall was quite enjoyable.'

James watched as the children lined up at various spots on the green. Mr Chrichton and Charlie had arranged for races within two age categories; for 3 to 6, and 7 to 11 year olds.

The green had several running lanes and three races were planned to start the afternoon off. The first, the egg and spoon race, had mums and dads, including Anne, scurrying around placing eggs on spoons and giving strict instructions to concentrate and not drop them. Once they were in place, Mr Chrichton quietened everyone down and held a hand up.

'On your marks. Get set.' The children instinctively got into race position. '*Go!*'

With family and villagers cheering on, the children sprinted with their eggs toward the finish line. It was a close run thing with Luke and Mark leading for the most part until the final few yards; but Georgina, Graham and Sarah's daughter, skipped past them at the last minute. Mr Bateson stood at the finish line wearing a home-made egg-shaped hat that stood over a foot tall. He held up a black and white checked flag and waved her across. Mark and Luke stared at her in disgust. Having a girl beat them was embarrassing and they stomped back to their parents.

Their disappointment was soon forgotten when Charlie yelled for them to come back. He handed out some old hessian sacks. 'Who's taking part in the sack race?'

The youngsters stretched their hands up high, insisting they wanted to take part and they jostled for position to make sure that Charlie and their teacher knew it. Gently handing their eggs over to Charlie, they raced to the start of the track and climbed into their respective sacks.

Beth let out a 'Phew,' and asked 'How many races are they doing?'

'Three to begin with,' said Anne. 'After this, they're doing the three-legged race. That'll wear them out for a bit. Our two certainly need to burn off some energy.'

'Th-then we break for the women's cake race. D-did someone bring the cakes?'

'They're with Kate by the bar there,' said Beth. The recipe the WI used ensured an extremely light, fluffy cake so that, when they were perched on upside down saucers, it would make for an exciting race. They hoped they wouldn't be dropped as the sponges were too nice to discard.

The next race was quickly underway and they looked on with hilarity as the children dashed up and down in the sacks. No sooner had that finished than they were sitting on the ground, each strapping their ankle to their partner's for the final race. James always enjoyed the three-legged race. No matter how proficient you were as a runner, people always came a cropper in this activity and this was no exception. The children giggled, fell over, tripped up and shouted their way down the track. Dads yelled encouragement and Mums shouted for their children to be careful and avoid breaking bones. Tommy and Susan were the winners in their heat and collapsed on the grass giggling. Mr Bateson dashed across to help the children to their feet and steered them away for the next race to begin.

Mr Chrichton shouted for the women participating in the cake run to come forward. Beth asked James to hold her handbag as she and Anne skipped across to join around twenty women. They each accepted their cake perched on its saucer; James noticed a few women press the sponge down to ensure it stayed in place.

'Right, ladies, a fair race please, no pushing or tripping. Once around the green, first one back with their cake still in place wins. If half your cake is missing or you drop it en route and have to pick it up you're disqualified. Ready?'

The women got into position. Stephen

turned to James.

'I-I notice Beth and Anne both have suitable f-footwear on. How is Mrs Silver going to r-run in those?'

James sought out Mrs Silver, a well-to-do yet eager lady who lived at the edge of the village. She wasn't always around for these things as most of her family lived in Berkshire but today she was here to be involved. He winced at the sight of her high-heeled shoes.

'That's an accident waiting to happen, isn't it?' He was pleased to see Philip was in the crowd should first aid be required.

Chrichton held a hand up. 'Ready, ladies? On your marks. Get set. Go!'

A cheer erupted as the women sped off. Mrs Silver immediately pulled up as her heels sank into the ground. Kate Delaney took an early lead, suitably attired in jeans and plimsolls; she sprinted ahead but slid in the far corner, causing her to lose the lead although amazingly she kept her cake on the plate. A few women slid in the far corner where the ground was still damp and bits of cake flew off their saucers. A few *oohs* and *aahs* went around the green as the women chased one another and occasionally slowed up to check their cake and reposition it. Anne got out in front and Mark and Luke yelled for her to keep on. Radley thumped his tail and barked as if he knew exactly what was going on. But Kate quickly regained her lost ground and, with a few yards to go, she leant forward to catch the win.

Donovan punched the air. 'That's my girl!'

James called over to him. 'She's pretty quick, isn't she?'

'That she is. Good athlete at school so she was. Represented Sussex in the county schools days.'

Impressed, James turned to join in the applause.

The women gathered to congratulate Kate and catch their breaths as Mr Chrichton asked for the gentlemen participating in the sack of apples race to step forward. James declined the invitation. He wasn't dressed for it and heaving a sack of Russet apples around the green was not his idea of a good time. Stephen put himself forward, along with Donovan,

Charlie and Graham. Pete Mitchell, who'd provided the apples, also joined them as they took their places. All in all around fifteen men lined up with their shirt-sleeves rolled up, ready for business.

Chrichton put his hand up. 'On your marks.' He glared at a few competitors. 'Stop jostling, no cheating. Get set. Go!'

The children, in particular, were shouting their lungs out to cheer their dads on. James grinned. He knew the men would be more competitive and there was certainly a lot of nudging and attempts to trip people up. Donovan stuck his elbows out on more than one occasion and Graham, the huge butcher, held a hand out as if he were about to do a rugby tackle. One man tripped and his sack of apples scattered across the grass. The men raced on with guffaws of laughter at their fallen competitor. The final twenty yards were a close thing between Donovan and Charlie, the latter getting a spurt of energy to win it by a whisker. Tommy and Susan raced across to hug their dad, who had collapsed on the floor to recover.

Applause rang out around the green for all the competitors. Beth and Anne, who had made their way back from the finish line, were grateful for a refreshing drink.

'That,' said Anne, 'has reminded me how unfit I am.'

'And me,' said Beth. 'My legs will be aching tomorrow, I'm sure.'

Mr Chrichton announced that the egg-rolling race for the children would take place next. Getting his breath back, Donovan handed out a selection of old wooden eggs, around six inches in length. Mr Chrichton gathered the children together and quickly went through the rules of the race and emphasised that they each must stay in their lane. They stood in a line and on Mr Chrichton's whistle rolled their eggs as hard as they could and chased them along the lanes to roll them again. The villagers roared with laughter as the eggs failed to roll in a straight line and the children veered off their lanes repeatedly and tried different ways to keep the egg from turning. Tommy had cottoned on quite quickly that the shorter the distance he rolled the egg, the more it stayed on track and he gradually edged ahead of the others and grinned proudly when he crossed the finish line in first place.

'I say, Charlie,' said James, 'your lad's something of a competitor, isn't he?

Charlie nodded. 'Loves his sport. He wants to have a go at the cricket and has asked for all the equipment but I can't afford it. He'll have to wait until he's older.'

'Why don't you bring him down to the club? He's old enough for the junior team. We'll get him kitted out and he can play there.'

Dorothy Forbes asked James and Beth to hand out the prizes. They began with the children and eagerly presented the cowboy and cowgirl outfits to the winners, along with various books, games and annuals to the runner-ups. They'd also purchased a few picture books for those who were too young to compete. With the children engrossed in their gifts, Beth presented a hand-made tea-for-two voucher for Elsie's café to Kate Delaney. James presented a small wooden barrel of

Easter beer to Charlie who announced that he'd be sharing this as he couldn't drink it all himself. A few men made their way toward him and held their glasses up, determined to keep him to that promise.

Mr Chrichton called for any children who wanted to play more games and the majority ran forward. The afternoon, as James expected, was a resounding success. The weather had behaved and another Easter weekend had been rounded off perfectly.

★   ★   ★

'A splendid day,' said James, as he slid into bed that night.

'A busy one,' replied Beth. 'Easter Monday takes such a lot of organising but everyone seemed to enjoy it. It looked as if the whole village had turned out; and the rain held off.'

He set the alarm. 'I'm going to be out of the house at nine o'clock sharp tomorrow and I'll be back at around one o'clock to pick you up. Unless you wanted to come with me of course.'

Beth picked up her *Woman and Home* magazine. 'I'd like to but I promised Anne I'd help Graham and Sarah with organising the fundraiser. We need funds in the events kitty. May Day is just around the corner and we have the fair to pay for.' She turned to him. 'Who's first on your list tomorrow?'

'First call I think will be to Reg Hyde, Terry's father. He's this side of Crawley. Then I'll call on his landlady and, last thing, I'll pop into the bus depot and see if I can catch this Danny and the ex-girlfriend, Shirley.'

'Sweetie, I do hope you get somewhere and that we'll find out who Belle is. I think she holds the key to this whole thing.'

He picked up his book, *Cocktail Time* by Wodehouse. 'Yes, I think you're right darling. I hope this time tomorrow, we'll be a lot further forward in our hunt for the elusive Jonathan.'

17

Reg Hyde was a stocky man with jowly cheeks and thinning, steel-grey hair combed straight back. He answered the door in his bus driver uniform and, James thought, very smart he looked too. This man was bulky, like a boxer, but not overweight and, even though he looked close to retirement, James felt he could probably hold his own in a brawl.

He held the door of his council flat open. It was a one-bedroom flat in a building at the end of a row of terraced houses. Fortunately, James had managed to get word to him about wanting to visit, via an acquaintance in the town. He was ushered into the lounge. The window was open and he detected a strong smell of Old Virginia tobacco. There was a black and white photograph of Reg and his wife on the mantelpiece.

'The man this morning said you wanted to talk about Terry.' His voice choked a little when he spoke his son's name. He sat down in a worn armchair and brought out a handkerchief. 'Sorry, your Lordship, but the news fair took me by surprise.'

There was a footstool nearby which James dragged across to sit on. 'You've no need to apologise Mr Hyde but I feel I need to expand on the reason for my visit.' He proceeded to go through everything that had happened, along with Mrs Dunhelm's insistence that her son be found to resolve what had happened. 'She's keen that justice should be done, even if her son is guilty.'

Reg sniffed. 'I'm not sure that I can tell you much.'

'I think you'd be surprised, Mr Hyde. Sometimes the most innocuous things prove relevant.'

''ere, d'you want a drink or something?'

'Not for me thanks, I've just had breakfast. Am I stopping you from going to work?'

'I'm due in at ten thirty but I tend to get there early to check my bus over.'

James assured him he wouldn't keep him long. 'What was Terry like?'

'Like any young man. When he was a lot younger, around fourteen or fifteen, he was a bit of a tearaway. Got into a few scrapes. His mother had died and he went off the rails, got in with the wrong crowd.'

'In what way?'

'Oh, minor stuff, shoplifting mainly. But he nearly got involved in a bank robbery.'

'Nearly?'

'He told me about it after we'd moved here and he'd grown up a bit by then. He got dragged in by a group of men, a gang they were but when Terry saw what they got up to, he backed off. Saw sense. He knew he would've crossed a line if he got caught doing that. Me and his mum brought him up to respect the law and he knows he let us down with some of that shoplifting stuff. I knew he'd carry on down that path if he kept those friends, so I had to make a decision. We moved down here and I got him a job on the buses. He'd been a conductor for a while and then qualified as a driver, same as me.

Loved it he did. The policeman that came here, Mr Lane, said he was found on the grounds of your estate, is that right?'

'I'm afraid so. It's taken a while to realise that it was Terry's remains. I know that DCI Lane is doing a thorough investigation and he's one of the best but what I want to know is, did he ever speak about a Jonathan Dunhelm?'

Reg licked his lips while he tried to recall the name. 'Nah, not that I remember. I never understood why he would've run off. It didn't make sense. If he'd died, I thought he'd have been found on a roadside or something. He loved his motorbike but, like a lot of bikers, he'd go too fast. He had a close circle of friends. He played the field where the girls were concerned but then started going steady with a lovely girl, Shirley — she works on the buses with Danny. He was Terry's conductor. They became good mates. Shirley was a nice girl; he got a bit more responsible when he went out with her but they split up about two or three months before he went missing.'

'D'you know why?'

'He didn't tell me but the gossip around the garage was that he'd taken up with some posh woman.'

'Did you get a name?'

'He only mentioned it once. Slipped out so to speak but it was unusual — Belle, Bella, something like that.' He stared at James. 'I asked Terry about it and I remember him going all soft and asking me to leave it. We had a good relationship, me and him, but he got all shy about this woman. *I'll tell you about it soon, Dad*, that's what he said. He seemed quite smitten, started smartening himself up when he went out.'

'You say this woman was posh. Do you think he was trying to pass himself off as coming from a different background — no disrespect to you, of course.'

'None taken, mate. Yeah, that could be it. He went down to John Colliers in Brighton and bought a suit that cost more than he could really afford. Looked right dapper in it he did. He wasn't a bad looking bloke either. D'you want to see a picture of him?'

James said he'd love to. It would be

good to put a face to the name. It made the whole thing more real and personal. Reg handed him a framed photo. The man staring back at him stood in a confident pose as he leant up against a wall, an assured smile on his face. He had short dark hair and wore a polo shirt and dark trousers. The short sleeves exposed muscles on his arms as if he boxed. James could envisage him developing the same build as his father as the years went on. He handed the frame back.

'I know he ain't no Clark Gable but he was a good lad, trying to make his life better. He had dreams too. Loved the buses but didn't just want to drive 'em, wanted to be an Inspector at the depot one day.'

'Very commendable,' James said, beginning to get a sense of the boy. 'And you say you're not originally from Crawley?'

'Nah, mate, we moved down from Morden, just south of London, when the New Town started. My wife had died, and we fancied a new start so we came down here and I got a job with the bus company. I think the move saved him from going down the wrong path.'

'When did he move out?'

'Decided before we moved down. We'd been offered a house but we didn't need all of that, and the garden, it was too much work. Terry wanted some independence so we asked the council for a flat for me and Terry rented in the town.'

'Did this friend of your son's, Danny, ever meet this woman or have any idea about where she lived?'

'Never met her, no, but I think he said she lived in one of the big estates just outside of Loxfield. Danny'll probably remember more.'

James knew the area well and although there were plenty of large houses out that way, it wouldn't take long to narrow the search down, especially with the name Belle or Bella. Although not unusual, it wasn't a name that cropped up that frequently.

'You should pop by the bus depot and see Danny. He's on this morning — he'll be able to tell you more than me.'

James asked if the ex-girlfriend would be in.

Reg raised his eyebrows. 'Shirley? Yeah, she'll be in but she won't have a good word to say about our Terry. She was well cut up about him breaking up with her. Having said that, I'm sure she'll be upset about the news. Time makes you feel different, don't it?'

'It does indeed, Mr Hyde.' James pushed himself up. 'Well, I'd best not keep you. You've been most helpful.'

'Have I?' He seemed surprised. 'Nothing'll bring my Terry back but at least I can give him a proper burial. I'm not a church person, your Lordship. Don't even know who our local vicar is.'

James assured him that the process was much easier than he might think and that he should simply visit the vicarage. 'Call in and speak with him. He'll liaise with the police and the funeral directors.' He handed Reg a business card. 'Be sure to let me know when the service is. My wife and I would like to attend and pay our respects.'

The kindness overwhelmed Reg and he struggled to keep his emotions in check. 'D'you know the one thing that upsets me? That I'll never see my son married nor have any grand-kiddies running about.' His eyes glistened. 'That's something we all expect isn't it, when you have children? That's the end of our family line now. Have you got kids?'

'Two boys, in National Service at the moment and nowhere near getting married; as far as I know.'

'You've got that to look forward to.'

James' heart went out to him. As he unlatched the front door, he turned. 'Mr Hyde, if you need to speak to anyone, if you're not coping, do contact me. A good friend of ours is a very modern vicar, not pushy where religious convention is concerned if you prefer it that way; he and his wife will be more than happy to spend some time with you.'

Reg nodded his thanks. 'I'm grateful, Lord Harrington. I know you're trying to find this Jonathan bloke but could you keep me informed please? I'd like to know what happened to my Terry.'

With an assurance that he would stay in touch, James bade him goodbye.

Before pulling away, he checked the

street map to pinpoint where the landlady, Mrs Wilkes, lived. It wasn't far. Within three minutes, he had pulled up alongside her house and introduced himself and his reason for visiting.

Mrs Wilkes was the kind of lady James could have easily picked up and hugged without even being introduced. She was a dumpy woman with wavy greying hair. Her eyes had a natural sparkle and her complexion was as soft as a marshmallow. She opened the door wide and welcomed him like an old friend.

'You come inside and I'll make you a nice cup of tea. The kettle's just boiled.'

James closed the door behind him and followed her through to the kitchen. Seen from the outside, the house was tall and narrow but the property went back a long way. The kitchen to the rear had been extended; three tables and chairs stood there. The smell of bacon lingered and, in the garden, shirts and undergarments billowed in the breeze.

'Poor Terry,' she said, 'such a lovely boy.'

She set a teapot on the side of the

dresser and spooned in tea from the caddy. 'He had a mischievous side to him but I didn't mind, I liked that about him, it was all part of who Terry was. But he did bring the girls back sometimes and I won't have that. Didn't have it then and I won't have it now.' A silky black cat poked its head around the door. 'Shoo away, Sooty, go on, you're not allowed in the kitchen.' She placed cups and saucers on the table. 'If I told him once, I told him a dozen times, no bringing back the girls. I could have clobbered him sometimes but I never had the heart to.'

James watched Mrs Wilkes. Tea-making was clearly an automatic process for her and her constant chatter was comforting. Her tone was soft and he could imagine her being everyone's favourite grand-mother. She placed the teapot on the table.

'I had him here for two years; my longest serving lodger he was and I got quite fond of him I did. Always gave me a cheery hello when he got in from the depot.' She sat down opposite him. 'Do you know what he did on my birthday, before he went missing?' She didn't wait for James to respond. 'A red rose. He gave me a big hug and says, 'This is for you Mrs Wilkes, you're like a mum to me'.' She pulled out a handkerchief from her apron and blew her nose. 'Such a shame, him turning up at your place. I couldn't believe my eyes when I read it in the paper. Poor Mr Hyde, he must be . . . oh, I don't know, it must have turned his life upside down.' She poured the tea. 'It's his only child, you know, and they lost Mrs Hyde years ago.'

James let her ramble on. It was clear that Terry was dear to her and he supposed that after two years of living under the same roof it was understandable for her to be upset. When he was sure that she'd exhausted her depiction of her fondness for the boy, he decided to move in with some questions.

'I know, from Mr Hyde, that Terry had an eye for the ladies but I understand that he had a regular girlfriend for a while; Shirley, was that her name?'

'Oooh yes, Shirley, pretty thing she was, worked on the buses. Still there she is. I see her now and again when I have to go further afield. You know, Terry used to let me get on his bus for free. Winked at me when I sat down and whispered it was on the house, and gave me a ticket just in case the inspector came on.' She smiled poignantly. 'He had a soft spot for me he did.'

James knew he was in danger of letting this turn into a general chat and tried his best to keep her on track. 'What happened between Terry and Shirley?'

'Well now, Terry was getting a bit fed up with Shirley. She liked routine, you see, liked to do the same thing every week; pictures on a Friday, coffee bar on a Wednesday, that sort of thing. Terry wanted something more and I think he found someone else. Started going out on the days when he wasn't seeing Shirley and dressing up proper gentlemanly. Polished his shoes, pressed his suit and shirt, told me not to wait up. Didn't come in sometimes until gone midnight.' She bristled but James could see that her kindness remained. 'I told him that's fine as long as he don't bring her in here at that time.'

'Did you ever meet her?'

'Ooh no. I didn't think it was terribly serious, just a fling. I got the impression that she was the next class up so to speak. Women like that don't tend to stay with boys like Terry.'

'What did you think when he went missing?'

'I thought he'd been killed.' She sat up with a start. 'Oh not murdered but just knocked down or something. I kept waiting for the police to bang on the door and break the news. I kept in touch with Mr Hyde but he never heard anything.' She shook her head. 'The police don't bother much when young men go missing do they?'

James had to agree. Their enquiries normally comprised a few interviews with friends and relatives and, if there was no success and no actual body found, they'd assume the man had gone off to do his own thing. But, from what Mr Hyde and his landlady had to say, that didn't sound like Terry. This young man had a plan in his life and people with plans tended to stick to them. His relationship with his father was a good one and he certainly seemed to have been settled here in his lodgings.

'Did you recognise any items missing from Terry's room after he'd gone?'

She offered him a slice of bread and dripping which he declined. She prepared a slice for herself. The chair scraped as she dragged it closer to the table.

'Something strange did happen. It was the night he went missing. He'd gone out. I think he was seeing that other woman because he was all dressed up lovely, had his hair all combed nice; anyway, off he goes. Don't worry Mrs Wilkes, he said, I'll be back later, not stopping over tonight. He winks at me and I said, go on with yer, and off he went. Remember like it was yesterday.'

'And he didn't come back?'

'No he didn't. It got to about ten o'clock that evening and, well, I was tired, I'd got other lodgers and they needed their breakfast in the morning. I normally wait until they're in and lock up but he still hadn't arrived. I didn't put the latch across. He had his door key so he could get in but I trusted him and I always worried a bit when he came back later than normal.'

'Did he do that often?'

'Oh no, dear. That night I went up to bed and peered out the window but he weren't there. My other lodgers were in bed and, well, that was it really until I got up the next day and he still wasn't here. His bed hadn't been slept in and it got to mid-morning and the telephone rang. It was the bus depot asking why Terry weren't at work. Well, I told them, I haven't seen hide nor hair of him since the night before and it fair put the wind up me. I telephoned Mr Hyde and told him and he asked around and no one knew anything.' She glanced behind as if making sure she wasn't overheard. 'But that weren't the strangest thing.'

James frowned. 'Oh?'

'Terry's bedroom door was open. I always push the doors at night to make sure they're shut properly and I did that with his just before I went to bed that night.'

'They have a key to their own room?'

'That's right, dear, yes. A key to the front door and a key to their own room. Anyway, the door was ajar and I went in when I got up in the morning and saw a drawer was open. The one that held his bank book and documents.'

'Was the bank book still there?'

'No, dear. Well I was that upset; him going off without telling me, and leaving all his clothes behind. Of course, I feel awful now having those thoughts when he was up at your estate, lying in a grave.' The handkerchief came out again.

James patted her hand. It must have been Jonathan who'd come in and taken the bank book. There were no keys on the body. He'd waited until everything was quiet here, come through the front door and entered Terry's room. It made sense to take the bank book; it gave the impression that Terry was still alive and, if Jonathan had put his own life behind him, he would need money.

''ere,' said Mrs Wilkes, 'I've still got a box of his things in a cupboard. I asked Mr Hyde at the time if he wanted them and he's never wanted them back; says it'll bring back too many memories and questions. I gave the clothes to a charity shop.'

She led him through to an outhouse where several bicycles and a wringer sat. She tapped a cereal packet. 'There, that's it.'

James edged it off of the shelf and peered in. It was a sorry sight. A few ornaments, a map of Sussex, photographs of his mum and dad, a swimming certificate and a table-tennis bat. He'd hoped to see a scrap of paper, a birthday card, something to indicate who this Belle woman was. He replaced the box on the shelf and asked if Terry had ever mentioned the name Belle or Bella.

'Ooh, no. Was that her name? This woman he was smitten with?'

They walked into the hall. 'Did Terry have any visitors at all prior to him going missing?'

'Only Shirley and Danny. His dad popped in now and again. Oh there was one man that came by once. Probably about a month before he went missing. Tall man he was, ever so handsome too. I

I'd have been forty years younger I could have fair taken to him.'

They exchanged a smile. 'What did this chap want?'

'Wanted to know about Terry; what he got up to and if he'd been in trouble. Odd questions they were and I said to him, 'ere, you've no right asking those questions, he's a good boy is Terry.'

'Did he identify himself?'

'He told me his name but I don't remember it now, just that he was a striking young man. He held out a card to say who he was but I didn't read it. He asked the sort of questions you'd expect the police to ask.'

James thanked her for her time. In some ways, he felt as if he were treading water but this visit had thrown up something far more interesting than he'd expected. Jonathan Dunhelm was the visitor pretending to be a detective of some sort. It was likely too that Dunhelm had entered the lodging house the evening Terry went missing. His thoughts led him to the notion of Jonathan killing Terry. If that was the case, he'd taken his keys and swapped identities by taking his bank book and, perhaps, his birth certificate. He started to get in his car but a sudden thought made him do an about-turn and return to the house. He knocked on the door.

Mrs Wilkes peered out. 'Oh dear, forgotten something?'

'Just a thought that occurred to me. I wondered if Terry Hyde had a passport?'

'No he didn't.'

'You seem very sure.'

Mrs Wilkes said she was very sure. 'We talked a lot over the breakfast table and I remember me telling him he should see the world. One of my lodgers had visited Italy and Terry said he'd love to travel and visit other countries. I said to him, why don't you then. He said to me, 'Mrs Wilkes, I need to get a passport and how am I going to afford to travel on a bus driver's wage?''

James thanked her for her hospitality and returned to his car. If Jonathan had stolen Terry's birth certificate, could he have obtained a passport?

On route to the bus depot, he stopped

off at a telephone box. A few minutes later, he piled coins into the slot and was put through to Gerald.

'You're in a rush, aren't you? I've only just started making checks.'

James apologised. 'I wondered if you could add something to my request.' He voiced his suspicion that a passport application might have been put through in the name of Terry Hyde. 'I've a feeling this Dunhelm chap may have skipped the country.'

Gerald assured him he'd add that to his list. 'I'll see you at The Moorings later.'

Satisfied he'd covered everything, James chose to walk to the bus depot. He had parked just off of the high street and the building was within sight. A number of green double-decker and single-decker buses were pulling out to start their routes and the cavernous garage itself smelt of diesel and oil, an aroma that James couldn't help but associate with his racing days.

A few enquiries at the entrance led him to a chirpy chap in his late thirties, smoking a cigarette. He wore a conductor's uniform and his peaked cap was

289

placed at a jaunty angle. He had a leather satchel over one shoulder and his trusty ticket machine over the other.

'Are you Danny, Terry Hyde's friend?'

The man dropped his cigarette and stamped on it. 'That's me. Who wants to know?'

'My name's Harrington, Lord James Harrington, Terry's remains were found on my land.'

Danny straightened his tie. 'Blimey. Sorry. How d'you do, Mr er . . . , your Lordship.' He adjusted his cap.

'Sorry, I didn't mean to land my title on you like that. It's just that I thought you'd recognise it from the papers.'

'Blimey, yeah, I couldn't believe it when I read that. We all wondered where he'd scarpered off to. That was the last place I thought he'd be.'

'I'll come straight to the point, Danny. I'm trying to trace this young lady that Terry was infatuated with.'

'Arabella. Posh bird.' He cleared his throat. 'Sorry, posh lady.'

'What can you tell me about her? Did you meet her? Did you see them together or see a photograph of her?'

'Kept that one close to his chest did Terry. He saw himself as a bit of a lady's man and he did all right for dates. Then he got keen on Shirley.' He jutted his chin. 'That's her over there.'

Across the garage, James observed a dark-haired, slim lady chatting to a driver. She waved when she saw them.

'I understood they finished their relationship.'

'That's right. Terry came in one day going on about this posh bird, sorry, lady, he'd met in town. Kept talking about her figure, her eyes, her hair, completely besotted he was. Bored me senseless with it but all he'd tell me was her name was Arabella. Shirley went up the wall when she heard he'd broken it off for this girl.'

'And you never saw her?'

'Once, I did, from a distance. I only saw the back of her and she picked him up in a flash car, an Aston Martin it was.' He sighed. 'It was all a bit odd around here the month he disappeared.'

'In what way?'

'Well Terry was acting as if he was the

cat that got the cream. Started trying to be a bit posh and he wasn't posh at all. I told him to stop trying to be something he wasn't. Then there was some bloke asking questions. I thought he was a copper at first, bit full of himself but he kept asking questions about Terry, personal questions that he had no right to ask. He didn't have any identification but he was too lah-di-dah to be a copper so I told him to come back when Terry was here but he never did.'

James described Jonathan Dunhelm. 'Is that the chap?'

'You don't need to describe him. His picture was in the paper, weren't it? That's the bloke they thought was in the grave. Well, that was the bloke who was asking questions.'

'Terry's father thinks you may know where Arabella lives.'

'Not exactly. I can tell you that she lived just outside of Loxfield. I'm sure he said the house was on the road between Loxfield and Charnley.'

James knew the area well and though it wouldn't take long to track her down

Loxfield was the largest of their three villages but there was a small community by the road Danny had pinpointed — that must be the area he was talking about. Surely, if she wasn't there, someone there would know her. A tap on his shoulder prompted him to turn.

'Hello handsome,' said Shirley. She nudged Danny. 'Who's this then?'

Danny glared at her and introduced James with his full title. 'I've got to go. My bus is due out but let me know if you need to ask anything else.' He turned to Shirley. 'Lord Harrington's got a few questions. It was his estate where they found Terry.'

Shirley flushed and apologised for being so forward. 'We wondered where he'd got to. I couldn't believe it when I heard.'

'You courted for while, is that right?'

She nodded and pursed her lips. 'Until I discovered I wasn't the only woman in his life. I could have killed Terry myself when he was here. He had me round his little finger, telling me I was his one love and that we could get married and have kids. I loved Terry, I really did and he just broke it off one day, telling me I weren't the one.'

'This is because of Arabella.'

'What sort of name's that? Terry Hyde don't belong with girls called Arabella. He was out of his league and he knew it. No smart suit is gonna convince a toffee-nosed family that he belongs with them.'

'When did he finish his relationship with you?'

'About a month before he disappeared.' She jerked her head at the depot. 'Did it in the canteen in there over a cup of tea. Couldn't even do it privately. I was having lunch and peeling an apple. I tell you I could have plunged that knife into him when he told me. We had a right old ding dong and I was waving that knife about and he was telling me to calm down. Calm down! How was I supposed to calm down after that? I'll tell you what I did do. He had mince and potatoes in front of him and I poured the lot over him, uniform and all. He had to go home and get changed.' She pulled herself straight.

'The depot supervisor had to come over and yank us apart.' She clenched her change bag tightly. 'I didn't do anything to him though.'

'You still feel the same way, after all of these years?'

'I was proper in love with him, Lord Harrington. I'm married now, got two kids, but you never forget your first love, do you?' She lit a cigarette. It was a cheap brand and the first curls of smoke caught the back of James' throat. 'And if you want to know if I killed him, I didn't but I had every reason to. I hated every bone in his body when he told me there was someone else.'

'What do you think happened to him when he went missing?'

'Off with that floozy, I reckoned. Are the police gonna be asking me questions?'

'I would imagine so,' James said, asking if she remembered where she was when Terry went missing.

'Over at The Sun having a few drinks. We had a leaving do for one of our girls and the landlord did a lock-in.'

A lock-in was arranged ahead of closing

time. To avoid any conflict with the law, customers paid for their drinks in advance. Once the doors had closed, providing no money changed hands, they could continue drinking. 'We finally staggered home about two o'clock in the morning.'

'Home being?'

She pointed. 'Just up the road there. That little row of terraced houses. I had a room there.'

The bus inspector yelled from the far side of the garage. 'Shirley, come on, the number 27's due out.'

'I'm sorry he's dead, sorry for his dad really but me going against Terry didn't last long. His dad's a lovely man and, to be honest, so was Terry. I hated him when he broke it off but I wouldn't have harmed him.' She mumbled a goodbye and made her way toward her bus.

James strolled back along the high street to his car. Terry Hyde had been a rogue, a minor criminal in his youth who had been doing his best to turn his life around. He'd mapped out a career on the buses and saw himself in the role of an Inspector. Perhaps the young man felt having someone on his arm from a higher social circle might have opened doors for him. It certainly appeared that he'd fallen in love with this woman. But did he have the gravitas to enter a higher social class? By all accounts, no. He certainly didn't appear to be a gentleman. Telling his girlfriend, in a crowded canteen, that there was no future for them was despicable in James' eyes.

And what was Jonathan doing, visiting the depot and asking questions about Terry Hyde? Who on earth had employed him?

It was almost midday — time to pop home for a quick snack with Beth and a drive up to London to meet Gerald. He hoped that his new acquaintance had managed to uncover some information.

18

The sunshine glinted off the Thames. Tug boats, tourist launches and barges chugged up and down the river; some were moored up alongside one another, bobbing up and down in the water. The tide was beginning to flow out and James caught glimpses of the black, oozing mud on the banks. Ships' horns and bells occasionally sounded and on the nearby bridge, a number of tourists were taking photographs of the iconic building next door to where they sat.

The terrace at The Moorings sat adjacent to that of the Houses of Parliament and gave them a wonderful close-up view of the architecture. The restaurant had become an exclusive pleasure for those with a little more money to spend and one that the Harringtons enjoyed far too rarely. James had brought Beth here when he'd first taken her to London before they were married. They'd arrived at a similar time for cocktails, caught the matinée of Noel

Coward's *Private Lives* and then dined at Simpson's-in-the-Strand, a favourite with the Harrington family.

The grandeur of the architecture of the Houses of Parliament left him speechless. The masonry work was exquisitely detailed and so much effort had gone into the sculpting and design he didn't think architects would ever have the time or money to produce that type of structure again. A lot of the original stone had been replaced — work which had only recently been completed. He turned to Beth.

'They started replacing that stonework back in the 1930s, you know. Only got around to finishing it now because of the War.'

'I remember them starting on that, don't you? It's certainly a building worth preserving.' She glanced over his shoulder. 'Oh, here's Gerald.'

Gerald, a tall, distinguished man dressed in a pinstriped suit and carrying a well-worn leather briefcase, strode toward them with his hand outstretched. 'Lord Harrington, Lady Harrington, how lovely to see you.'

James stood and pushed a chair out for him. 'Lovely day for it.'

'Certainly is. Am I late?' Big Ben rang out to signal two o'clock and Gerald commented that he couldn't have timed it better if he'd tried. 'Have you come up for the day or is this a special trip?'

Beth explained that James had got his teeth into something and that this was a visit simply to meet him. Her eyes went heavenward. 'He's been asked to look into the matter privately, so he's been beavering away interviewing people all morning.'

Gerald raised an eyebrow. 'Your reputation perhaps? Are you becoming known as the real-life Lord Peter Wimsey?'

James grinned. 'I don't think my sleuthing skills are as refined as Wimsey's. But it's certainly intriguing. You got the gist of things from our telephone conversation.' He ordered three vodka Martinis.

'Goodness, steady on,' said Gerald, 'I have to go back to work — got a meeting in a little while.'

'I'm sure one won't hurt.'

'I'll be asleep at my desk.' Gerald pressed the lock of his briefcase and lifted the leather flap to pull out a legal pad. 'I jotted everything down so I wouldn't forget.' He made himself comfortable and they chatted until the waiter arrived. With the drinks in place, he gave them a crooked smile. 'I have to say, I can understand why you think this is intriguing. You have your work cut out.'

James caught Beth's eye. She was as fascinated as he was but, for a split second, he forgot about the enquiry as the spring sun emerged. The glare had accentuated the navy blue in the dress she wore. It had the style of Dior; indeed, it may well have been a Dior. He remembered her bringing it back after a shopping trip to Liberty's the previous year.

Beth playfully kicked him under the table. 'Wake up, James.'

'Sorry, you were saying? Intriguing?'

Gerald pulled out a document. 'Right, first things first: your Jonathan Dunhelm chap was registered dead about five years after he went missing.'

'Is that a little quick? I thought you had to wait longer.'

'Not always. Depends on the circumstances. Dunhelm was rich, powerful and, presumably, easy to track down if need be. His bank accounts were never touched although he did make a couple of substantial withdrawals a few weeks before his disappearance. His property remained at the family home, his business deals were still ongoing courtesy of his business partner. The police eventually confirmed that he was missing, presumed dead.'

Beth asked if any life insurance had been paid out.

'There was a policy but it was never claimed.'

'I guess because Mrs Dunhelm wanted to believe he was still alive.'

James sipped his Martini. 'So Jonathan is registered dead. He's managed to bury his identity so to speak. How about Terry Hyde?'

Gerald's eyes lit up. 'Ah, well now, that is interesting. Terry Hyde was showing as alive and well at the time Jonathan was declared dead. His bank account was closed in the spring of 1951 and I couldn't, for the life of me, trace an address for him so I widened the search a bit. After you telephoned, I did a check with the passport office and a passport was issued to him in August 1951.'

James almost leapt from his chair. 'Aha. Now where was that passport sent?'

'Yes, thought you'd ask that and I'm afraid it's a dead end.' Gerald flicked through a few papers. 'He put his address down as a pub. I contacted the said establishment and they'd never heard of him. But then the pub had changed hands a few times and they've always had rooms to let.'

Although he felt a little deflated, James was sure of one thing. 'He's gone abroad hasn't he?'

'Yes, I did a bit more digging and checked with the airports and shipping people to see where he'd gone.'

'Don't tell me it's Mexico.'

Gerald gave him a queer look. 'Mexico? No, why would you think he'd gone there?'

James waved the question aside and

asked him to continue.

'He went to New York on the *Queen Mary* and had an airline ticket issued at the same time to take him to Boston.'

James glanced at Beth. 'Your old stamping ground.'

'You're from Boston?' said Gerald. 'I detected an accent but never knew from where exactly.'

'Born in Boston and lived there until I was sixteen. I came over here for finishing school and never went back.' She gave James a coy smile. 'A certain gentleman caught my eye.'

Gerald's eyes darted between the two of them and he cleared his throat. 'Mm, quite. Well, I'm afraid that's where the trail goes cold. I don't have a contact in Boston. I can certainly try to find out but it may take some time.'

Beth wondered if the girl Belle had also gone with him. 'Do you know if Jonathan, sorry, *Terry* travelled with a woman?'

'The passenger manifest suggests he was alone.' He delved into his briefcase again and brought out a thicker document. 'I have it here. I thought you might ask something like that.'

James enjoyed his Martini as he watched a large boat steam toward the old docks further down the river. Black smoke billowed from its chimney. After a few minutes of reading and flicking papers back and forth, Gerald put the documents down.

'No woman travelling on her own except a couple of elderly spinsters, not according to this anyway.'

'Perhaps she travelled by air, to avoid suspicion.'

'Goodness, that would take some investigation. I mean, you don't even have a surname, do you?'

James shifted in his chair. 'I don't at the moment but I'm pretty sure I'll have one later today or certainly tomorrow.'

Beth frowned. 'How can you be so sure?'

'The community on that road between Loxfield and Charnley is tiny. There can't be more than one Arabella living there.'

Gerald agreed that this would certainly help matters. He finished his Martini and gathered his things. 'I've another meeting and it's at the other end of Parliament. Will you excuse me?'

James and Beth did so with a promise to arrange dinner in the near future. They ordered a second Martini and remained on the terrace for a further couple of hours. It didn't take long for them to decide to recreate their first visit together and dine at Simpsons-in-the-Strand before returning to Cavendish.

★   ★   ★

When they arrived home, Beth picked up several letters from the doormat and leafed through them. 'This looks like a letter from your sister.' A sturdier envelope with airmail stickers caught her eye. 'Oh, heavens, I think we've finally received Meg's letter.'

James followed her through to the lounge where he poured them each a whisky and soda. He read the short letter from his sister and announced that she'd invited them down for the weekend. 'That'll be fun, we haven't seen them in a while.'

He reached down and turned the television on. It was now early evening and one of their favourite comedy shows, *Whack-O!*, was due to start.

'I knew it.' Beth held an invitation card up with glee. 'Meg Craven is getting married.'

He sat down beside her and read the gold lettering announcing that they were cordially invited to Meg Craven's marriage to one Michael Howard III. 'How wonderful.'

Meg had been flown over from Boston to be a flower girl at their wedding. She'd been three years old at the time and Beth always wondered whether she would ever marry and settle down. She'd turned out to be a real socialite and preferred swanning from party to jazz club and back again whenever she could. This Michael Howard III must have tamed her.

Beth rested her elbow on the back of the sofa. 'How lovely of her to think of us. I always said that when she got married, we'd make the trip. We could visit Great Auntie Constance.'

James groaned. 'Oh lord, do we have to? She does nothing but complain.'

She grinned. 'She'll be at the wedding and we need to stay somewhere. She lives in a rambling old house in Kingston, about an hour south of Boston, so it'd be ideal.' She waved the invitation. 'And the wedding is taking place nearer to her house than to Boston.'

James felt his stomach sink. 'Can we not stay in a hotel?'

Beth laughed. 'It'll only be for the wedding. We'll be out most of the time so you'll only have to put up with her at breakfast.'

He examined the card and winced. 'Did you look at the date?'

She said she hadn't and began planning who to visit. He pulled the envelope from the pile and checked the post-date. 'This has been winging its way to us for several weeks.'

Beth caught her breath. 'We haven't missed it, have we?'

'It's a week on Saturday.' He pushed himself off the sofa and flicked through the pages of their diary on the sideboard.

'We'll have to postpone a dinner with Herbie.'

Herbie Harrington was his flamboyant cousin who ran an antique and art emporium in an exclusive part of London.

Beth told him they could easily rearrange that and then sat up with a start. 'Goodness, I have to get an outfit; we need to buy a gift and book the flights! Is there a flight direct to Boston?'

James settled her down and promised to get onto Thomas Cook and ask them to make the arrangements. 'Why don't you telephone Meg now? It'll be the middle of the day over there. You can tell her we'll be there and then get onto Great Auntie Constance.' As she made to go, he grabbed her wrist to stop her.

'What is it?'

'Darling, if we're going all that way, let's stop in Boston for three or four days and see the sights.'

She gave him an enthusiastic nod but, when she got to the doorway swung round. 'You want to try and find Jonathan Dunhelm, don't you?'

His attempt to conceal innocence failed

miserably. 'Don't you?'

Beth admitted that it would be churlish not to do some delving. 'I'll ask Meg if she or her intended have any contacts who can help us.' Her eyes lit up. 'This is exciting isn't it?'

James settled back on the sofa and swigged his whisky. This certainly was exciting. The discovery of the skeleton was surprise enough and now they were heading to Boston on the trail of the man who stole Terry's identity. He got up to replenish his glass. A sudden feeling of gloom descended upon him. 'What a shame we have to stay with that confounded Great Aunt,' he mumbled.

The theme tune to *Whack-O!* began but his mind whirred with ideas and chores. He'd have to contact Thomas Cook and sort those flights out and, the next day, he must try to find Arabella. Their visit to Boston would be more successful if they knew the full name of this elusive beauty who appeared to lure men like mint humbugs attracted elderly ladies.

19

Bert had joined them for breakfast. 'Just passing,' he'd said with a glint in his eye, while holding out fresh eggs from the farm down the road.

James did think his friend had rather a cheek just landing on the doorstep like that but such was his personality it didn't take long for him to be chuckling along with his suggestive laugh. And a cooked breakfast was always the perfect start to the day.

'Beth says you're off to Boston, mate, is that right?'

'Correct. We have a society wedding to attend which should be rather fun.'

'And you're on the trail of the missing Jonathan too.'

James gave Beth a wry look. He loaded his fork with the last of his crispy bacon and mushrooms while Bert asked if he wanted any company.

'I could carry yer bags for yer. They love a Cockney accent over there, don't they? I could get people talking about things — maybe find out a few bits and pieces about this Jonathan geezer.'

James pushed his plate away and told him he was welcome to come if he had a couple of hundred pounds to spare. 'I'm certainly not paying for you.'

His friend puffed his cheeks out. 'Strewth, is that 'ow much it costs? I could go betting for a few years on that. Nah, you're all right, I'll stay here.'

'If you've nothing on, you might want to help me hunt down this Arabella woman. We've provided breakfast so you can help with some donkey work.'

Bert gave a quick nod. 'Yeah, why not. I'll do that providing you drop me off at the train station after. I'm meeting Gladys tonight.'

Beth's beaming expression quickly changed when Bert waved a fork at her. 'Don't you start. I told you already, we're just friends, nothing else.'

She raised her eyebrows and told him not to be so boorish. 'If you like the woman, why not just say so. We all think you're a couple.'

'We?'

She nodded. 'Us, the Merryweathers, Charlie, Donovan and Kate. It's evident you're smitten with her.'

Flushed, Bert ordered them both to change the subject.

James did so, saying that he'd spoken to the lady at Thomas Cook who always made their travel arrangements. BOAC, she had explained, could get them to Boston via New York and that they'd be travelling First Class. He verified the arrangements and the dates they required a hotel in Boston with a promise to call in with payment later that day.

Keen to make use of Bert, he ordered his friend to stop dawdling. Bert grabbed the last remaining piece of toast and followed him out to the Austin Healey.

Within ten minutes, they'd pulled into a lay-by on the road between Loxfield and Charnley.

Bert peered through the windscreen and screwed up his face. 'Is this it?'

'I believe so. Danny described the road and the community and this is really the only place it could be.'

Ahead the road circled to the left where

he knew it simply dipped and continued on to Charnley with no further housing on the way. He knew this area was tiny but he hadn't realised exactly how, having only ever driven through it. The only visible signs of life were a garage, a pub and, further down the road, a church. He hoped Arabella was a member of their congregation.

Bert climbed out of the car. 'I'll go and 'ave a word with the garage lot, shall I?'

'I'll try the pub on the bend. Wait for me there.'

Locking the car, he saw two women gossiping further along a side road but, other than that, not a soul was about. The publican's name was above the door. Mr Percival Bardon. Knowing this establishment wouldn't be open until lunchtime, he was loath to disturb him but needs must. He gritted his teeth and used the cast iron knocker. A man on the other side of the door cursed the disturbance but then he heard a lock being slid back. A key turned and the door swung open.

The man scrutinised James but didn't speak.

'Mr Bardon?'

A nod.

James decided to use his full title. 'Lord Harrington. I'm sorry to disturb you but I wondered if I could have a few minutes of your time?'

Using the title tended to have one of three effects as far as James was concerned. People bent over backwards to accommodate you, couldn't care less about you or made very little effort to be polite. Percival Bardon slotted into the latter. Although he was civil, that civility did not extend far.

'I wondered if you knew a resident here by the name of Arabella? I'm afraid I don't know her last name. I believe she'd be in her mid-thirties by now, quite a well-to-do lady.'

Percival's expression didn't change and it was clear he had no idea what James was talking about.

'What about your wife, would she know?'

'She's not here. This woman, she definitely lives in this village?'

'Well she did about ten years ago, yes.'

The landlord grunted. 'We've only

been here two years. I ain't never heard of an Arabella. Anything else?'

James opted to simply thank him and try the vicarage. Where pub landlords were concerned, how different that man was to Donovan. James made his way to the bend in the road where he saw Bert strolling toward him.

'Any luck?'

'Nah, mate. The bloke that runs the garage is away this week. He'd probably know because he's been here for years but his sidekick there is 'opeless. He lives at Handcross and don't really know anybody here.'

James groaned and told him he hadn't had any success with the pub landlord. He nudged Bert toward the church. 'Come on, let's try our luck with the vicar. At the very least, he should have some parish records to look at.'

It was ten o'clock and the vicar was pruning roses in the garden. When he saw them approach he stopped what he was doing and said a warm 'Hello'. He had thinning grey hair and a gentle aura about him. James made the introductions and went straight to their reason for visiting.

The vicar took his gardening gloves off. 'Arabella. Gracious, that's a name I haven't heard in a while.'

'You know her?'

'Oh yes. Well, used to know her. Doesn't live around here anymore. Upped sticks and disappeared.'

James' stomach did a minor somersault as Bert asked the vicar if he knew where.

'I'm afraid I don't. Is it important?'

'It is rather,' said James. 'We're trying to get to the bottom of something quite complicated.'

'Well you'd better come in then. I'll see if I can help. Wife's inside making a pie. She'll be able to contribute, I'm sure.' He held a hand out. 'My name's Ron Stokes.'

He beckoned them around to the back of the vicarage where the garden extended out some way and demonstrated that Stokes was a man who loved gardening. Roses, colourful shrubs and a variety of containers had been arranged in an orderly way and James couldn't see a weed in sight. On the expanse of lawn were half a dozen orchard trees.

'Strewth,' said Bert, 'this is big for a vicarage, in'it?'

'One of the biggest. Normally we get shunted into a little cottage. The garden was half the size originally but the land from where we're standing to the end there was just rough ground. The council kindly allowed me to use it. On the understanding, of course, that it remained their property. We've been here for quite a time now and I think, and pray, that they've forgotten it's under their jurisdiction.'

A woman of a similar age to Ron limped out. She had a slightly deformed foot and walked with a stick.

'Doll, this is Lord James Harrington and his friend, Bert Briggs.' He turned to James. 'If you don't mind me saying, you seem a bit of an odd friendship — from opposite ends of the spectrum.'

Doll ushered them all in to the kitchen while James explained how he and Bert had met.

Stokes appeared impressed. 'That's what you call a friendship.'

His wife added that those were the best

318

kind. 'If you can see past backgrounds and like people for who they are, not where they come from or what they look like, you're high up on our list of good folk.'

As they sat down, James discovered that Ron knew Stephen Merryweather from the odd church-gathering. 'You've quite a community in Cavendish, haven't you? Difficult to do that here, we're mainly farms and manor houses.'

'I take it that Arabella was from the latter?'

'Oh yes, lived about a mile away in Woodridge House.'

Doll pressed pastry into a pie-dish and popped it in the oven. 'There, that's done.' She joined them at the huge oak kitchen table. 'Now I remember quite a bit about Arabella because she started getting quite rebellious, do you remember, Ron?'

'I do. Her uncle confided in us frequently before he died.'

James thought he'd lost track. 'I'm sorry, her uncle?'

Ron held a hand up. 'I'm the one who

should apologise. I think we're jumping around the story. It's probably best if we start at the beginning.'

'Before you do that,' said Bert. 'What's this Arabella's last name?'

'Oh, same as the house, Woodridge.'

Doll said that if they were going to discuss Arabella, they would need sustenance. To Bert's delight, she produced a Victoria sponge worthy of a shop display and a pot of fresh coffee. With everyone settled, James invited Ron and his wife to tell their story. He looked forward to listening to the vicar, not least because he had a wonderful speaking voice. He could imagine that even if Ron read the back of a cereal packet, his audience would be glued to their seats.

'The Woodridge family lived in the house I spoke of until around ten years ago. The family are not a traditional Sussex family like yours, Lord Harrington. They moved to the area in the mid-nineteenth century and had that house built. I believe they made their money in the north of England, with the textile industry and moved here to be in cleaner air and, for reasons I could never establish, get a better education. I mean, the schools in the North are just as good. Anyway, during the next century, the men of the family became doctors and surgeons. One of the Woodridge women was part of the Suffragette movement — chained herself to the railings along with Mrs Pankhurst and her like.' He mumbled that that sort of behaviour was most unbecoming of the female race.

'Don't go off the topic, Ron,' said Doll. 'He always gets on his high horse about how women should behave.'

James afforded her a quick smile and asked Ron to continue.

'We moved to this parish just before the war. 1936 it was. We got to know Arabella's parents. They were strict church people; here every Sunday come rain or shine.'

'What were they like as people?'

There was a long pause and Ron shifted in his chair. James looked at Doll. 'I appreciate this may be difficult, but what you have to say may be important.'

Doll made a face as if she was sucking

321

a lemon. 'Too posh — hoity, toity, they were.' Ron started to say something but she insisted on continuing. 'Oh, they were nice people in their way, always said hello and helped the church out if we were short of funds but they were not a welcoming couple unless you had money.' She pointed to James and Bert. 'This would never have happened with Mr Woodridge. He'd have never walked in here with someone like Bert. Far too posh to have someone like Bert with him.'

'Unfortunately, Mrs Stokes, there are still many of my ilk who continue to be like that.'

Bert slapped him on the back. 'Lord H is a unique man, Doll.'

James thanked him for the compliment. Fortunately, his own parents were a world apart from the Woodridges. Harrington Snr had always reminded his children that they were extremely fortunate. And with Grandma Harrington spending a lot of her time with their cooks, swapping recipes, the family had become unusual for their time. James had a vivid memory of one man falling out with his father because of it. 'Shouldn't mix with people outside your status,' was the phrase used. He cut into his sponge.

'Is their outlook relevant to what happened to Arabella?'

'Oh yes,' replied Doll. 'You see, the Woodridge family always married well. Always had plenty of money and made sure any would-be husband was suitable.'

Bert nodded his understanding. 'I take it Arabella took up with a bloke that weren't suitable.'

'Mmm,' said Ron. 'It all became very upsetting and chaotic. Arabella confided in our daughter several times. They're the same age. Her parents didn't know she came here but she did.'

Doll emphasised that even in their position, they were not deemed to be suitable people to socialise with.

'Only when needed,' Ron added. 'Arabella had met a man. They were courting and she'd taken a shine to him. I remember her giggling with Mary — that's our daughter — saying that her father would explode if he knew she had eyes on someone working on the buses.'

James nudged Bert. 'That'll be Terry.'

Bert asked if Arabella had mentioned the name. The Stokes said that she had. Ron continued.

'Well, then, something dreadful happened. Mr and Mrs Woodridge were killed in a train crash. They were in Switzerland, on holiday, and we understand the train simply ran away with itself. Crashed into a siding. About thirty people killed. It was in all the papers.'

'Ye-es,' said James, 'I seem to recall it.'

'Mmm, a tragedy. But that's when the Uncle got involved.'

Doll explained that Aubrey Woodridge, Arabella's uncle, was cited in the will as taking ownership of Woodridge House and he became her guardian until she turned twenty one. 'Arabella was only twenty and didn't inherit anything until she was twenty one. So Aubrey moved to Woodridge House.'

'And,' said James, 'I presume he continued with the Woodridges' opinion that Arabella should marry within their own social circle.'

They explained that three months after

the death of her parents, Arabella had begun to date the man called Terry. Ron highlighted one particular visit.

'She brought him to Woodridge House to meet her uncle.' He checked with Doll. 'Well, we had two variations on a theme, didn't we?'

James frowned. 'Two variations on a theme?'

Doll apologised for the phrase. 'What we mean is, we were the people they turned to. Arabella spent time with Mary pouring her heart out about this Terry and how her uncle treated him. And Aubrey, as soon as Terry's first visit was over, was straight round here. I can't imagine that the young man had even reached the bus stop.'

'Blimey,' said Bert. 'I bet that made for an interesting afternoon. What did the uncle 'ave to say for 'imself?'

Doll poured more coffee. 'Spitting with rage, he was. Accused that man of being a money-grabber, a thief, a crook, a tramp; he didn't have a good word to say about him. Questioned his niece's sanity, ordered her to stay in the house and told her he wouldn't let her out without a chaperone.'

Ron linked his fingers together. 'I took Aubrey into my study and asked him exactly what the problem was. He was bandying all these accusations about but I told him to explain why. Was Terry a thief? Was he a tramp?'

What a calming influence that must have been, thought James, and what a sensible thing to do. To take the emotion out of the scene and stick to the facts. 'And what did he say?'

The vicar announced that Aubrey Woodridge did calm down. He had no proof that Terry was a thief, a crook or any of those things. He let out an exasperated sigh. 'He said *But he's a bus conductor for God's sake.* I knew if I told him what I thought, I'd just annoy him so I suggested it was just an act of rebellion. After all, the girl had lost her parents, she'd been shunted from one wealthy suitor to another. I wondered if this was just her way of having some fun.'

His wife added that Ron had told Aubrey not to react like he did. 'To do so would just push Arabella further away. Let the girl have her fun, I said, let her get it out of her system, and it will probably all just fizzle out.'

Sound advice, thought James. Bert asked what Arabella had told Mary.

'You'll have to understand,' said Ron, 'that I overheard this. Had I been in the room, they would have scurried off somewhere else. You know what young women are like if their fathers are about.' He rested his elbows on the table. 'Arabella was smitten with this Terry. It was obvious in the way she spoke. She'd never met anyone like that before. I had the impression the feeling was mutual, although I know of no man who set eyes on Arabella and didn't fall in love.'

'Oh?'

'Beautiful she was. If we were to compare her to someone now, we would be reminded of the actress, Natalie Wood.'

'Cor, she's a smasher,' said Bert. 'D'you think she was just playing 'im though?'

Ron tilted his head. 'Playing him?'

'Rich little girl with a plaything. She's found herself a rough diamond, someone that excites her and treats her different to the way rich blokes do. She teases him and gets him to fall in love with her. The relationship is all a game to her. She knows it's going nowhere but he excites her, doesn't treat her like a rich little princess.'

The vicar knew exactly what he meant but was quick to object. 'I don't think it was that, Mr Briggs. I may be wrong but the tone I heard in Arabella's voice was not one of playing games. There was no sarcasm; this was a woman who had found love for the first time. I believe you may be right that Terry was a rough diamond and that it excited her but she really did swoon over him.'

'When was this?' asked James.

Ron asked Doll, who remarked that it must have been about three months before she disappeared.

'And this infatuation continued?'

'Oooh yes,' gushed Doll. 'Well, then it became fascinating. The uncle got a private investigator in.'

Ron told his wife she was jumping too

far ahead. He explained that the uncle visited them nearly every other day to express his concern and worry about the relationship.

'I believed he was exaggerating but he feared he had no control over his god-daughter and, of course, with every week that went by, she was closer to coming into her inheritance and being able to do what she pleased. She was young enough to be naive and innocent but too old to be disciplined. All he could do was implore her to see sense. Over the next few weeks, she began to speak of marriage.' He placed his hands together as if in prayer. 'I thought he'd have a heart attack, he was that angry. We sat here, at this table or, I should say, *I* sat. He paced that floor so much I thought the lino would wear away.

'She can't marry him, he said, her parents would turn in their grave. He has no money, no prospects, no manners, he's not a gentleman, it'll be a disaster. He didn't wait for my advice, not that I had any. But then an odd thing happened.'

James caught Bert's eye. The pair of

them were so engrossed in the domestic life of the Woodridges, they wondered what on earth could have happened next. Did Arabella and Terry marry secretly?

Ron continued. 'The day after this floor-walking episode, he told me he'd solved the problem. He'd hired a private investigator. I don't know who, he didn't say, but he said he was a friend of a friend of a friend; that sort of thing. He was going to prove to Arabella that this man was no good for her.'

'And how long before she disappeared was this?'

Doll remembered it as being about two months. 'And then, of course, Aubrey Woodridge died.'

Ron nodded and explained he'd had a heart attack. 'He wasn't a well man and I'm sure this contributed to his passing. To feel such impatience and anger wasn't good for the heart.'

'What 'appened to the 'ouse?' said Bert. 'Was she the only Woodridge left?'

Ron said that she was and that she had remained in the village for a short time and then disappeared. 'It was after she became twenty-one and had the estate in her name. No one knows where she went — she left no forwarding address. Any mail was redirected by the postal service. About three months later, the house was sold and I presume the proceeds were sent on to her.'

James breathed in deeply and let out a long sigh. He asked a few more questions: was there anything else they could tell them? Were there honestly no other relatives? Did they know the solicitor involved in the house sale? Ron and Doll were clueless about most issues but did know the solicitor was not a local one.

'I believe she may have used one in London; probably one her father used but I'm afraid I wouldn't know who that would be.'

James asked for details about Arabella; her age, the full address in the village, the approximate time she went missing and when the house was sold. He then asked if they'd be kind enough to allow him to use their telephone.

Ron directed him through to the narrow hall where he perched on a slim wooden chair and began dialling. After a few minutes, he was put through to Gerald Crabtree.

'This is becoming a regular occurrence, Lord Harrington. You have me on another mission?'

'I'm afraid so. I hope you don't mind me pestering you but if you can find this out for me, I'll treat you to lunch at Mirabelle's.'

Mirabelle's had become a popular haunt in London, frequented by Winston Churchill, Orson Welles and even Princess Margaret. He received a delighted 'Well, in that case!' down the telephone. James gave him all of the information he'd received from Ron Stokes.

'If you're able to track her down or find her on a flight or shipping passenger list I'd be extremely grateful. I think DC Lane will be too.'

'Leave it with me.'

Passing on their gratitude to Ron and Doll, he and Bert made their way back to the car.

'Blimey, that were a right productive visit, weren't it?'

'It was indeed. We're certainly getting more of an idea about things now. Where d'you want to be dropped off?'

'A bus stop but not here — it's out the back of beyond. Can you drop me in Haywards Heath? The buses are more frequent there.'

'Indulge me, for a moment.' He drove down the road that led to Arabella's family home and came to a halt by the entrance. Two concrete pillars had the name of Woodridge House chiselled artistically into the masonry. It was an impressive home, the sort many privileged families had built back in the 19th century; square and imposing with a long drive. A brick wall surrounded the entire property.

'Blimey, I'd 'ate to live there. Rattling about like a pea in a bucket.'

James let out a laugh as he turned the car around. They went over their discussion with the Stokes and were more convinced than ever that Terry Hyde had been killed because of his love for Arabella. Bert insisted that Jonathan was to blame.

'Stands to reason,' he said as he expertly rolled a cigarette. 'He's done him in, stolen his identity, got a passport under a false name and buggered off to America with his one true love. If that don't scream of guilt, I don't know what does. Crime of passion, mate, crime of passion.'

James had to agree. Jonathan and Arabella, or Belle as she was known, were likely to be living in New England. The sale of the family home would have brought in a considerable sum of money. He wondered what they were doing. Was Jonathan back in the property business? Did they have children? Did George have some sort of jurisdiction to arrest them in America? He thought not. Jonathan was still a free man, years after committing murder — would he continue to be at liberty for the rest of his life? And what of Belle — would she be an accessory to murder? Did she know that Terry had lost his life? Perhaps she was unaware of it all. Perhaps, though, she had helped dispose of his body.

After dropping Bert off, he decided to take the Austin for spin and arrived home

334

around an hour later.

Beth swung the front door open to greet him. 'I heard the car draw up.' There was an aura of anticipation about her, as if she had a secret to tell.

He pecked her on the cheek. 'Come on, darling, what is it? I can tell you have something exciting going on. What do you know?'

'I know you had a successful trip.'

He closed the door and gave her an incredulous look. 'How on earth do you know that?'

'I know because Gerald's just telephoned. He said it took him less time than he thought. He went for the most obvious records first, not thinking he'd find anything, but he did.'

James raised his eyebrows and waited.

'She's living in Wiltshire.'

'Arabella? In Wiltshire?'

Beth gave an enthusiastic nod. 'According to Gerald, she began living there eight years ago.'

'No sign of Jonathan?'

'That's all he could find out but he managed to get a telephone number.' She handed him a piece of paper. 'Fiona's invited us to stay for a few days. Why don't we descend on her this weekend and pop across to visit Belle?'

He shrugged his jacket off. 'What a splendid idea. I'll telephone Fi now. Regardless of whether we can stay or not, we'll try and arrange a visit to Belle.'

It took no time for his sister to confirm the date, announcing that it was the weekend of a big agricultural show so much of their time would be there as she and her husband, William, had entered some animals into the best of breed competition. He then told her about Arabella and was delighted to hear that Fiona knew of her.

'How on earth do you know her?' asked James.

'I said I knew of her, you idiot, I don't know her. She attends quite a few of these farming and country fairs. We're there with our animals and she's there with a friend doing a craft stall. The most interaction I've had is a nod of recognition or a polite hello, how are you type of conversation.'

'Male or female?'

'What?'

'The friend, male or female?'

'Female. Why all the questions?

James went through his investigations with George and the mysterious identity swap.

'Really, James, you are infuriating. Let George get on with his job and stop interfering.'

Once he'd finished chatting with her, James prepared himself for the next conversation. After a brief pause, he dialled Arabella's number and a few seconds later, the telephone was answered.

'Is that Arabella? Arabella Woodridge?'

'Yes?'

James introduced himself. 'I wondered if my wife and I could call in later this week, perhaps Friday? You were acquainted with a gentleman by the name of Terry Hyde, is that correct?'

A short silence followed before Belle answered. 'Goodness, I haven't heard from Terry in years.'

'There's a reason for that. I'm afraid the young man died nine years ago.'

He heard a short intake of breath. 'Oh my goodness, how dreadful! He was such a dear man, I had quite a crush on him. What happened?'

'It's rather a long story. I need to speak to you on a separate matter, although it is loosely connected to Terry. Is it convenient for us to visit?'

'Of course. Friday you say. It's a busy day; I have the agricultural show to go to, perhaps we could meet there; although . . . hold on just a moment, let me check my diary.'

'We're also going to the show if that's helpful.'

After a lengthy pause, Arabella suggested they come to her house. 'I live opposite the entrance to the showground. Why don't you park your car here and we'll walk across. Shall we say ten o'clock? I know if we meet in the ground, I'll be too distracted as I'm helping friends out on a stall.'

'Splendid. We look forward to seeing you then.'

He replaced the receiver and Beth stared expectantly. 'Well?'

'Friday, ten a.m.'

'Never mind that, how did she react?'

'Difficult to say. She appeared shocked to hear about Terry.'

'Are you going to let George know?'

He pulled a face to indicate that he'd rather not. 'I've nothing to tell him yet. Let's wait until we speak to Belle and, when we get back, we'll invite him to dinner.' He picked up his jacket and took Beth's stylish macintosh off the hook. 'Come on, let's lunch at Harrington's and we'll call in and see if the Merryweathers can join us. Didier has trout on the menu.'

The telephone rang and he answered it to discover Stephen on the other end.

'You must be a mind-reader,' James said. 'We're just popping over to Harrington's to lunch. Do you want to join us?'

After a quick consultation with Anne, Stephen accepted the invitation. 'We'll s-see you in a few minutes. Terry Hyde's funeral is on W-Wednesday at midday. I popped in to see his father earlier and he asked me to l-let you know. It's at St

John's church in Crawley. We thought we'd c-come along with you if that's all right.'

James scribbled it down and ended the call. He felt good about the prospect of attending the service and of being of some support to Reg Hyde. Something about the man made him want to help in whatever way he could. He wondered how he would feel if they had to bury one of their sons. Just the thought of it sent a shiver through him.

He joined Beth in the lounge and felt as if they were, at last, making progress. He couldn't wait for Friday to come round and to finally meet the woman who, to all intent and purposes, was the reason for one man being dead and another leaving the country. She was the key to moving forward. But was she a killer? Was she involved? Women had been known to be cool and calculated when committing a crime. Was Arabella such a woman?

But first, they had to pay their respects to Terry.

20

The service was a short one: the vicar delivered a poignant sermon full of compassion along with a selection of prayers, as well as leading the congregation in two hymns that Reg remembered his son singing in the school choir. The only family members by the graveside were Reg and an elderly aunt who found it hard to hear what was being said. James, Beth and the Merryweathers stood to one side and a dozen colleagues from the bus depot were gathered together, in their uniforms, reflecting on the passing of their friend and colleague. Mrs Wilkes, the landlady, sniffed and had her hankie close from the beginning, the occasional shake of the head emphasising her disbelief about what had happened. Reg remained stoic throughout and stayed close to Danny who seemed to be a great support to him.

During the last prayer, when all heads

were bowed, James scanned the individuals by the graveside. There had been a good turnout and he sent up a silent prayer of his own to give thanks that Terry was remembered so well. He was somewhat startled to see the man standing by the line of trees that surrounded the church. What on earth was he doing here? The man, dressed appropriately in a black suit with his eyes closed, was Pip Logan. As if he knew he was being watched, he suddenly looked straight at James and immediately appeared uncomfortable and James could understand why. What had prompted him to attend? Did he have some connection to Terry Hyde? Was this a killer tying up loose ends? He returned his attention to the vicar and tried to quash his unwelcome thoughts.

'Amen' was murmured. Beside him, Reg made sure he greeted everyone who'd attended. Most of them he knew from the bus depot; some, like Mrs Wilkes, were simply acquaintances. Others were strangers or friends from drinking in the same pub and this was the category where Pip Logan announced himself as being.

'I didn't know him at all well, Mr Hyde,' said Pip confidently, 'but I thought he deserved to be remembered.'

Reg thanked Pip and moved on. James excused himself and made his way through the overlong grass towards Pip. 'A friend from the pub? Is that what you're claiming to be?'

Pip steered him away and groaned. 'I made enquiries about when the funeral was and thought I'd show my respects. I don't know what the hell has happened or how Jonathan was involved or if he even *was* involved. But, whatever happened, Terry Hyde deserved to be remembered. In my mind, I feel that I'm representing the Dunhelms.' He had a look of despair about him. 'I'm not sure that Mrs Dunhelm would have wanted me to come. It was instinct that brought me here, nothing else.' He sought James' assurance that he'd done the right thing.

James gave a brief shrug. 'I've no idea. It's commendable in some ways but in others, completely inappropriate. Perhaps when all of this is tidied up and Jonathan is found, you may want to come clean with Mr Hyde.'

'Good idea. Listen, I'm glad you're here, I didn't open up about everything when you came to visit.'

'Oh?'

The young man shuffled his feet. 'Look, Jonathan's my oldest and dearest friend, I don't want to get him into trouble but, well being here today, seeing Mr Hyde so upset . . . ' He made sure he wasn't overheard. 'I'm sure it was Terry Hyde that Jonathan was investigating. We went out for a drink one night and Jonny had sunk a few and got a bit chatty. He spoke about this Belle woman and how wonderful she was. But then he mentioned a chap that he'd been asked to look into. Told me the man had a criminal past, came from a working class background and deserved to stay there. I can't help but think that it was Terry.

'The thing is, Lord Harrington, he didn't say this but I got the impression that Terry and Belle were an item. Just little things he said that suggested this chap wasn't good enough for such a beautiful woman and if anyone was going to court her, it would be Jonny. He reckoned this Belle woman was in love with both of them.'

'You think Jonathan exaggerated the details of Terry's past to gain her affection?'

'It's the sort of thing he'd do. I may be putting two and two together and making seven but after you left the other day I sat down and thought about it. It's a long time ago now, of course; my recollection may be wrong.' He met James' eyes. 'Have you found out who this Belle girl is?'

James said that he hadn't. As much as he liked Pip and thought him to be an honest and law-abiding citizen, he wasn't entirely sure how much he could trust him. Was Pip feeding him correct information? It sounded genuine but as he was Jonathan's best friend, he might be leading him in a false direction. He said himself that he would still be his friend even if he had murdered someone. And to pitch up at Terry Hyde's funeral . . . well, something about that seemed strange.

Keen to play down the investigation, James told him that the police were working on the case. 'The trail for Jonathan appears to have gone cold at the moment. We're taking a short break in Boston. We have a wedding to attend.'

James studied Pip's reaction but there was nothing to suggest he'd put the young man on his guard.

'Boston in America or up in Lincolnshire?'

'America. My wife's family are Bostonians and the bride was a flower girl at our own wedding.'

'Delightful.' He held out a hand. 'Good to see you again, Lord Harrington. I'd best get over and say goodbye to Mr Hyde. Enjoy Boston. It's a big city; full of history and wonderful scenery.'

'You've been?'

He nodded. 'A few years ago now. I think you'll love it.'

James watched as he strolled away and wondered whether Pip had visited Jonathan there. He hoped Beth's friends had been able to secure some contacts who traced missing people. He'd passed on the details of Jonathan's new name, his travel plans and final destination in New England. Fingers crossed, a snippet of information would reveal his whereabouts.

A few minutes passed before Beth brought him out of his musings. 'Why are you standing all alone here?'

The Merryweathers joined them as he recounted his conversation with Pip and how he hadn't divulged anything to him about the investigations or their additional reason for visiting Boston. Anne remarked that this was very disciplined of him. 'I'm afraid I'm a soft touch where this Jonathan man is concerned. He looks so adorable and his friend does too. I'd find it difficult not to let things slip if I was standing next to such a handsome man.'

Stephen muttered his annoyance. 'S-sometimes, Anne, you really sh-should have a little more decorum.'

Beth linked arms with Stephen and told him not to worry. 'Most women will swoon over someone like Pip Logan. He is an attractive man. Give Anne her moment of fantasy.' She grinned. 'You must have had a crush on someone.'

All eyes were upon Stephen.

James suggested he should simply admit it. 'I had a thing for Rhonda Fleming way back when.'

Anne proudly announced that Frank Sinatra was someone she'd have cocktails with while Beth opted to put Cary Grant for her pin-up. Stephen, looking a little pressurised, let them know that Ava Gardner was quite beautiful and swiftly changed the subject.

'When a-are you off to B-Boston?'

James went through their travel plans. At Harrington's the previous evening they'd had a good chat about their findings to date and their friends were more than a little intrigued about the whereabouts of Jonathan.

'Th-this is a little out of the ordinary isn't it? I mean, normally you don't know who's committed a crime; but this one w-well, it seems likely we know. We simply don't know where he is.'

'Yes, more of a where-is-he than a whodunnit.' He nudged them toward Reg Hyde. 'Come along, let's say goodbye to

Reg and be on our way.'

Anne slipped in alongside him. 'I do hope you find him, James. It's a terribly callous thing, isn't it? To put a young man into a shallow grave and simply leave him.'

James pondered on the thought. It certainly was. Anne's compassion gave him a surprising spurt of purpose. The next few days would, he hoped, prove to be fruitful with a meeting with Belle and the chance to track down Jonathan Dunhelm.

21

Arabella Woodridge greeted James and Beth with a warm smile. She had emerald green eyes and thick chestnut hair. It was cut into a chic, feminine style. She wore blue jeans and a pale blue and white gingham shirt with the top three buttons undone. James could see why the Reverend Ron Stokes had likened her to the actress, Natalie Wood. If ever someone could have stood in as a double on a film-set, she could have.

She invited them in and led them toward a room to the right of the square hallway. They found themselves in a large living room with a view out to the front of the building and the road ahead. It was an impressive, detached thatched cottage with small lattice windows, one of several on the outskirts of the small market town of Malmesbury. James remembered from his school history lessons that Malmesbury Abbey had been the final resting place of Ethelston, the first king of England. The cottage was located opposite the huge expanse of land that was being used for the agriculture and livestock show. Beth remarked that she could imagine a photograph of it on the front of a biscuit tin.

Belle agreed. 'That's what sold it to me. My family lived in a huge prison just outside of Loxfield. I hated it there. Too many rooms with servants and what have you. I kept telling my parents to get into the twentieth century.' She swept her arm around. 'I hope you don't mind walking and talking. I really need to get going. I'm afraid, I've left myself a little short of time. I just need to get my jacket.'

James asked to be forgiven but wondered if he could use her bathroom.

'Of course. Follow me, it's opposite my room.'

On the landing, he nipped into the toilet. When Belle had told them they'd be going to the agriculture show straight from her house, they'd decided to seize an opportunity to study whatever rooms they could for signs of Jonathan Dunhelm. The bedroom, for James, was the most obvious place to look but, with Belle getting her jacket that would be impossible. He opened the medicine cabinet which gave up nothing. One toothbrush, one comb, one set of towels. He lifted the top off of the wicker wash basket but there were no male garments inside.

He tapped his watch and counted the seconds as they ticked by. Belle was still in her room. How long did it take to pick up a jacket? Frustrated, he flushed the toilet and went downstairs to join Beth who gave him a helpless shrug and whispered that she'd found nothing in the lounge. A door slammed upstairs and Belle trotted down to join them.

'All set?' She swung the door open and ushered them out.

As they crossed the road to the show ground, James stuck to a wide variety of what he felt were safe topics: weather, holidays, entertainment and the current news. Fiona had already given them tickets to enter but he wasn't surprised to see her standing at the entrance. He went to introduce Arabella and couldn't hide his surprise on learning the two had met the day previously in the village.

'It was nice to get to know each other a little better,' said Fiona.

He suppressed a grin. Fiona was as interested as him about this little mystery.

Fiona handed them a map of the showground. 'We'll be at the arena in around an hour, showing our cattle. Do try to make it. Christian would love to see his aunt and uncle cheering him on.'

Beth assured them they would be there.

Crowds were already flocking in and although it was a nice day, the grass had yet to dry properly. James was pleased they'd worn country tweeds and walking shoes. With so many people milling about, it wouldn't be long before some areas became soggy underfoot.

As they passed through the entrance, James spotted the large arena in the distance, surrounded by a number of marquee tents where, Belle explained, the animals were groomed before being judged. He detected the meaty smell of sausages and realised they were close to a large tent where farmers sold their produce. Many had plates of samples on offer to passers-by. He made a mental note to return here before they went back to Fiona's. He always loved to buy local produce and some of this looked delicious.

Belle suggested they head to a far corner behind a pen displaying rabbits and guinea pigs. She had an exhibitor's pass and there was a small refreshment area there for traders. She emphasised that she had to make sure they didn't run over time. 'I have my own things to do but that gives us an hour. This is a little out of the way, I know, but it's a bit quieter.' They sat on folding chairs and ordered coffee and fairy cakes.

'Belle, do you mind if we get on to the business in hand?'

She smiled. 'Of course. You carry on. I have to admit that I've often wondered where Terry was. It was such a shock to learn that he'd died. But he wasn't old, that's the odd thing. He was the same age as me. When you said he was dead, I assumed a motorbike accident. That wouldn't have surprised me, I always told him he shouldn't tear around the bends like he did.'

'I'm afraid it wasn't an accident, Belle.

This was definitely murder.'

'I simply can't believe it. Not Terry.'

Beth explained that his remains were found on their estate and how they, and the police, had been pursuing an investigation based on the identification found on the body.

Belle screwed her face up in confusion. 'I'm not sure I follow.'

'Whoever killed Terry covered it up,' said James. 'We and the police were led to believe the body in the ground was that of Jonathan Dunhelm.'

'Oh,' she answered nonchalantly, 'who's he?'

'You've not heard of him?'

She shrugged. 'I haven't although for some reason the name is familiar.'

'The police later discovered that it wasn't Jonathan in the grave. Whoever killed Terry had planted Dunhelm's items on the body. Jonathan's mother is beside herself and has asked me to try to track Jonathan down.'

Belle proffered the iced fairy cakes. They each took one. 'And you thought he was here?'

'You seem to be at the centre of things, Miss Woodridge. Is it still Miss Woodridge, or have you married?'

'It says Woodridge in the telephone book so a spinster I am. Oh, how I hate that word. I always think of elderly ladies in knitted shawls and bonnets.'

Beth stirred her coffee. 'I'm surprised. You're a beautiful woman, Belle, you must have many admirers.'

A sheepish grin crossed Belle's face. 'I do have someone. We're hoping to get married next year. We're actually shopping for an engagement ring next week.' She delved into her handbag and brought out a small photograph. 'Lars. He's Swedish. Works for a pharmaceutical company in Bristol.'

The photograph showed a studious-looking man with blond hair and black-framed glasses. Beth commented that they would make a handsome couple.

'I've waited a long time for the right man to come along.'

'I understand from Terry Hyde's work friends,' said James, 'that you were courting for a while.'

She let out a nervous laugh. 'I'm not sure that I'd call it *courting*. I was being a little rebellious; I think that was more like it.'

'Rebellious?'

She settled back in her chair. 'I was twenty and bored senseless. My parents kept loaning me out to every Charles, Rupert and Julian who had money and who was potential husband material. They loved money, Lord Harrington, so much so that they would settle for status over happiness.' She lit a cigarette and gently exhaled smoke above her. 'They were dire, absolutely dire. We'd go to dinner parties and exclusive opening nights at the theatre — all very glamorous and all incredibly mundane.'

James caught Beth's eye. This is what Bert had hinted at, Terry being a rough diamond who'd taken her fancy. He sipped his coffee and immediately regretted it. It was bitter and half-cold. 'So Terry coming along offered you something different?'

She teased her hair and crossed her legs in a seductive way. James could quite understand how men fell for her. Her voice was like treacle, soft and sensuous. 'Terry was a breath of fresh air. He'd parked his motorbike too close to my car and I couldn't get out. I was quite ready to tear him off a strip but he moved it, opened my car door and made an exaggerated bow. He had a leather jacket on and I remember him having an arrogant look about him. I told him he should be more careful about where he put his bike and he said something like, it's a good job I haven't got a tank, they're not so easy to move. Then he invited me to a coffee bar to apologise for upsetting my delicate constitution.' She chuckled at the memory. 'I knew he was making fun of me but I was curious.'

She tapped the ash from her cigarette onto the grass. 'He told me to climb on board. I couldn't believe it! I'd never ridden a motorbike in all my life and he didn't offer to help, just told me to jump on. So I did. Wrap your arms around me he said. I remember laughing my head off. If my parents could see me now, I thought, they'd have a fit. We raced off and he took me about a mile down the road to a grubby coffee bar and we had milky coffee in glass cups.' She closed her eyes as if reliving an exquisite memory. 'Oh we had such fun. He didn't put on airs and graces and he treated me like a shop girl. I liked it. I liked being treated like an ordinary woman instead of the Queen of Sheba.'

Beth asked how long she'd known him.

'A few months. I met him a couple of times a week. We went to the cinema and he took me to places I'd never dreamed of going to before.'

James questioned what sort of places.

'Cheap cafés to have burger and chips. It was divine. And he took me down to Brighton on his bike and we had fish and chips on the beach and shared a bottle of ginger beer, drinking from the same straw. Mother would have been livid.'

'Goodness,' said Beth. 'Did your parents get to meet Terry?'

A resigned look crossed her face. 'That's when it all went sour.' Belle went on to describe her frustrating and strict upbringing by a mother and father who were obsessed with their position in society and more concerned about what the neighbours would say than their daughter's happiness. 'They died in an accident but my Uncle met him. Uncle Aubrey was my guardian and Terry was such a dear the day they met. He knew he had to make a good impression so he went to a tailor and purchased a lovely suit. He was a sweetheart for doing that and he posed awkwardly in it but he did his best.' She scowled. 'Of course, that wasn't good enough for Uncle.' She asked Beth if they had children.

'Twins; they're doing their National Service at the moment.'

'I suppose you have to keep up appearances too. At least you have an excuse, you're a Lord and Lady. My parents were just normal people trying to be something they weren't.'

Beth glanced at James. 'Well, I guess we do have a status, but I'd like to think we'd accept any choice that our boys made.'

'Lucky them. I was told in no uncertain terms to ditch Terry and to stop being a *silly little girl*, in my Uncle's words.' She brushed a crumb from her jeans. 'Did you know how my parents were killed?'

James said that he did. 'The local vicar mentioned your Uncle who I understand also passed away.'

'He was a sweet dear but quite elderly. More forgiving than my parents. When he realised the romance had gone on for more than a couple of weeks, he decided to have him investigated. I thought it was all very amusing. So did Terry. Terry said he'd nothing to hide. He'd told me about some petty crime business when he was younger but that was all in the past. Anyway, Uncle went ahead and employed some acquaintance . . . *oh*!' She turned to James. 'That was him.'

'Who?'

'The man Uncle employed. That was Mr Dunhelm, I'm sure of it.'

'You met him?'

'Once.' Belle detailed the first introduction and how this Jonathan man had assured her he would remain unseen and simply collate information and feed this back to her uncle. 'I didn't see him again. He provided the details to Uncle and . . . ' Her eyes glazed. 'It appears Terry wasn't being as truthful with me as I thought. He'd been more involved in theft than I had thought and I think I came to my senses.'

'You confronted him about it?'

'I broke all ties. I don't mind lowering my standards but it was silly of me to consider carrying on. Terry had it in him to steal. He knew I was wealthy so I'm not sure that I could have trusted him. As much as I rebelled against my background, I had to be realistic and there are men out there that my parents would have approved of. Lars is one of those men. Not stuck up but someone that I can trust and be comfortable with.'

Beth asked how Terry had reacted.

'As you would expect, Lady Harrington. He was angry. Wanted to know what this investigator had told me. Ordered me to go to the police myself and check. In between all of this, my uncle died. Oh I couldn't stand it. Terry kept pestering me, following me everywhere. That's when I decided to start my life over. I hated that house at Loxfield and I had nothing to tie me there, so I sold everything and moved away. Cut ties completely with everyone and never went back. I never told anyone where I was going, I didn't want Terry following me.' She caught her breath. 'But I can't believe someone killed him. Poor Terry. I suppose he came up against the wrong element.'

'I'm afraid he didn't, Belle. Terry had changed his ways. He hadn't been in trouble with the police since he was around fourteen years old.'

He observed her as she gathered her thoughts and her tone became more assertive. 'I couldn't have trusted him. In short, Lord Harrington, I grew up. I realised that I needed to be more responsible. If I'd have married Terry, I couldn't be sure that it would have worked.'

Beth commented that when one chose to marry, one ran the risk of problems later in life. 'People change. Fortunately most grow old together but some grow apart. That's the risk you take when you commit yourself to marriage.'

'If I met Terry today, I might well have

wanted to share my life with him. I'm more mature now. Nine, ten years ago, I was a rebel and out of control. That's no foundation for a relationship.'

'You're absolutely sure you only met Jonathan the once?' asked James. 'He didn't ask you out, want to get to know you better?'

She bridled at the suggestion. 'Absolutely not. If that's the man you're looking for, he certainly isn't here.' She collected her things. 'I'm afraid I must be running along. My friend has a stall in the craft tent and I said I'd help her. I'm sorry to hear about Terry but I'm afraid I can't help you with your quest to find this Mr Dunhelm. What possessed you to think he'd be here, I don't know.'

She dashed off a little too quickly for James' liking. He turned to Beth. 'Damn and blast, we're getting absolutely nowhere.'

Beth reached across and squeezed his hand. 'We're a lot further ahead than we were a few days ago. I may be wrong but what I don't understand is that Jonathan was bowled over by this woman yet she says she hardly remembers him. They must have met more than once, surely.'

'Perhaps Belle is not being entirely truthful. She may have seen Jonathan a few times and then decided he wasn't the man for her. In between times, he's coshed Terry and got himself in a pickle for no positive gain.'

They left their drinks and made their way to the judging arena where Fiona, dressed in a white coat, was showing her prized Highland Cattle. She'd entered three for the judging and, although he was not a farmer, James always had a soft spot for this breed. Their long horns and flowing coats made them unique. Fiona's son, Christian, helped her lead them around. Finally, those showing their cattle paraded them in a straight line where the judging became more exacting. Everything was examined, from the hooves and teeth to their posture and stance. The head judge announced the first, second and third prizes. Fiona clapped enthusiastically on being given a yellow rosette for second prize.

James and Beth joined in with the applause and made their way over.

Christian, who had converted Fiona's smallholding into a much larger enterprise, beamed from ear to ear. 'Uncle James, Auntie Beth, we got a Second, fantastic!'

James stroked the enormous bull standing in front of him. 'Well done. Does that help with your business?'

'I'll say. A prize-winning bull is a money-earner. He's covered most of our stock so we need to let him go and get another in. This'll put a few pounds on the price.'

Fiona agreed, in her booming voice. 'This boy of ours is making a good job of the farm, James. I'm terrifically proud of him.'

'Where's your husband disappeared to?'

'William's taking part in the carriage driving in the next arena. Mad as a March hare, that one. Get himself killed one day.'

Beth laughed. 'That's quite a thrilling ride. Don't you ever want to sit up top with him?'

Fiona stared at her with a look of

horror, stating that this was the last place she'd want to be. 'Do you?'

'I'd love to.'

James admired his wife's adventurous spirit and asked if it was possible for her to sit up top. Within ten minutes, Fiona had marched them across to where the event was taking place and Beth was ensconced next to her brother-in-law.

'Goodness, it *is* high up isn't it,' said Beth, grimacing at James.

He looked up. It certainly was. They had four eager horses ready to take them through the course, stamping the ground impatiently. 'For goodness sake, hold on tight,' He said.

William gave her a few instructions about what to hold onto and, if the worst happened, how to jump off. She let her handbag fall into Fiona's waiting arms as William slapped the reins and the horses trotted off.

Fiona heaved a sigh. 'She's game, your wife, but as mad as William. Come on, let's get a snifter. I could do with one. How did you get on with that woman? Find anything out?'

'I'm not much further forward than I was before I met her. I honestly thought she'd be married to him and the search would be complete.'

'Nothing in the house?'

'Nothing. No male presence as far as I could see. I popped up to the bathroom and rummaged through the medicine cabinet but just perfume and the usual women's toiletries there. No razor or shaving brush. Beth found photographs of her parents but, funnily enough, none of this Lars chap she's engaged to. I thought there'd be more about him in the property.'

'What about her first husband?'

James gawped at her. 'She's never married, Fi, what're you talking about?'

Fi shouted out an order for two brandies and turned toward him. 'I thought she'd been married before.'

'What makes you think that?'

'When I saw her today, she had her hand by her face. Did you not notice her fingers?'

'What about them?'

'The third finger of the left hand, the

marriage finger. There are rings missing, James. You can see the skin was slightly paler. At least I think it was that finger. Perhaps I was wrong.'

James chewed his lip and then grinned at his sister. 'You see! You are just as inquisitive as me. Are you sure about the rings? You only met her briefly.'

Fiona shrugged and told him to believe it or disbelieve it as he chose. 'You're the one trying to solve a puzzle.'

There was no record of a marriage where Belle was concerned. Gerald had established that she had not changed her name, that she'd remained Arabella Woodridge. He excused himself from Fi for ten minutes and dashed over to the craft tent. Perhaps Belle could clear this up.

He found her helping her friend out on a stall selling embroidery and cross-stitch. She appeared surprised to see him and took him to one side where he asked if she had ever been married. She frowned.

He held his left hand up. 'Looks like you have a ring there normally.'

'You're observant. I normally do. Lars

gave me his mother's opal and diamond rings and I wear them on this finger. I take all my jewellery off when I'm washing up; they're probably by the sink.'

He apologised for being so intrusive and strolled back to Fi who held his drink out for him. 'You look like a man down on his luck.'

He returned to his seat. 'I still think she's the key, Fiona. I may get George to telephone her.'

Fiona ordered him to put it all from his mind and enjoy the day. Beth skipped over, elated with having completed the carriage driving without the need to leap to safety. He half-listened to her but couldn't help but think about Belle. Was she telling him the truth about that ring? Who would put rings on their marriage finger if they weren't married? Perhaps it was fashionable to do so. There was no sign of a man living in her cottage or even visiting. He had no real reason to doubt her, but why did those doubts persist?

He hadn't time to revisit her that day. Jonathan wasn't there and she'd think it odd if he kept pestering her. They had to drive back to Cavendish that afternoon and pack their bags. Boston awaited them. A society wedding and, hopefully, a fruitful discussion with the family records people in the city. He hoped their visit or a chance comment would unlock the whereabouts of Jonathan Dunhelm. Beth was right: they were a lot further forward and he felt tantalisingly close to a breakthrough. He chuckled to himself as they stopped by the food tent to buy some sausages. He's probably right on the doorstep.

22

They'd arrived in Boston the day before the wedding, after a comfortable journey on one of the new Comet airliners. The air hostess in First Class had treated all her passengers like royalty and the pair of them had spent an enjoyable few hours playing cribbage and drinking cocktails. It was certainly a wonderful way to travel. James had arranged for transport to take them to the small town of Plymouth in Massachusetts where Beth's Great Aunt Constance lived. He'd never been keen on her because she generally complained about most things but he couldn't fault the welcome. It must have been twenty years since they'd last seen each other and he thought that perhaps she had mellowed with age.

She lived in a substantial red clapboard house; a traditional New England style property with the nearest neighbour being half a mile away. The property was surrounded by tall spruce trees and in the midst of the copse was a triple garage that housed just one car. Like Rose and Lilac Crumb, Constance made do with the car she'd driven since she'd learned to drive, a 1925 Franklin Sedan. He didn't understand how the thing remained on the road but she drove it everywhere including the fifteen miles to the church.

Meg, the tiny flower girl at their wedding, now beamed radiantly at her own wedding and what an occasion it was too. James hadn't realised that her family were of Irish descent and he was delighted to see that she'd incorporated this into the celebrations.

The wedding took place in a quaint wooden chapel where Meg and Michael Howard III exchanged vows in front of the congregation. A number of replica shamrocks and four-leafed clovers were hung at the end of each pew and Meg's dressmaker had sewn emerald green silk into the hem of her dress. The church was full and, as with many Irish families, there appeared to be a huge extended family from distant baby cousins to elderly great-grandparents. Beth recognised a few of Meg's friends and, of course, Meg's parents, but other than that, the Harringtons were welcome strangers.

The reception took place at a hotel in Plymouth overlooking the Atlantic. Many guests made a point of greeting James and Beth to include them in the celebrations. Meg had apparently asked everyone to make a fuss because they'd travelled a long way and they were special people. When the guests heard they were titled, the welcome became more hearty, with many asking if they had ever been to Buckingham Palace.

Over the lobster and crab salad and sips of champagne, James and Beth patiently answered their questions and did their best to turn the attention back to the wedding. James hated talking about himself so much, thinking it selfish and egotistical, but he had difficulty in deflecting the well-meant interrogations. They managed to squeeze half an hour in talking about Meg's ancestors who, he learned, were from Dublin in southern Ireland.

He turned to Beth. 'Isn't Donovan from Dublin?'

Beth, enjoying the succulent lobster tail, nodded. 'I think so although it's quite big, isn't it? Are you thinking he may know the family?'

'We could always ask. What a small world it would be if they knew one another.'

'Say,' a guest interrupted them. 'Are you a real Lord?'

James held back his frustration and gave the man his full attention. 'I am indeed but it's simply a title and nothing else.'

'Would you and your wife please come and have your picture taken with us?'

He and Beth obliged and afterwards he steered her toward Meg. 'Let's move about a bit. It may stop all this fuss.'

Meg spotted them and hugged them both. 'I'm so pleased you could make it. I couldn't believe it when you telephoned. I thought the invitation had gotten mislaid.'

'It was late arriving,' explained Beth, 'that's why I thought it best to telephone. But we're here now. I suppose we're not going to see much of you.'

'We're flying to Hawaii first thing tomorrow but we're staying until the last minute tonight. You know we have a traditional Irish ceilidh, don't you?'

James noticed Beth's American accent becoming more prominent as the evening went on. He'd discovered that with a number of people from the various regions. Whenever Donovan returned from Ireland, his accent was thicker for a couple of days. He wondered if, when he spent time among his peers, his own speech pattern became more clipped. The groom approached him. He wore a tailored grey suit, white shirt and a patterned tie. His dark brown hair had been well cut and his smile beamed broadly.

'Sorry I haven't got around to saying hi. Meg was so excited you were coming over. I think she'd have forgiven everyone else saying no as long as you were going to be here. She was your flower girl, right?'

'Correct.' He left Beth speaking with Meg. 'This is the sort of thing that makes one feel a little old. Meg, I believe, was around three years old when we married and stole the show. Now she's a stunning lady about to embark on married life. Where did you meet?'

'We both attended Bates. Met in our first year and it felt as if we'd known each other for years.' He explained that he was now working for the government. 'I'm not a popular man, Lord Harrington.'

'Call me James, please. You made that statement with a glint in your eye. I take it you are well thought of.'

'I work for the IRS.'

'Ah, that's the tax office, isn't it?'

'That's right. I got accredited as an accountant and I intend to set up my own accountancy business but Dad thought it would be good to be an employee for a couple of years.'

'Sound advice. One of the best things my father taught me was to see things from all sides. Everyone has a story, a background. If you're to be an employer, try your hand at being the employee and see how it is.'

Michael agreed and observed that their respective fathers probably would have got on.

'You are Michael Howard the third, I understand, so I presume your father is the second.'

'Correct. My family are accountants and have no imagination. When we have kids, I intend to steer clear of giving my boy a number.' A waitress passed with a tray of drinks. He lifted two glasses of champagne and handed one to James. 'Say, Meg was telling me you were over here for another reason. You're trying to track someone down.'

'Mmm, someone who's proving to be extremely elusive and under suspicion of murder.'

'Wow, that sounds a little more exciting than adding up a tax return. Did Meg put you in touch with someone?'

'I believe one of your guests is going to help us. I understand they work in one of the records offices.'

'Oh yeah, that'll be Chad Jenkins.' He pointed across the room. 'That's him over there with the brunette.'

James didn't know whether Chad and this woman were a couple but he couldn't have imagined a more unlikely twosome.

The brunette was slightly taller than Chad and wore stilettos and a silk two-piece suit that accentuated every curve. Her red hair was stylishly dishevelled and cascaded over her shoulders.

Chad, by comparison, was a thin, wiry individual with thick black-rimmed glasses and a severe haircut. If someone had told him Chad was a scientist or seeking a cure for cancer, it wouldn't have surprised him. He appeared to be a serious individual and far older than the mid-twenties age-group that Michael referred to. Michael excused himself and explained that he and Meg must circulate.

James caught up with Beth. 'D'you think Meg will remember to introduce us to Chad or should we just go over?'

'Leave it a while. The ceilidh's starting soon so I can go over and ask him for a dance.' Her brow knitted. 'Is that his wife?'

'I'll ask her for a dance at the same time and we can find out.'

Meg and Michael had hired one of the best Irish ceilidh bands in the area. There were seven members in total, each playing a variety of instruments, from guitars and fiddles to the traditional accordion and Bodhran drum. A caller stood at the front. They made a start by blasting out a few jigs and reels to get people in the mood and, after fifteen minutes, invited the bride and groom along with their guests to come onto the dance floor. The first dance would be the simple 'Waves of Tory'. James led Beth onto the floor alongside Chad and his partner.

The caller talked them through the steps and, in a couple of minutes, the dancing began and over the next hour, reel after reel, jig after jig, it continued until there was a break. Many of the guests drank as if their lives depended on it and independent dances were taking place in the bar adjacent to the main floor. The traditional Irish stout, Guinness, flowed from the pumps and a number of the men had moved on to Bushmills whiskey, another Irish favourite. Jackets and ties were discarded, ladies slipped their shoes off and some of the older relatives began rubbing their sore feet, deciding they could dance no more.

James steered Beth toward the bar and ordered two tall glasses of Cinzano and lemonade. They found a quiet space where they flopped down into two armchairs.

'Oh James, I'm not sure I'll be able to get out of this. I never thought sitting in an armchair would be so divine.'

James slipped his shoes off and wiggled his toes. 'I feel as if I've been running for days.' He picked up a discarded invitation and fanned himself. 'We're going to have to ingratiate ourselves with Chad before the end of the evening.'

'Meg caught me a few minutes ago when you were dancing with her mother. She's bringing him over when she gets a chance.'

He fondled her hand. 'Glad you came?'

'Oh yes, it's been wonderful.' She mentioned what had been the highlights for her and how lovely it was to see some old faces and to stay with Great Aunt Constance. 'I know her opinions can grate but she's quite a dear.'

He tipped his head toward the dance floor. 'She's certainly fit for a pensioner.'

Constance, although suffering with arthritis, was determined to enjoy the dancing and had proved popular with the younger generation who all took it in turns to partner her. She wasn't such a bad old stick, James thought and recollected that his aversion to her was triggered many years ago. She'd annoyed him with her views on foreigners and his friendship with Bert. The decades had gone by and he felt more tolerant of her now and had actually enjoyed the previous evening when they'd arrived. Age had, perhaps, made the pair of them more tolerant. She didn't seem quite so offensive and he didn't think he took her comments to heart as much as he used to.

Meg approached with the studious Chad Jenkins. 'Chad, this is James and Beth, Lord and Lady Harrington.'

Chad pushed his glasses up the bridge of his nose and seemed not quite sure whether to bow or shake hands. James spared him his embarrassment and held out a hand.

'Good to meet you Chad. Please don't stand on ceremony, we're quite happy with James and Beth. I understand you're the chap in the know where the family records are concerned.'

'That's right, sir,' he replied. 'Meg let me have all the details that you'd passed on. How long are you in Boston for?'

Beth explained they were in Plymouth for the next two nights and then staying at the Sheraton in Boston for the following night before returning home. Chad reached for his wallet and brought out a business card.

'Well, I managed to find out a few things for you but I've still some digging around to do. If you can get to City Hall around eleven on Monday — that would be great.'

'I say, Chad, we're also wanting to know if there are any name changes associated with this individual. Are you able to check that too?'

'Yes sir. I have a colleague in the Probate department so, providing he stayed in the Boston area, we should be able to come up with something.'

James took out his fountain pen and jotted the arrangements down on the back of the card. 'You have a stunning lady on your arm, Chad, is that your wife?'

Chad grinned. 'No, sir, that's my sister.'

Beth gawped. 'Your sister!'

The young man chuckled. 'I know, we don't look like we're from the same family, right? She's the spitting image of my mother and I take after my dad. I don't think I'll end up with a lady as beautiful as sis.'

Beth told him not to put himself down so much. 'There's a good woman for every good man, Chad, your time will come.'

'Look at me,' James said. 'I'm no Cary Grant but I managed to nab a rather lovely wife.' He squeezed Beth's hand.

'You sure did, sir. It was good to meet you sir, ma'am. See you on Monday.'

The rest of the evening seemed to rush by and before they knew it, Meg and Michael, accompanied by a fiddler, were winding their way under an arch of arms to their awaiting car. Friends had tied a number of ribbons and tin cans to the back bumper and fixed a banner announcing 'Just Married' to the rear window. The guests waved until the car was out of sight and then drifted in to finish their drinks and think about going home. The band members loosened their ties and packed up their instruments.

Great Aunt Constance hobbled over to them and handed James her car keys. 'I really don't think I can put any pressure on that accelerator. Will you be a dear and drive us home?'

James held an arm out for her to lean on and escorted her to the old automobile.

'It don't go any faster than thirty so don't go too fast. I know you like speed, but you can't do that in this old thing.'

Beth gave him a knowing look as she got in the back. James studied the many switches and buttons on the dashboard as he sank into a worn leather seat that had lost its cushioning long ago. Constance stabbed a finger.

'There, that's where the key goes, there. I thought you knew about cars. If you don't know how to drive this thing, you'd better let me do it.'

And there she was, James thought. Her impatience was lying beneath the surface all this time. He gave her his best smile and started the engine. Fortunately, when they arrived home, Constance was ready for bed and after James had mixed up a hot chocolate for her, she retired.

Beth, mindful of the potential fragile relationship between James and Constance, had made specific arrangements for the following day. She split her time between a shopping trip with Constance and spending the afternoon with James. James said he would do some fishing in the morning. With he and Constance being separated most the day, the evening went well and was surprisingly enjoyable.

The next day, he and Beth bade Great Aunt Constance farewell with a promise from Beth that she would write soon and send copies of the photographs they'd taken.

On the road to Boston, James thanked Beth for her patience. 'I don't know what it is about that woman but more than an evening with her and my nerves begin to get frayed. I was fine on the first day but then my tolerance was tested.'

'I know what you mean. She isn't a patient person, that's for sure.' She shifted in her seat. 'On a brighter note, the likelihood of you seeing her again is pretty remote.'

That evening, they checked into their room at the Sheraton and took some time to examine their surroundings. James picked up a coloured card.

'There's an advert here for a rather lovely seafood restaurant.'

The telephone rang; they wondered who it could be. James picked up the receiver. 'Hello?'

'Lord Harrington?'

'Yes?'

'Chad Jenkins here, sir. Just wanted to make sure you'd arrived safely.'

'Jolly decent of you. Everything in place for tomorrow?'

'Yes sir. I have everything I need to show you so I wondered if you'd prefer to meet somewhere other than a boring office.'

'Where did you have in mind?'

Chad suggested a traditional coffee house just around the corner from the historic State House. 'It's called Johnson's coffee house and reading rooms. You can't miss it. It's a glass fronted building on the corner. How about meeting in the afternoon? That gives you time to explore the city in the morning.'

After ending the call, he told Beth of the change in plans. 'This looks as if it will be an exciting day.'

'I certainly hope so.'

He changed into his pyjamas. This Chad Jenkins chap had some paperwork to show him. He hoped it would lead him to Jonathan Dunhelm. He also hoped the missing man hadn't upped sticks and taken a jaunt to the West Coast. If he had, he would have to leave it in George's hands. But what a coup if he were able to confront Dunhelm on his doorstep here in Boston! Beth asked him what he would say if he did confront him.

'I've absolutely no idea. I can't make a citizen's arrest in America, can I? I could be an innocent and simply explain that his mother was asking after him, before passing everything on to the authorities. I'll have to think on my feet if the situation arises.'

23

James and Beth rose early and spent the first few hours of the day walking the length and breadth of Boston and its harbour. They began at Faneuil Hall, the historic merchant selling point where they learned that the locals were petitioning to have the tired building restored. From there, they threaded their way over ancient cobbled streets to several sites relating to the American Revolution and the legendary folk hero, Paul Revere.

The camera never left James' hand as they admired the architecture and statues and spent a reflective five minutes in the Old North Church. From there, they went across to Copps Hill and examined archaic lichen-covered gravestones dating back centuries.

As they wandered toward Boston Common, Beth reminded James they had the fundraiser to look forward to at the end of the week.

'I'd forgotten about that. I understand Graham has taken charge of the event. Makes a nice change to take a back seat, doesn't it?'

The majestic State House was situated opposite the Common and James took some time to photograph it at various angles. They marvelled at its neo-classical style and James likened it to old Roman temples with its colonnades and long steps at the entrance. The centrepiece was its golden dome with a gilded pine-cone at the top. James asked Beth if that was symbolic.

'If my history lessons serve me correctly, that represents the forests that helped the settlers survive.'

He continued snapping and a young couple kindly asked if they would like a photograph taken of the pair of them. They posed in front of the building before Beth insisted James had taken enough photographs of this structure and steered him across the Common.

James decided to use up the last few pictures on his film on the coffee house. It was far too beautiful to ignore. The frontage was incredibly ornate and eye-catching. The borders of the main stained-glass window displayed colourful images of cups, steaming coffee jugs and swirling plants on a trellis. Above the window, gold lettering spelt out 'Johnson's Coffee House, established 1910'.

'What a splendid building. Have you been in here, Beth?'

'Oh yes, all Bostonians come to Johnson's at some time or another. This used to be a meeting place for us on a Saturday morning. It doesn't look as if it's changed one iota.'

James opened the door and was immediately welcomed by the aroma of coffee. Staff behind the counter busied themselves concocting all kinds of coffee variations and, behind a glass cabinet, was a wide variety of cakes, pastries and cookies on offer. It was a convivial gathering place where groups and individuals could enjoy the ambience, read newspapers and books or chat with friends and acquaintances. He spotted Chad in the corner. The young man was right. This was certainly better than meeting in a town clerk's office.

Chad had secured a table in the corner, by the window. Their view encompassed Boston Common and gave glimpses of the magnificent State House through the trees. A waitress attended them, offering an assortment of coffees along with an optional extra of vanilla essence.

Beth studied a jar on the side. 'Is that cinnamon powder?'

'Oh yes, that's a popular extra that we can either stir in or sprinkle on your cake.'

James licked his lips. 'That sounds delicious. We don't have anything like this in England.' He and Beth perused the menu. 'I'll have a coffee with some double cream and a splash of vanilla too.'

Beth smiled. 'I'll have the same. And what are those scrummy cakes over there?'

Chad turned as the waitress offered a number of pastries and doughnuts together with her recommendations. 'Would you like a sprinkle of cinnamon on a Danish pastry? That's a favourite with our regulars.'

James salivated at the thought and after a quick consultation, put an order in for all three of them. He slid the menu card, sugar and spoons to one side and suggested they wait until the drinks arrived before getting involved in the serious business of missing persons. They spoke about the wedding and the pros and cons of living in Boston. Beth, in particular, was surprised by how some things had changed.

'But I'm pleased to see that the football stadium at Harvard is exactly the same as I remember — cold and draughty. My parents used to take me there and it was always freezing.'

Chad agreed as the waitress returned to the table with their mugs of steaming coffee and flaky pastries. With no risk of interruption, James rapped the table.

'Now, Chad, what have you got for us?'

'Well, sir, I think I have everything you're looking for?'

Beth gave a silent clap of the hands as Chad peeled open a brown envelope and brought out a few papers.

'The name that you wanted me to look for was Terry Hyde and you confirmed the date that he landed in New York and that he took transportation to Boston either that day or within the following few days.'

James nodded.

'Fortunately, we only have one Terry Hyde arriving into New York. My colleague there managed to secure a copy of his airline ticket to Boston.'

'Goodness, how efficient.'

'Yes sir. The documentation he completed when he entered the country showed that he rented an apartment in the centre of Boston.' He drew out a copy of Terry's plane ticket and address details.

James took it from him. 'Is he still there?'

'No sir,' Chad responded with authority. 'He stayed there about two months and then sort of disappeared.'

'Oh no,' James put his head in his hands and felt Chad tap his arm.

'But we found him again,' he said with a smile. He brought out another document. 'When you mentioned name changes, I got in touch with my colleague in the Probate area and ran a few dates past him. He was able to track an official change of name. This person provided a birth certificate and other documentation to prove who he was.' He handed James and Beth the document.

They examined it. Terry Hyde had changed his name to Frederick Smith.

Beth slid the document back to Chad. 'What happened to Frederick Smith?'

'Well, ma'am, Mr Smith moved to another area of Boston, not far from here actually and stayed there for around four months. Then he changed his name again.'

'Good Lord!'

Chad slid another document across. 'He became Alastair McKee.'

'And did you trace him?'

'Well, then he changed it again.'

James and Beth stared at each other as Chad began searching for another document while explaining that he had then booked passage back to England.

'By plane?'

'Yes sir, he went back the way he came, via New York. This would have been about a year later.'

'So,' said Beth, 'Mr McKee, or whatever his name is, is now back in England?'

'Yes ma'am. I guess you'll need to talk

to the contact you have at Somerset House about his whereabouts, unless he's changed his name again.'

James fidgeted in his seat, itching to find out this latest name change. Jonathan Dunhelm must have been getting awfully confused. Switching to Terry Hyde, then Frederick Smith, then Alastair McKee and, a few months later, to a fourth alias.

'Chad, if he travelled back I presume he had another passport? Could he apply for another passport over here?'

'I don't think so. It's a British passport so I'm pretty sure he'd have to go through your own passport office. If he did get another, he sure didn't get one through official channels. I got in touch with the authorities and a passport was not issued for him under any of these names. I can tell you that he travelled back using the latest alias which I'll find in just a moment.'

Beth asked James if it was easy to fake a British passport. He shrugged and said he really needed to speak to Bert about something like that. 'The passports are handwritten though; a good forger could easily change things about.' He swung round to face her. 'But don't they just cross the name out and write the new one on? When Fiona got married she sent her passport off to be changed and she got the same one back with the new name written on.' He nodded an affirmation. 'That's right and there was an ink stamp inside showing the date it was amended.'

'It can't be difficult to forge a stamp,' said Beth adding that she didn't think anyone would scrutinise it that closely.

Chad suspected this would be the case. 'Whatever he did, he got onto the aircraft.' In frustration, he drew out all the scraps of paper and documents from the envelope and leafed through them. 'Where did that go? I know I had it with me. Hey, here it is.' He slid an authorisation for name change toward James.

The name left him speechless. He slid it to Beth.

'Oh my goodness!' she said. 'How can that be?'

He smiled. 'Jonathan Dunhelm is an ingenious man who has thought things through.' He held the coffee up, sniffed the mixture of coffee beans, vanilla and cinnamon and took a sip. A feeling of satisfaction followed the coffee down to his stomach and he felt like the dog who'd nabbed the best bone from the butcher.

'Well, sir, it looks like you have things tied up by the expression on your face.'

'I certainly do.' He thanked Chad for being the one to tie up the loose ends for him.

The young man finished his coffee and pastry and announced that he should get back to work. He handed the envelope and documents over. 'These are all copies. I'm taking a risk giving these to you but Meg assures me you'll hand them to that Inspector you know. Sure was good to meet you sir, ma'am. Good luck with your hunt although it sounds like you know exactly where to go.'

'We do indeed.'

'You have my card. Perhaps you'd let me know how it went.'

Chad waved goodbye and left them to it.

Beth heaved a sigh. 'How on earth did we miss this?'

'All down to appearances and we fell for it. Come on, let's get back to the hotel and pack.'

'Are you going to telephone George?'

'No need to rush. I'm sure he's still busy with those canal murders. We'll do it when we get back.'

Later that day, James settled back in his First Class seat but sleep refused to come. His heart beat a little faster than normal and he hoped George would allow him the pleasure of witnessing the arrest.

24

James sat alongside George in an unmarked police car which was parked some distance away from the house they were monitoring. He folded the *Telegraph* to a more manageable size and commented on the sub-heading. 'You're getting quite a bit of publicity for solving those canal murders, George. Your name's mentioned here a few times. That must be a feather in your cap.'

George continued gazing through the windscreen. 'I must admit I was pretty pleased with myself. Couldn't have done it without the rest of the team but I did feel I'd done some good detective work.'

'You'll have this little mystery under your belt too, once today's over.'

It was midday and showers had swept in from the west. His friend reached behind for his Thermos flask. 'Tea?'

'That'll break the monotony,' said James who was beginning to feel stiff from two hours of sitting. 'I don't think I'd be cut out to be a policeman, George. If I could have entered the force directly at your rank, it might have been acceptable.'

'Stick to what you're good at, James.' George said, adding that he did make for an impressive amateur sleuth. He handed James two plastic mugs and poured out the tea. 'You know, when you first stuck your nose into my business over that farmer's death a couple of years ago, I could have throttled you.' Securing the flask, he took his mug and sipped it. 'Although you were actually annoyingly persistent, you did well, apart from nearly getting yourself killed, of course.'

'How long do you think we're going to have to wait?'

George quickly put his mug in the footwell and grabbed a small pair of binoculars. 'Not long at all. I think that's him.'

He passed the binoculars across. 'That's him all right,' James said, focussing. 'Even the beard doesn't disguise him.' He watched the man open the front door and enter. George picked up his police radio.

'Camber 1, are you receiving?'

'Yes, sir.'

'We're about to go in. Do you have the rear entrance covered?'

'Yes, sir, Carstairs and Sillitoe are by the back gate.'

He replaced the receiver and opened the door. 'Right, come on.'

James followed George up the narrow pathway. The tension felt unbearable; part of it was excitement and adrenalin, another part of him hoped that Jonathan Dunhelm wouldn't be prepared for this and be ready to greet them with a revolver. George rapped the door knocker firmly. A man's voice shouted out.

'I'll get it. It's probably the glazier. He said he'd be round today.'

The door swung open.

James studied the man in front of him. He hadn't changed much at all from the photograph. He was a little older of course, but behind the beard, those same striking looks were there for all to see.

George showed his warrant card. 'Jonathan Dunhelm?'

The man started but quickly regained

his composure. 'No, I think you must have the wrong address?'

'I don't think so, sir.' George took out the paperwork he'd kept for this visit and leafed through it. 'Although I must apologise: I was forgetting that I was originally trying to locate Terry Hyde.' He flicked through to the next page. 'Then I understand it was Frederick Smith; then Alastair McKee.' He straightened his shoulders. 'But I believe I now need to address you as Laurence Woodridge.'

'Who is it, darling?' Belle came to the door, froze, then dragged Jonathan back. Her attempt to slam the front door was thwarted as George dipped his shoulder to take the force.

James pushed him through and they dashed along the hall and into the kitchen where PC Carstairs had positioned himself at the back door. He held his truncheon with grim determination.

Jonathan held his hands up. 'All right. All right.'

Belle snatched a rolling pin and went for the constable. Jonathan pulled her back while James twisted the weapon from her hand and put it out of reach.

She glared at him. 'How could you have possibly known?'

'I didn't. Not to begin with. Aside from what I discovered on my holiday in Boston, something about our visit here nagged at me. I'd given you plenty of notice about my visit. We'd spoken on the telephone and I believe my sister may have divulged a little too much when she met you in the village. And the story had hit the national papers so it was inevitable that you'd be on your guard.'

He pulled out a kitchen chair for her. She and Jonathan both sat down.

'When we spoke on the phone, you wanted to meet away from the house. Then you suddenly changed your mind and wanted us to meet you here. You had no reason to do that. We're opposite where we were going to meet. I think you wanted us here to give the appearance that you lived alone. I looked around the bathroom and it was devoid of any connection to Jonathan. The same in the lounge. You conveniently waited until I came out of your bathroom and went downstairs before

404

you emerged from your bedroom, presumably to ensure I didn't check anywhere else.'

She crossed her arms with a sneer.

'And that business about the ring.' She instinctively covered her fingers. He gently manoeuvred her hands onto the table, where he could clearly see a wedding, engagement and eternity bands. 'You see, when you wear a ring all of the time, the skin is paler. It's a give-away. The paleness of the skin here means you had more than one ring. I take it you did, eventually, get married, perhaps in another country.'

'No. We couldn't chance the authorities tracing us. We did everything but sign the paperwork.'

Jonathan held her hand tight. 'She had nothing to do with this.'

George begged to disagree. 'She's an accessory if nothing else.'

He smoothed his hair back. 'I've already made a statement. I wrote everything down because I knew it'd come to this. We saw the papers, my picture plastered all over the place. I grew this beard years ago because I knew it couldn't last. I hadn't dug that grave deep enough.' His angry eyes sought out George. 'How the hell did you find out about all of these name changes?'

George shrugged. 'It didn't take long once we'd discovered it was Terry Hyde in that grave. You left a clear paper trail.'

His shoulders fell. 'My statement's upstairs in the bedroom.' He moved towards the door but George ordered him to stay where he was. 'I'm not having you disappear on me again.' He jerked his head at James who trotted upstairs to the bedroom.

On entering the room he could see why Belle wouldn't have wanted him in there. Three large photographs of the couple adorned the walls. A smaller, framed photograph of Celia Dunhelm sat on one of the bedside tables, on what he assumed to be Jonathan's side. Sliding open the drawer, he brought out two pages of foolscap paper, dated the day the nationals had run the story of the discovery of the body. He returned to George and handed the statement over.

After reading them their rights, PCs Carstairs and Sillitoe handcuffed the couple and took them through the rear entrance to the waiting police car. George slid the statement toward James so they could both read it.

Statement of Jonathan Dunhelm

This statement is my confession to the murder of Terry Hyde on 8th April 1950.

I was the Chairman of Dunhelm Developments, a business inherited from my father. I was rich, bored and seeking adventure. When Father died, I took his place in the company. I couldn't sell it, as Mother would have been devastated and I didn't want to let her down. I kept the business going for a few years but eventually asked Jack Pemberton to run it on a day to day basis so I could pursue other things. Quite frankly, I wanted rid of the whole thing. I fantasised about having a new life, one that brought excitement and danger. I thought about returning to the air force but something else took my interest.

I fancied myself as a private eye. I loved the idea of having the odd scrap here and there. I knew it wouldn't pay any money but that wasn't what drove me. I had money. This was simply fun. I liked the idea of it and ended up stumbling upon something I'd never really experienced. Love.

I was contacted by Aubrey Woodridge to find out about the boyfriend of his niece, Arabella Woodridge. The boyfriend's name was Terry Hyde and he was, in the uncle's words, unsuitable for his niece. Aubrey introduced me to Arabella and told her what he had arranged for me to do. I understood she wasn't happy about it but then we met and things changed.

I took her to Martell's in Brighton for dinner to discuss what I had been asked to do. She knew that in order to move the relationship with Terry forward, she'd need her uncle's blessing. At the same time, although nothing was said, I felt a spark between us and she did too. She touched my hand that night and began flirting with me. By the end of the evening, I felt that Terry had become less important to her.

I made enquiries about the boyfriend.

On March 7th 1950, I spoke to his colleagues at Crawley bus station. On March 10th, I spoke to his landlady. On 14th March I spent the day following him and wondered what on earth Belle saw in him. He appeared to be a rough chap with no etiquette or social skills.

Aside from my reporting back to Mr Woodridge, Belle and I met several times and each time our feelings became more all-encompassing, beyond anything we'd experienced. A day away from her seemed like a lifetime and she told me that she felt the same. But, she said, she needed an excuse to break it off with Terry. He was obsessed with her and she thought it might be difficult to shake him off.

I reminded her that Terry had a past. He'd committed minor acts of theft. If he had that in him, then he was untrustworthy. I reminded her of her position; did she want adventure, travel and love with me, a man she had feelings for and plenty of money to do what she wanted? Or did she want to spend her life married to a bus driver who she would quickly tire of? She didn't take much convincing. We were in love and any feelings she had for Terry had evaporated the day we'd met.

But Terry wouldn't take no for an answer and he kept following her, checking up on her.

On 8th April 1950, we dined at 6 o'clock at Martell's and at seven o'clock I spotted Terry Hyde on the street. I knew he'd be there. I'd seen his bike in my rear view mirror on the drive down. He'd seen us at the table and I deliberately leaned over to kiss Belle. I thought that would get his back up and he'd simply accept things and disappear. But it didn't work out that way. He confronted us outside the restaurant and I told him to go home.

Unfortunately, he had other ideas. He followed me — collared me after I'd dropped Belle home. We had a blazing row. He was a pretty strong chap but I was a bigger, fitter man than him and I punched him good and hard. He fell and when he went to get back up I picked up a hefty rock and brought it down on his head. I confess I was not expecting to kill the man. I felt his pulse and tried to resuscitate him but without success.

I thought about telephoning the police and pleading self-defence but I knew the sort of trouble I was in. This was manslaughter at the very least and I didn't want to be found out. I had plans for my life and that included Arabella. I couldn't let that be taken away from me.

Then it dawned on me that this was a way out of my humdrum existence. This was exciting. This was my opportunity to be someone else. I could swap identities with Terry.

I bundled him into my car, went home to get a spade and took what money I had there. Then I drove. It wasn't until I saw the sign for Harrington's that I remembered there was a huge wood there. I drove as deep into the wood as I could, parked and carried the body the rest of the way. I dug a grave and put Terry in there. I knew his body wouldn't be found for some months, possibly years, and by then I would have a new identity.

I put my wallet and watch on him and took his door key. At around eleven, I went to his lodgings. It was easy to get in as the landlady was asleep and I had a rummage round his room. I found some money, bank book and a birth certificate. That's when my mind really started to work. I searched everywhere and couldn't find a passport. That was my next move. I took all of his documents and bank books. Terry Hyde would be my new persona.

My only concern was Mother. I knew she would be beside herself with worry and for that I feel an absolute heel and continue to feel that way. The only thing I could do was leave a clue. I got back to my rooms to pick up any other spare cash and I collated a few bits of music — titles that didn't interest me at all in the hope that she would work it all out. Mother is alert and astute and I honestly thought that these items would give her a clue that I wasn't dead. It was a risk but one I was prepared to take.

At ten o'clock on 9ᵗʰ April I visited

Belle and confessed. It was then that I realised that Belle truly loved me. She said she would support me no matter what — so I continued with my plans.

I moved away, drew money out of Terry's account and put in for a passport. On May 7th 1950, I received my passport in the name of Terry Hyde. I had it delivered to a pub that a business acquaintance ran. Belle had turned twenty one and she sold the house and moved to Wiltshire. To be perfectly sure I would not be found out, I told her that I'd have to leave the country for several months and return with another identity. I took myself off to New York and made my way to Boston.

In New England, I changed my name. Belle joined me for a week's holiday in July. She told me that the search for Terry had died down. I told her that we would sit tight for a few more months and that I would return home in November. I finally took the name Woodridge — if it was necessary, I could simply tell people I was Belle's brother.

When Terry Hyde's body was found,

I warned Belle that our dream might be coming to an end and I prepared this statement.

The phone call from Lord Harrington was a surprise. Although Belle thought it best to meet at the agricultural show, I was here and I suggested to her that they call in here first. We cleared the house of anything relating to me. We put all of my photographs, books and toiletries in the bedroom. When she returned from the fair, she told me that the police might be visiting so we kept the house clear of my presence.

Belle is innocent of all wrongdoing. I take full responsibility.

George sat back and brought out his pipe and tobacco. 'Love is a terribly strong emotion, isn't it?'

James agreed but wondered whether this was more about obsession. 'I've no doubt they were in love but to help cover up what appears to be an accidental killing? I'm not sure that many wives or lovers would do that. Beth certainly wouldn't — she'd march me to the police station and tell me to do the right thing.'

'Perhaps. But Jonathan had never felt like this about any woman in his life. He was, and is, a selfish man who is only interested in personal gain. The man dotes on this woman. He's bored and along comes this striking lady who is equally selfish and tired of her mundane existence. They live off excitement, don't you think? She probably enjoyed this as much as he did. They don't have children; probably too self-engrossed to have them. Arabella is as guilty as he is.'

James slid the statement toward him and scanned the details. He frowned.

George puffed on his pipe and asked him what the matter was.

'This. This statement, it's too exact.'

His friend slid his chair forward. 'What d'you mean, too exact?'

'I mean can you remember exactly what you were doing last month on a particular day at a particular time? Take three Sundays ago. What were you doing at four o'clock?'

George sat quietly for a few moments. 'I wasn't working, I know that much.

Four o'clock. I usually have lunch around two so I was probably snoozing. I generally listen to the wireless.'

James clicked his fingers. 'There. You've generalised. You know what you were doing but you can't be certain, you're telling me you normally do this, you usually do that.' He slapped the statement. 'How can Jonathan possibly remember exact times and dates? This was written two weeks ago about events that took place years ago. And Jonathan's put all these plans in place before even confessing to Belle. And the music, he didn't just gather that music up from his rooms. Celia said herself if wasn't his taste so where did that come from? And how did he have time to think up such elaborate clues to tell her he was still alive? He wouldn't be able to do that if this killing was a sudden and accidental blow to the head.' He twisted in his seat. 'And don't forget that Jonathan had withdrawn a large sum of money before he'd disappeared.'

George allowed his pipe to fall into his hands. 'He's covering up for her, isn't he?'

James gave an enthusiastic nod. 'That

statement is too perfect. I believe she dealt the fatal blow with that rock. And I think she planned to kill him.'

'What makes you say that?'

'She'd worked out their plan or they'd worked it out between them. I don't believe Jonathan went home a second time. I think he'd thought out those clues before they went to dinner. They knew Terry would follow them. They formulated a plan. Whatever they needed to bury a body was already in the car. And Terry was wearing his best suit that night. He wouldn't have done that to ride his motorbike. I think he was lured.'

'You may have something there. Come on.'

'Where're we going?'

'You're going home. I'm going on to the local police station to question Arabella.' He squeezed James' shoulder. 'Good work, James.'

25

'Roll up, roll up,' Graham shouted, to everyone within earshot. He tied his butcher's apron at the front and held up a long carving knife. 'Hog roast rolls for a voluntary contribution. Tip your change in the bucket.'

James had made the field adjacent to their house available for the fundraiser. They'd used it during the Guy Fawkes celebrations and it lent itself to a gathering like this. Beth, Anne, Helen and Kate had spent the day decorating the trees that surrounded the field. Although Easter was over, they made use of the yellow and white bunting left over from the games day. It was draped from branch to branch, along with an assortment of small fairy lights.

The WI had set up a number of trestle tables to sell items of jumble, books, crafts and homemade jams and pickles. Donovan had set up his mobile bar at the far end of the field and Rose and Lilac Crumb staffed the cake stand alongside Elsie. By the side of each table was a bucket labelled 'Contributions', the proceeds of which would help fund the next festival on the calendar. Didier approached Elsie's table to sample some of her baking.

Stephen manned a small table just by the entrance and handed out a number of leaflets about events at the church. These last few weeks, he'd started to think about ways to draw people in and had discussed them with James. The congregation in Cavendish was always good but they both knew the distractions that kept people away. What with the wireless, television, sports and different activities, the vicar needed to work hard to ensure his flock continued to attend church.

James studied the leaflets: Sunday School, Board Game afternoons, Bridge Club, The Teachings of Jesus, Cavendish Players and the new activity, the Cavendish Choir. He smiled. This last club had come about after Beth and Anne's visit to the WI during their holiday in Cornwall.

He waved the leaflets. 'You're certainly

making good use of the church and hall, Stephen.'

'And t-to good effect,' he replied, adding that all of the events had a number of supporters. 'A-and this is a p-perfectly splendid way to r-raise funds. What is the next festival?'

'We have May Day coming up and, of course, the cricket season starts shortly. I have my work cut out with a new event at Harrington's. GJ and Catherine have asked to run a special art weekend. We have the steam fair and classic car day next month and Bob Tanner said that might combine nicely with a folk day.'

Stephen shook his head. 'I don't know h-how you find time to fit everything in. And r-run Harrington's too.'

George strolled toward him, holding one of Graham's pork rolls. He leant forward to take a bite and licked up the apple sauce that began oozing out at the bottom. Beth and Anne joined them as James was quick to ask about his questioning of Belle.

'Didn't take much for a confession to come out. Once we told her Jonathan could hang, she dissolved into tears and it all came pouring out. They'd discussed a new life together, a new adventure and with them being people who have no compassion for others, they thought Terry could provide that for them. The talk about swapping identities was exciting, she said.'

James opened his eyes wide in horror. 'They had no thought of Terry's family and friends?'

'None whatsoever. They'd set it up so that Terry thought he may have a chance of getting Belle back. That's why he was all dressed up. They got him to follow them from the restaurant to somewhere a bit remote, away from prying eyes and Jonathan laid into him. Then she said that she simply picked up a rock and hit him.'

Anne shuddered. 'How cold-hearted and despicable.' She turned to Beth. 'Have you spoken with Mrs Dunhelm?'

Beth's hand went to her chest. 'That was the most difficult conversation. She insisted she wanted to know everything regardless of the outcome but I have to say that my heart went out to her.'

Donovan passed by with a tray of beer.

James grabbed a half pint of ale. 'She was devastated, of course.'

'W-will they hang?'

'Not up to me, but it was premeditated,' said George. 'I do all the work and the judge and jury get the deciding vote. If it were up to me, they'd both be on the end of a rope or in jail for life. Arabella admitted that some of the music Jonathan left for his mother was hers and they had it in the boot of Jonathan's car. It proves premeditation. The pair of them were deceitful in the extreme.'

'Well she deserves everything that is coming to her,' added James.

'And all for love,' said Anne. 'Such a shame that the thing we all need and treasure can make people turn so vicious. Does Terry's father know what happened?'

James assured her he did. 'We popped in to see him earlier and gave him all the details. He'll never get his son back but at least he knows the truth now.'

'A-and he's been able to give his son a worthy send-off.'

Beth asked who Lars was. 'You know, the photograph that Belle showed us.'

'An acquaintance and nothing else,' said George.

'Oi, oi,' Bert's voice carried across the field. They turned to see him walking arm in arm with Gladys. 'I 'ear you've gone and solved the mystery of the buried remains and,' he turned to George, 'you're plastered all over the newspapers with that canal business. They must be considering you for promotion?'

George winced at the idea. 'Not me, I don't want to be stuck behind a desk all day.'

Gladys took in the celebrations with a beaming smile. 'This is lovely, ain't it? What's it in aid of?'

James explained about the fundraising and how everything on offer could be purchased for a contribution only. 'From a penny to whatever you can afford and, of course, you need to attend some of these functions too. I say, you and Bert are seeing a lot of one another lately. Is this getting serious?'

She blushed and a coy expression crossed her face. 'You know Bert would 'ave your guts for garters asking me questions like that.' She sidled in closer. 'But yes, I think we are getting a bit serious. I don't push it because I know what he's like but I 'ope one day he'll think about us in the long term, you know. I mean, we're not gettin' any younger.'

Elsie's stall was close by and she offered Gladys an elderflower cordial. James dropped a few coins into the bucket and invited Gladys to enjoy the afternoon. As he turned he bumped into Charlie and his children. The young librarian gave Tommy and Susan some change and told them to go and buy something. He commented on James' expression.

'I didn't realise I had an expression.'

'You look pleased with yourself, like the cat that's got the cream.'

James steered him through the side gate and onto the gravelled drive. 'Actually, I am pleased as punch. Come and have a look at this.'

He dragged Charlie to the garage and opened the wooden doors where a 1907 Mercedes stood. The paintwork gleamed and the nickel plating shone. Charlie blew out his cheeks and stroked the panelling.

'Blimey, where'd you get this from?'

'Mrs Dunhelm wanted to auction off some of Jonathan's cars. He gave her a list of those he wanted to keep. The man is too sure of himself. Convinced he'll charm the jury into a short sentence.'

Charlie shook his head in disbelief.

'Anyway, she told me off for putting a bid in — let me have it at a good price for finding her son. She's a beauty isn't she?'

As Charlie circled the vehicle, James held up a letter from the Royal Automobile Club. 'I thought I'd enter her into the London-Brighton run in November and show her at the steam and classic car rally next month.'

They returned to the field where the fundraiser was in full swing. To his amusement, the curmudgeonly Professor Wilkins had paid Bob Tanner *not* to sing for five minutes. In his place, Mr Bateson gave a rendition of some odd little folk song about a charabanc.

James snaked an arm around Beth's waist. 'All's well with the world again.'

'I can't help but feel sorry for Reg Hyde and Celia Dunhelm. That young couple didn't think of the consequences, did they?'

'I would imagine all murders are the same. It's only after the event that people look back and consider what they could have done differently.' He took her hand and let his gaze settle on the fields leading to Harrington's and the forest beyond.

'Let's hope there's nothing else unpleasant buried on our estate.'

Didier, who seemed to appear from nowhere, piped up. 'Only the wild garlic and mushrooms, *oui*?'

James chuckled. '*Oui*, Didier, only the wild garlic and mushrooms.' He held up his glass. 'Cheers.'

THE END

See over the page for Grandma Harrington's Hot Cross Bun and Sherry Trifle recipes. For more information on the Lord James Harrington series of books, please visit: www.lordjamesharrington.com
Follow me on Twitter @cosycrazy.

Grandma Harrington's
Hot Cross Buns

(As traditional yeast is hard to come by,
use the instant/easy-blend type)

HOT CROSS BUNS — Serves 8 people

1lb 2oz/500g white bread flour
A pinch of salt
One teaspoon of mixed spice
One teaspoon of cinnamon
2oz/50g caster sugar
2oz/50g butter
5oz/150g mixed fruit
Just under half an ounce/7g of easy-blend
   yeast
7fl oz/200ml milk
2 eggs

For the crosses:
Three tablespoons of plain flour
Up to two tablespoons of water

Put the flour in a bowl and stir in the salt,
mixed spices, cinnamon and sugar.
Add the butter and rub in with fingers.

Stir in the dried fruit and yeast.

Warm the milk and beat the eggs. Then stir these into the mixture.

As with bread, use your fingers or a utensil to form a moist dough.

Take the mixture from the bowl and cut into eight.

Shape as buns and place on a baking tray. Cover with a linen cloth and leave in a warm place to rise for one hour.

Heat oven to Gas 7/220C.

For the cross: Mix flour with water to make a paste. Cut into strips and place on the buns as a cross.

Bake for 15 minutes

Best served toasted with butter.

SHERRY TRIFLE

(Grandma Harrington never really stuck to a strict recipe for her trifle so this really is from memory only!)

For the base, she used raspberry or strawberry jam Swiss Roll, sliced and arranged in the base of a large bowl. If Swiss Roll was not to hand, she would use segments of Victoria sponge.

Once in place, douse with a generous helping of sherry or brandy.

Then, make up a raspberry or strawberry jelly (jello) and pour over the sponge. Place in the fridge to set.

Once set, make some custard, either from scratch or use a packet, allow to cool a little and spoon over the jelly. Allow to set.

Next, whip up some double cream and spoon over the custard.

Sprinkle with hundreds and thousands or sliced raspberries/strawberries.

Serve and feel your waistline expand!!

We do hope that you have enjoyed reading this large print book.

Did you know that all of our titles are available for purchase?

We publish a wide range of high quality large print books including:
Romances, Mysteries, Classics
General Fiction
Non Fiction and Westerns

Special interest titles available in large print are:
The Little Oxford Dictionary
Music Book, Song Book
Hymn Book, Service Book

Also available from us courtesy of Oxford University Press:
Young Readers' Dictionary
(large print edition)
Young Readers' Thesaurus
(large print edition)

For further information or a free brochure, please contact us at:
Ulverscroft Large Print Books Ltd.,
The Green, Bradgate Road, Anstey,
Leicester, LE7 7FU, England.
Tel: (00 44) 0116 236 4325
Fax: (00 44) 0116 234 0205

MYSTERY OF THE RUBY

V. J. Banis

According to legend, the Baghdad ruby has the power to grant anything the heart desires. But a curse lies upon it, and all who own the stone are destined to die tragically, damned for eternity. When Joseph Hanson inherits the gem after his uncle's bizarre murder, his wife Liza is afraid. Though his fortune grows, he becomes surly and brutal. And suddenly Liza knows there's only one way to stave off the curse of centuries — she must sacrifice her own soul to save the man she loves.